Tropical Judgments

A novel by

David Myles Robinson

International Standard Book Number 13: 978-1-60452-100-9
International Standard Book Number 10: 1-60452-100-7
Library of Congress Control Number: 2015941661

BluewaterPress LLC
52 Tuscan Way Ste 202-309
Saint Augustine Florida 32092

www.bluewaterpress.com

This book may be purchased online at -
http://www.bluewaterpress.com/tropical

Printed in the United States of America

Also by the author

Unplayable Lie
Tropical Lies

Tropical Judgments

One

A untie Irene Kamaka put both hands on her lower back and stretched, arching her back as she did.

Hazel, her cousin, chuckled good-naturedly. "Think we're getting too old for these long gigs?" Hazel asked.

Irene finished her stretch and then bent over to pick up her ukulele in its case. "Five hours *is* a long time," she said, "but I can't see myself stopping. You either, for that matter." Her eyes twinkled playfully and she sought out their other cousin, packing up her bass. "Or Eleanor."

Irene kissed both cousins on the cheek and turned to walk out of the now almost empty restaurant where they had performed for a private party. "You like go get one drink at the Mai Tai Bar?" Eleanor called out. Her Pidgin English phrasing sounded melodic. "It's still early."

Irene reflexively looked at her watch. It was eight-thirty. Most of the shops and all of the restaurants in the Ala Moana Center were still open. "*Mahalo* my dears, but no. I'm beat. One drink would probably put me to sleep." She walked out into the warm night.

There were few cars left in the parking lot on the *makai* side, the ocean side, of the shopping center. She carried her ukulele case in her right hand and her black patent leather purse in her left. At fifty-nine, Irene was gracefully morphing from a stunning former Miss Hawai'i into a Polynesian grand dame. She wore a long sleeve fitted *mu'umu'u* that allowed the audience to see her swaying hips when she did the hula. It was a subtle dark blue floral pattern with white piping. Around her still elegant neck was a purple orchid *lei*. On her graying head was a hand crafted *haku*, a veritable crown of flowers. The laugh and smile lines in her nut brown face were said to be proof of her constant good humor and love of life.

Irene squinted briefly as the headlights of a passing car crossed her face. She could hear the rush of cars on Ala Moana Boulevard, but close by the only sound was the soft click of her heels on the pavement. She hummed a song about Nanakuli. The night air was soothing and had a slight winter crispness to it, probably something only *kama'ainas*, locals, would notice, she thought.

Her tan Mazda was twenty feet ahead when she heard a sound behind her. She began to turn when she was struck across the side of her face with something hard. She could hear a bone crack in her cheek a millisecond before she felt the piercing pain. She yelped in pain and fright. At the same time, someone was grabbing at her purse. She instinctively tried to hold on to it.

"Come on, *tutu*, let go your fucking purse." The voice was young, angry, and mean.

Irene relaxed her grip on the purse and it was yanked free, but still she was struck again. Her nose felt like it had been crushed and blood was spurting out, running onto her *lei* and staining the printed flowers on her *mu'umu'u*. Then she felt herself being dragged away from the direction of her car, back toward the building.

She was hit again on the side of the head, near her left eye socket. She dropped the ukulele case and tried to cover her head, but she was dizzy, disoriented, and in terrible pain. She was crying and thought she was screaming, but she couldn't hear herself. The next blow knocked her down and she couldn't catch herself with her hands. She hit her head on the asphalt, then everything went black.

Two

"Pancho." The voice was deep and distinctive.

"Hello, Your Honor." Pancho McMartin was frantically trying to figure out why Judge Makena was calling him. As far as he knew he had nothing pending with the Judge. Had Pancho screwed up somewhere? Maybe another judge had complained? Judge Makena was the Administrative Criminal Judge in charge of all the other Honolulu Circuit Court judges presently sitting on the criminal calendar.

"I need you to do me a big favor, Pancho."

"Certainly. If it's something I can do, it would be my pleasure."

Judge Makena chuckled. "Oh, it's something you can do, all right, but I doubt you'll find it to be a pleasure. I want you to represent Jackson Steele on a court-appointed basis."

Pancho had been leaning back in his desk chair, his trademark cowboy boots resting on his large rosewood desk. He took his feet off the desk and sat up straight.

"Isn't he the guy charged with the murder of Auntie Irene Kamaka?"

"That's right."

"What's wrong with the public defender's office? They have several top notch people who can try murder cases."

"Bob has a conflict. Auntie Irene was his cousin and their families are close." Bob Taniguchi was the head Public Defender, and when one attorney in the office had a conflict, the entire office was deemed conflicted out.

"Okay, but why me? I'm not even on the court appointment list. There are plenty of guys on the list who would love to have a high profile case like that." He paused. "Not to mention need the money."

Judge Makena chuckled again. The two went back many years. They had been good-natured adversaries when the Judge had been a prosecutor. "Not so anxious to kiss up to me now, are you, Pancho?"

Pancho laughed. "Good one, Judge. I'll admit I would love to remain in your good graces, but I'd be lying if I said I wanted to represent the guy charged with murdering one of the most beloved icons Hawai'i has ever had."

"I can't say that I blame you, Pancho, but I really do want you to do this for me. As you know, this Steele kid is black. Irene Kamaka was everyone's favorite symbol of old Hawai'i. As you said, she was beloved. There have been threats against Steele, some of them with pretty strong racial overtones; unusual for Hawai'i. The NAACP, such as it is here, has become involved. There will be a lot of people watching this case closely, for various reasons, I might add. I want someone defending the kid whose credentials and experience can't be criticized. I don't want to give anyone the chance to play the race card."

"There's no one on the list?" Pancho was racking his brains to try to think of some experienced attorneys on the court appointment list. The problem was that the court appointment fee was so low that any attorneys who could make it on their own simply didn't sign up.

He could hear Judge Makena sigh. "Trust me, Pancho, I've scoured it. I have three former PD's who are experienced, but one is already involved in a pretty big murder case. One was just diagnosed with colon cancer. And the third is, as far as I'm concerned, a walking malpractice case. It's just a matter of time before he gets suspended, or even disbarred."

Pancho realized he was holding the phone with a death grip. He relaxed his left hand on the phone and ran his right hand through his long brown hair. This was not a case he had the slightest inclination to take. During his last big murder trial he'd started having panic attacks. At first, he thought he'd been having a heart attack, but after all the tests came back negative, his doctor diagnosed panic attacks. Since then, he had turned down one high profile murder case and had only recently admitted to those closest to him that he'd been having attacks. He absently rubbed his chest. This seemed like a no win situation, but he couldn't see how he could refuse the Judge's request without doing serious damage on that front.

"You realize, Judge, that this is going to wreak havoc on my practice."

"I do, Pancho. That's why it's such a huge favor. I won't forget it, and I'll make sure the CJ knows the sacrifice you'll be making. You'll get whatever you reasonably need, including fees for your private investigator, what's his name, Drew?"

Pancho didn't hide the big sigh of resignation. If the CJ, the Chief Justice, was on board already, Pancho didn't see that he had much of a choice. "I have a feeling I'll need Drew more as a bodyguard than as an investigator on this one." Drew was a huge Samoan former NFL lineman.

The Judge laughed. "I'll get the paperwork started. Thanks, Pancho."

Pancho mumbled a goodbye and hung up the phone. He leaned back in his chair again and wondered what the hell had just happened.

Three

At the 300-hundred acre ranch in Kamuela, on the Big Island of Hawai'i, Bobby Lopaka sat in his study behind his huge roughhewn desk. In front of him, sitting in various stages of relaxation around the room, were his three most trusted advisors — his fifty-three-year-old son, Emmet, and his longtime friends, Buddy and Napoleon.

At eighty-one, Lopaka was still a big, dynamic man, an imposing figure even without his reputation for merciless violence. He was light-skinned and his oversized face was dotted with freckles and moles. His features had enough Polynesian, along with his name, to assert his 'Hawaiianness' when it served him to do so. His light green eyes were chameleon-like in their ability to either put someone at ease or scare them to death.

Lopaka took a sip of the bourbon he always seemed to have at hand. "So what the fuck is up with that little *popolo* kid killing Irene?"

Buddy Ahlo, who had not aged as well as his boss, coughed into his arm and spoke in a raspy voice, evidence of sixty years of smoking. "Looks like the cops have the black kid cold. Our man on the homicide team said they have his fingerprints on the purse."

Emmet, whose nickname was 'Rigger' from his days as a top outrigger canoe racer, snorted in disagreement. "Then where's the shit she had in the purse and da kine, the ukulele case?"

Buddy shrugged, not taking offense. If Bobby was the CEO of the organization, then Rigger was the COO, making most of the day to day decisions. That meant that the younger Rigger was also Buddy's boss. "The cops think there was an accomplice who got greedy and bopped the *popolo* kid on the head and took off."

Napoleon, a dark-skinned, almost pure Hawaiian who had a full head of white hair and who, at seventy-two, still surfed and paddled canoe whenever he had time, rarely spoke unless spoken to, so Bobby Lopaka almost missed his quiet utterance.

"What'd you say, Nappy?"

"I said the detective on the case is a lazy fuck-up. Always has been. I watched him move up through the ranks of the HPD despite himself. He was even on our payroll for a while back in the eighties."

"Who's that?" asked Rigger.

"Bryson Wong."

Buddy nodded. "Yeah, I remember him. You mean he's head of homicide now? My guy didn't tell me that. What happened to Frank Nip?"

"Nip retired last year. The new Chief promoted Wong about six months ago."

"What's this fucking state coming to?" said Rigger, to no one in particular.

Bobby cleared his throat, a message to get the discussion back on track. "So Nappy, do you think this cop, Wong, screwed up the investigation?"

Napoleon looked at Buddy and seemed to shrug. "Buddy would know more about that than me since he's got a guy in homicide. But my guess is that Wong got the little *popolo* kid with his prints on the purse right outside the bathroom and decided that the case was solved. If they're looking for their assumed accomplices, I doubt they're working too hard."

Bobby swiveled to his right and stared out the huge picture window overlooking rolling, emerald-green pastureland. A light fog sat close to the ground and seemed to heighten the green of the grass. There was a time when Bobby's 'legitimate' business empire extended to various state-wide businesses. He owned the largest security guard company in the islands, never failing to get a contract on which he had bid — airport, stadium, Blaisdell Arena — you name it and Bobby Lopaka's agency provided the security.

It was said that he had a big piece of most of the Waikiki Beach concessions and that he controlled much of the live entertainment in

Waikiki. The tour companies would get huge kickbacks for bringing the busloads of tourists to the showrooms controlled by Lopaka.

As the purported head of Hawaii's organized crime syndicate, Bobby Lopaka's power at one time had even reached as far as Washington Place, the Governor's Mansion. Key legislators, bureaucrats, and cops were all on his payroll.

Perhaps the most troubling rumor, however, was that one of the most high profile criminal defense attorneys in town had bribed a Circuit Court judge in a murder case involving one of Lopaka's trusted lieutenants, Buddy's godson. Although a jury found the man guilty, the previously well-respected judge overruled the jury verdict using the power of JNOV, judgment non obstante veredicto, the English translation being 'judgment notwithstanding verdict,' almost unheard of in criminal cases. The judge resigned in the uproar that followed and proceeded to drink himself to death in record time. The defense attorney moved on to become a wealthy tort lawyer, taking criminal cases only when Lopaka 'asked' him to.

When a couple of extremely brave investigative reporters began a series of articles about Lopaka, his business empire, and his alleged association with organized crime, Bobby rode out the storm by keeping a low profile, then slowly began to divest himself of all the businesses with the exception of his ranch. It was a good decision. His name showed up less and less in the news, and within five years he was all but forgotten by the public. Since then, Bobby and Rigger Lopaka focused on gambling, drugs, and some prostitution.

Bobby realized he had not been following the discussion by the three men about the murder. He turned away from the window and refocused on the room and his lieutenants. "I want to find out what happened. If the *popolo* boy had an accomplice, then let's find him. If he didn't do it at all, then let's find out who did. We don't need this *kine pilikia*."

Four

Pancho McMartin's heart sank when the guard escorted Jackson Steele into the small interview room in Module Five of the O'ahu Community Correctional Center. All he had known about Jackson before this meeting was that Jackson was a nineteen-year-old African-American. What he saw as Jackson eased his thin and bony body into a chair across from Pancho, was a mean-looking boy.

Jackson's mouth was turned up on one side into a permanent sneer. His nose was flat and almost bestial looking. There was an ugly round scar on his right cheek. Although his eye contact with Pancho was intermittent and fleeting, his dark gray eyes were strange, almost haunting. His eyebrows were unnaturally thick. His nappy hair looked unkempt and matted. His skin was African black, almost purple. Pancho's first thought was that if looks were any indication, this kid would be found guilty as charged.

Pancho cleared his throat and fiddled with his pen for a moment before speaking. "My name is Pancho McMartin and I've been appointed by the court to be your attorney. Do you understand what you've been charged with?"

Jackson looked up at Pancho for a second and nodded, then looked back down at his hands. "Yeah. They say I murdered some woman."

Other than the slight body, Jackson's voice gave Pancho the first indication of how young the kid was. *Meanness is an old-looking trait,* thought Pancho, but the voice sounded young, slightly high pitched and soft, kind of Michael Jackson with a Mississippi accent.

Pancho gave Jackson his standard rap about attorney/client privilege and how the process worked before cutting to the chase. "So, Jackson, I'm going to ask you if you killed this woman. If you did, I'll still be your attorney, but I will never put you on the stand to testify. If you did it, I want you to explain to me exactly what happened so I can figure out if there were any facts we can use to help you." He paused, watching Jackson closely to see if he understood. Noticing the pause, Jackson looked up at Pancho and nodded before looking back down at his hands.

"Okay, now, if you think it will help your case by telling me that you didn't do it when you really did, you're wrong. It'll make matters worse in the long run. So the cardinal rule here is never, ever lie to me."

Jackson looked up again and Pancho saw something in his eyes. "I don't never lie, Mr. Martin."

"It's McMartin, but you can call me Pancho if you want. Okay, so, tell me, Jackson, did you murder Auntie Irene Kamaka?"

Jackson made a face, like he was thinking. "How come you gots such a funny name, Pancho? Are you a Mexican?"

Pancho smiled. "No, I'm not. The short story is that I grew up in New Mexico, in Taos, which is near Santa Fe, and my parents had some weird idea that giving me a Latino sounding first name would make me fit in better at school, which was mostly Hispanic." He shook his head from side to side. "But of course that was just silly. In fact, it had the opposite effect." Pancho stopped smiling and stared hard at Jackson. "Now, are you going to tell me what happened? Did you murder Auntie Irene?"

Jackson again looked down at his hands resting on the scarred metal table top and for a few seconds he didn't say or do anything, then he slowly lifted his head and met Pancho's look straight on. "No, sir, I don't think I did that, sir. At least I ain't never done anything bad like that before."

To Pancho, the innocence of the voice belied the scary looking face.

"What does that mean, you don't *think* you did that?"

"It means what I said, Mr. . . . . Pancho. I sure don't think I would have done anything like that."

Pancho realized he hadn't really been breathing, had assumed that he would hear a confession, and now he took a deep breath. He ran his left hand through his hair. His sharp featured, tanned face looked puzzled.

"Jackson, you've got to help me out here. I need to know what happened. Do you not remember? Is that why you don't know what happened?"

Jackson looked back down at his hands as he spoke. "Yeah. I don't remember. I passed out, and when I woked up and walked out of the bathroom the cops arrested me."

"Why did you pass out, Jackson? Had you been drinking?"

"No, sir. I don't drink none."

"Drugs?"

Jackson shook his head. "Never done drugs neither. I don't know why I pass out, Pancho; I just do."

Pancho made a note on his legal pad. "So this happens a lot?"

Jackson seemed to shrug with his whole body. Although he was still looking down, Pancho could see that his eyes were closed. His right hand, resting on the table top, closed into a fist, then relaxed, then closed again. Finally he shook his head, as if finishing a conversation with himself, and looked into Pancho's eyes.

"You gotta understand, Pancho, I wasn't even 'sposed to be born. My mama wanted to 'bort me, but she was real religious an' all and her pastor told her 'bortion is a sin and she had to have me." Jackson's tone was matter-of-fact, totally devoid of emotion.

Pancho was caught off guard. "Why did your mother want to abort you?"

"'Cause I am from the seed of a terrible monster who raped my mama over and over again, then kilt her own parents right in front of her." Jackson said this as if he had memorized it and was reciting it by rote, but his voice cracked and Pancho felt a tightening in his gut.

"How do you know all this? Did your mother tell you she didn't want to have you?"

Jackson shook his head vigorously. "No, sir. She wouldn't do that. She may not have loved me none, but she treated me just fine and she wouldn't have told me nothin' like that. It was my Aunt Clio what told me all about it." He pronounced 'aunt' as 'awn't'.

"Mama was only seventeen when that happened. I don't blame her none. She should've been allowed to 'bort me. That just wasn't right what the preacher made her do." He paused, and Pancho realized that he was beginning to see beyond the terrible visage. It was Jackson's eyes that were telling Pancho the real story. The strange, haunting look that Pancho had felt when he first saw Jackson was, in reality, that the eyes were young, hurt and sad.

"So mama raised me up best she could what with not wanting me an' all. She and Aunt Clio took me to church three days a week. The preacher tol' me that I was the son of the devil and that I would someday have to pay for sins of my father."

Jackson paused and gave Pancho a strange look, his forehead scrunched up, his eyes squinted, and his thick eyebrows came together almost as one. "Why'd he make mama have me if he knew I was the son of the devil? I don't understand that at all." He looked around the room, as if there might be someone else there. Then he shrugged and continued his story.

"The rest of the time I was pretty much on my own. I went to school some of the time. I was made fun of a lot at school, 'cause I'm so ugly an' all I guess." He paused and rubbed at his left eye, like there was something in it. "Plus, I'm not real smart. So I sometimes didn't go to school and I'd just go for long walks, mostly out to the country where there weren't nobody around. I got bad grades an' all, but mama didn't care and I didn't care, so it weren't no big thing."

Pancho wasn't sure where this was going, but he sensed it was best to let Jackson tell the story in his own way.

"When I was 'bout thirteen or so, I started having blackouts. The first one happened when I was 'bout five miles out of town, walking along a farm road. I liked to look at the cattle and sheep an' all. I liked horses the best. Anyway, next thing I know I was lyin' on the ground and I didn't know what happened. I was out for a while, but I don't know how long. But when I woked up I just got up and dusted off my clothes as best I could so's I wouldn't get yelled at when I got home." Jackson closed his eyes and stopped talking. Pancho would come to understand that this was Jackson's way of gathering his next series of thoughts.

"Aunt Clio said that my blackouts were God's way of punishing me for being the ill-gitimate son of a monster. She said it's called 'sin' something."

Pancho sighed and looked away from Jackson for a moment. He wasn't exactly sure what Jackson was trying to tell him. All he knew was that there was a monumental shift going on in his mind about how he felt about this kid.

"Do you love your Aunt Clio?" Pancho finally asked in a gentle tone.

Jackson shrugged noncommittally. "She all right, I guess." He looked down at his hands, as if he had just made a terrible confession. Pancho believed that was exactly what had just occurred.

"You won't get mad at me if I contradict your aunt about some things?"

Jackson looked at Pancho, his bushy eyebrows knotted. "What's that mean?"

"It means that I'd like to tell you that your aunt is wrong about some things. But if you don't want me to, I won't."

Jackson seemed to think about it for a moment before he shrugged his bony shoulders again. "It all right."

Pancho nodded and continued to keep his voice soft, his tone gentle. "First of all Jackson, what you say you have is called 'syncope' and is pronounced sin-ka-pee. It has nothing to do with sin or with you being a sinner. It just means that you suffer from fainting spells. Has any doctor examined you and told you why you faint?"

Jackson shook his head. "Nah, not really. The church people made mama and Aunt Clio take me to the 'mergency room one time when it happened at church. That's when the doctors told them I had that sin— whatever it is. But mostly when I come to, everyone just asks if I'm all right and when I say yeah, they go on their way."

Pancho felt like screaming and crying at the same time. *How could these people, his own family, have treated him like this?* "Okay, if it's all right with you, I'm going to ask to have a doctor come and examine you. I'm no expert, but I know that fainting spells can be dangerous and I want to make sure you're okay."

Jackson looked like he started to say something, but instead he nodded.

"What is it?" asked Pancho.

"It's just that I ain't got no money and 'surance to pay for doctors an' all."

Pancho smiled. "Don't worry about that. I'll take care of it." He allowed his smile to fade away and, although he kept his tone gentle, he leaned in toward Jackson. "Jackson, why are you telling me about your mother and about what your aunt thinks about your fainting spells? You don't believe that nonsense about you being the devil or being a sinner, do you?"

Jackson looked quickly away from Pancho. Pancho could see the bandage on the back of Jackson's head where he had hit it on the bathroom floor before being arrested. There was a small patch of red on the white gauze, a rising sun. Somewhere off in the distance Pancho heard an echoed shout, indistinct as to content. When Jackson turned back to face Pancho his eyes were moist. It was the first real emotion Pancho had seen from Jackson.

"All I knows is that me being borned ruint my mama's life. Every time she looked at me I reminded her of that bad night. That's why she had to make me leave. Like I said, I don't blame her none."

"But you don't believe God is punishing you for what happened to your mother, do you?"

Jackson breathed out heavily, his flat nostrils flaring. He wiped at his eyes, but this time, he did not look away. "I don't know, sir. I don't wanna think so. I knows my Aunt Clio thinks like that, or something like that. The preacher said I gotta pay for what happened to Mama. I'm bad seed. That's all I know."

Pancho felt like he wanted to take Jackson in his arms and hug him and tell him that his mama and his aunt and his preacher were all full of hateful shit and that he wasn't responsible for anything that had happened to his mother, but, of course, he couldn't do that—and he still had to try to figure out if Jackson murdered Auntie Irene.

"So what happened on the night you were arrested? Why are you unsure about whether you killed Auntie Irene?"

Jackson closed his eyes and rubbed both hands aggressively over his nappy scalp. Dandruff fell like tiny snowflakes.

"Why's she called Auntie Irene? She can't be everyone's aunt."

Pancho chuckled. "In Hawai'i, it's a term of respect. In Auntie Irene Kamaka's case, she was loved as a singer and hula dancer, and I guess we all kind of felt like she was part of our family, our *'ohana.'* "

Jackson was silent, thinking, then he said, "So that's why everybody's so mad? They think I kilt one of their family?"

"Tell me what you remember about that night, Jackson."

"That's the thing Mr. . . . I mean Pancho. I don't remember much of anything. I walked over from the park to the Ala Moana Shopping Center like I always did. I liked to use the bathroom over there by those restaurants near the elevator."

"Longhi's and Morton's?"

"Yeah, I guess that them. Anyway, at night, before they close down, they're cleaner than the park's bathrooms. So if there's no security around, I go there and clean up a little and use the toilet. Then I liked to walk around the shopping center. I like looking in windows at all the stuff."

"Did anything happen before you went into the bathroom?"

Jackson shook his head. "Not that I can remember. But I don't remember even getting to the bathroom that night. The last thing I remember is walking up the ramp to the top floor of the parking lot on my way to the bathrooms. Then, next thing I know, I'm on the floor of the bathroom. I must have fainted an' hit my head on the concrete floor 'cause I was bleeding from my head. I got up an' put a wet paper towel on my head an' just as I walked out of the bathroom I got stopped by the police."

Jackson's gray eyes were pleading, a sharp contrast to the rest of his face. "Honest, Pancho, I know I'm a bad person an' all, but I don't think I would've beat someone to death like they say I did."

Five

Pancho felt physically and mentally exhausted by the time he returned to his office from his interview with Jackson. Susan, his longtime secretary, looked at him with an expectant look on her face.

"That bad, huh?" She got up and followed him into his office where he tossed his soft leather briefcase onto the couch and plopped down in his chair.

"Yeah, but not in the way I was expecting." He leaned back and rubbed both his temples with his fingers. Susan sat in one of his client chairs while simultaneously sticking loose strands of her gray hair back into the practical bun, held in place with a black lacquer chopstick.

"The kid's a mess," said Pancho. "He's so psychologically damaged from the way he was treated by his family that he isn't even sure he didn't kill Auntie Irene."

He told Susan the story. When he was done he could see the outrage on her craggy sixty-six-year-old face. Her olive-green eyes seemed to darken and narrow, causing the deep lines in her forehead to become even more pronounced.

"Part of the problem," Pancho continued, "is that the kid looks naturally mean. His face is fixed in a permanent look that says 'I'm gonna kill your honky ass.' And on top of that, he's pretty damn ugly."

"Well, meanness and ugliness often go hand in hand," said Susan. "People who've been told over and over again how ugly they are tend to get a chip on their shoulder."

"Yeah, I guess I agree. Jackson is ugly and mean-looking, but I have this strong gut feeling that even though he's been brainwashed into thinking that he's some sort of bad seed, he really couldn't hurt a fly."

Pancho and Susan sat silent for a few moments, each lost in their own thoughts. When they heard the phone ringing in the outer office, Susan jumped up and went to answer it. Pancho swiveled in his chair to look out his floor-to-ceiling window overlooking Honolulu Harbor. It was a gray and windy day and there were whitecaps, even in the harbor. A Matson barge was being towed out of the harbor, laden with supplies for the neighbor islands. The intercom buzzed and Susan's ex-smoker voice said, "Drew's on his way in."

***

Thirty minutes later Drew Tulafono, Pancho's best friend and private investigator, sat across the desk listening to Pancho once again tell Jackson's story. The huge Samoan shook his head in disgust when Pancho finished.

"Man, that sucks big time."

"More than that," said Pancho, "it's heartbreaking. Every time I tell the story I think I'll get used to it, desensitized. But instead I just get more and more upset and angry."

Drew nodded. "That's who you are, man. That's what makes you such a passionate advocate. But . . ." he hesitated for a beat. "Are you sure you're up to this, Paunch? I mean, the stress is going to be off the charts."

Pancho knew Drew was trying to be diplomatic. He smiled grimly.

"You mean can I hold my panic attacks in check? I honestly don't know, man. It's kind of scary. But shit, this is my life. This's what I do for a living and it's what I love. I've already turned down one big case. I can't live in fear that I'm gonna pass out, or whatever, in court. Shit, if I do that I may as well find another line of work. I think it's time I got back in the saddle."

Drew slowly nodded. "Okay, man, what do you want to do? How do you want to handle this?"

Pancho ran his left hand through his hair. It caused his long brown hair to look disheveled, wild even. "Let's prove he's innocent. Let's prove the cops screwed the pooch big time on this one."

"Are you gonna play the race card? You gonna claim the cops racially profiled the kid?"

Pancho shook his head. "I don't want to go there. Besides, how do you argue that when they have Jackson's prints on the purse? No, I want you to do a full blown investigation on this one. Don't assume the police were thorough. Start from scratch and see what you can dig up. Witnesses. Possible accomplices. Security cameras. I know Ala Moana Center has a lot of security cams spread around. Let's see if there are any near the murder scene and the bathroom where Jackson went." He paused. "Go wherever the investigation takes you."

Drew raised his dark bushy eyebrows. "You want me to go full-time on this. Who's paying?"

Pancho waved a hand dismissively. "Don't worry about it. Judge Makena and the Chief Justice owe me big time for taking this case. Makena promised me whatever I need." Pancho looked up from the legal pad on which he was doodling and stared hard at his friend. "Whatever the court doesn't cover I'll cover out of my own pocket."

Drew rose slowly from his chair, grimacing slightly at the obvious pain which Pancho knew came from his bad knees. "Don't worry about it, bud," Drew said. "We're in this one together."

Six

Emmet "Rigger" Lopaka had two sons. One, Vincent, had such a severe case of autism, he required twenty-four/seven care. The other, Winston, was handsome and intelligent and was capable of unfathomable violence. He was Rigger's right hand man.

Winston sat across from Scotty Gouveia, the owner of Paradise Security Systems, a company Gouveia had bought from Winston's grandfather, Bobby. Winston's unwavering glare sent shivers down Scotty's spine. Scotty was aware of Winston's proclivities. He'd once witnessed Winston slowly and methodically break every single finger on both hands of one of Scotty's employees. The unfortunate man's gambling habit had caused him to fall heavily into debt. When he didn't pay on time, Winston had gone happily to work. After that incident, Scotty, a pretty heavy gambler himself, never again gambled in Hawai'i.

"So," said Winston in a soft, calm voice. "We asked you to watch out for her that night and instead, you let her get robbed and murdered. Any comment?"

Scotty could feel his face flush and he looked away toward the window air conditioner that suddenly sounded like a jet engine. He looked back at Winston, then coughed into his hand. His throat felt dry and his heart was thumping hard. He shrugged. "I put a guy on her, just like you asked me to do. But he's disappeared. I don't know what happened. Believe me, I'm trying to find out."

Winston raised his eyebrows. "Your bodyguard disappeared? What the fuck, Scotty? What does that even mean? You trying to tell me that the little *popolo* boy off'd your bodyguard, too? And hid his body?"

Scotty shook his head, which felt like it was about to explode. His mouth felt like it was full of cotton, and he looked around for the bottle of water he usually kept on his desk, but it wasn't there. "I don't know, *brah*. Honestly. When I heard Auntie Irene had been murdered at the Center, the first thing I did was try to get hold of the guy I assigned to her. But his cell phone is off and he didn't report to work the next day, or since."

"Who was it? Anyone known to us? You think he was in on it?"

"It wasn't anyone you'd know," said Scotty. "Just a guy who's been with me for about five years and has always been trustworthy." He held up his hands in submission. "There is no reason for me to think he'd be a part of something like this."

Winston stared at Scotty for a few beats, as if evaluating the integrity of Scotty's statement. "I want his name and address and everything you know about him."

Scotty nodded vigorously.

"And what about the surveillance tapes? Do they show anything?"

Scotty's affirmative nodding turned to negative shaking. He had a vision of himself as a doll with a bouncing head that people put on their dashboards. He felt stupid and scared, more scared than stupid, if truth be told. He swallowed and tried to generate some saliva. "I've gone over the tapes and I haven't seen anything unusual. My guy followed Auntie Irene from the gig, but there's no coverage shortly after that."

Winston grunted. "Lemme have copies of those as well." He sat back in his chair as Scotty jumped up and almost ran to his office door to bark instructions to his secretary.

When Scotty was settled back in his desk chair, Winston looked around at the small, fake wood-paneled office with the loud air conditioner and fixed Scotty with a hard look. "Work with me, Scotty. We want to find out exactly what happened." He paused and began to rise. "And trust me on this. If we find out that you fucked up in any way, or fucked us in any way, you can kiss your *okole* goodbye."

Scotty couldn't summon up enough saliva to wet his mouth to reply before Winston was gone.

Seven

"Mrs. Steele?"

"Yes, who's this?"

"My name is Pancho McMartin. I'm an attorney in Honolulu, Hawai'i and I'm representing your son, Jackson."

"Honolulu? In Hawai'i?" It came out 'hy-why-ee.' "Like that TV show?"

"Yes, ma'am. In Hawai'i, just like where *Hawai'i 5-O* takes place." Pancho cleared his throat. "Ma'am, I'm representing your son, Jackson, for murder."

Pancho thought he heard an intake of breath, but the woman said nothing for several seconds. Then she said, "Who he killed? And why you calling me? I don't have nothing to do with him no more."

"Mrs. Steele, I don't think he killed anyone. I've been assigned by the court to represent him. I thought it might be important for you to know what's happened. I'd also like to know a little more about him, since I need to know as much as I can to effectively represent him."

The line was silent again, but he hadn't heard her hang up.

"Mrs. Steele? You still there?"

"I here," she said. "But I still don't know what this has to do with me, or what you want from me. I ain't got no money to help him."

"I don't want any money from you, Ma'am. And I don't want anything from you except whatever information you can tell me about him. I want to help him." Pancho decided to take a gamble. "I understand why you don't want to talk about Jackson or have anything to do with him, and I understand how hard this call must be for you. But I need to know as much as I can. Has he ever been in trouble before? Is he a violent man?"

"How you know why I don't want to talk about him?" Her voice was harsh and accusatory.

"Jackson told me the story about . . . about his conception."

Once again the line was silent. When she spoke again, her voice was soft, and it sounded to Pancho like she was trembling. "He . . . he told you that? How he know any of that? I never tol' him nothing."

"Do you have a sister named Clio?" Pancho's tone was gentle.

"What she have to do with any of this?"

"Apparently your sister told Jackson the story about how you were raped and how your parents were killed. She told him that you had wanted to have an abortion, but that your church, your preacher, wouldn't let you do it. So you raised him. Your sister Clio told Jackson that he was a bad seed, that he would have to pay for what his father did to you and your parents."

"No, she—"

Pancho felt bad for what he was putting on this woman, but he plowed ahead. He had a client to represent. "Jackson has blackouts. You know about that. I'm going to have a doctor examine him, but I think they're probably psychological. He had a blackout on the night of the murder and he doesn't remember anything. That's why I need help, Mrs. Steele."

Pancho didn't talk into the silence that seemed to go on and on. He had ambushed Jackson's mother, and it was pretty clear she hadn't known that her sister had dumped all her baggage onto the boy. He imagined she was crying, but he didn't know. He finally spoke.

"You should know, Mrs. Steele, that Jackson doesn't blame you for anything. He knows you wanted to abort him and he thinks you should have been allowed to. He understands how hard it was for you to look at him and see your assailant."

Pancho heard what sounded like an effort to choke back a sob, then, away from the phone, he heard her blow her nose.

"What that boy doing in Hawai'i?" Hi-why-ee. Her voice, when she finally spoke again, was small, docile even.

Pancho realized that he had been holding his breath and now he held the receiver away from his head so she wouldn't hear his sigh of relief. He knew that the fact she had finally asked a personal question about Jackson, no matter how trivial, was a good sign.

"Jackson said he spent a lot of time traveling from city to city, trying to find work. When he had no job he lived on the street or in shelters. He said he would ask people where there were plenty of jobs or else where it was warm enough to live outside. He eventually heard about Honolulu. The weather is warm all year long and even in the bad times the unemployment rates are usually not too high. He said he also heard it was an okay place for black people. So he took some of the money you had given him and bought a one way ticket to Honolulu."

Pancho paused just long enough to catch his breath. He knew he was talking fast, but he wanted Mrs. Steele to hear about Jackson before she shut him out again.

"He'd been in Honolulu about six months before this happened. He hasn't had the best time of it. Jackson knows he's not the best-looking kid and, despite what he heard, there is prejudice in Hawai'i just like everywhere else. We're just a little more polite about it most of the time. So he spent a lot of time on the streets or at a shelter called Institute for Human Services."

"But he still blacking out?"

"Yes, Ma'am. It's kind of scary in fact. Most of the work he gets, when he gets work, is labor work. If he passed out on a jobsite he could get hurt." Pancho stopped, hoping she would ask more questions, hoping she would get involved. Seconds passed. He was about to give up and start talking again when she spoke.

"So what's all this 'bout some murder? That boy was always gentle as a lamb. He never been in no trouble." For the first time her voice sounded like Jackson's. The soft and melodious Mississippi accent was without the hard edge of suspicion and hostility.

Pancho was sitting at his office desk. He closed his eyes, smiled, and nodded slightly. He told her everything he knew.

***

"I don't know if I got through to her or not," said Pancho. He was lying on his bed in his Diamond Head apartment, his hands clasped behind his head. His girlfriend, Paula Mizuno, was resting her head on his chest, which was tanned and muscular and had just a sprinkling of brown hair. The February sunset beyond the open lanai doors was a cacophony of reds, oranges, and purples. The two were naked. Except for the respite of their recent lovemaking, Pancho couldn't seem to think of anything except his new client.

Paula stirred, sitting up against the bed's backboard. It was warm, and she made no attempt to cover her exquisite breasts. Her brown nipples were still erect. "I wouldn't be too hard on her, Pancho. I mean, we can't begin to imagine what she went through, let alone being forced to raise her attacker's son." She sighed and stroked Pancho's long hair. "I suppose she thought that by making Jackson leave she would finally be able to put everything behind her, although how she thought she was just going to ignore the reality of her son is beyond me."

Pancho closed his eyes, enjoying Paula's soft caress. "I know, and I'm sympathetic to her situation, but if I need her help to save her son, I'm damn well going to push for it."

The two were silent for a few moments before Pancho sat up, took a long look at the quickly fading sunset, and gently kissed each of Paula's nipples; then he looked into her dark oval eyes and ran his right hand over her jet black, short cut hair. In Hawai'i, Paula would be referred to as '*hapa haole*,' which meant part Caucasian, even though the reality was that, like most mixed races in Hawai'i, it was much more complicated than that. Paula was mostly Japanese and *haole*, but she also had some Hawaiian, some Portuguese, and some Filipino blood. It was, to Pancho's eye, a perfect blend.

"Let's walk into Waikiki for dinner," said Pancho. "Maybe with all the people around, I'll think about something besides my new little albatross named Jackson."

Eight

Jackson Steele had been indicted by the Grand Jury, which meant there would be no preliminary hearing and Pancho would have no chance to learn how strong the case against his client was until the prosecution began to comply with his discovery requests. Historically, the prosecution dribbled the evidence to the defense in painstakingly slow bits and pieces. It was frustrating, but Pancho usually didn't get too upset about it. After all, he reasoned, even the prosecution had to have some fun sometime, and messing with the defense attorney was pretty much the only fun they could think of.

The arraignment and plea following the indictment was held in Circuit Court the following week and was a *pro forma* event where Pancho entered the plea of 'not guilty' to the charge of Murder in the Second Degree on behalf of Jackson. Nonetheless, the press was out in force. As Pancho made his way out of Ka'ahumanu Hale, the brown, monolithic Circuit Court building on Punchbowl, a tight cadre of reporters moved with him, like a rugby scrum, shouting questions and sticking microphones in his face. When he finally stopped at the bottom of the steps the reporters went quiet to allow him to speak.

"My client is innocent, and both he and I express our heartfelt condolences to the family of Auntie Irene. I ask all of you to please reserve your judgment until all of the facts come out in court. In the meantime, I've heard of some troubling reports of racial unrest as a result of this case.

Again, I beg everyone in this wonderful state to prove why we are called the Aloha State. We're all angry over this senseless and violent crime, but please do not jump to conclusions, and please don't react in any way that Auntie Irene herself would find abhorrent. Thank you. I will have no further comments on the case until trial."

Pancho walked off alone, ignoring the contrails of shouted questions which blew away in the mild trade winds. When he got to Queen Street, he took off his blue linen sport coat and slung it over his shoulder. The wind whipped his pastel blue tie. His cowboy boots, worn with blue jeans and a white dress shirt, clacked softly on the pavement. His longish hair, worn to just below his collar, blew with random abandon.

Just that morning Susan had come into his office shortly after he'd arrived and tossed the *Star-Advertiser* onto his desk. "Have you read the paper yet this morning?" she asked, although Susan was well aware that he never read the paper before he got to the office.

"Something of interest I should know about?"

She nodded grimly. "Page two. A couple of black kids at Radford High were beaten up by some locals. They said they did it for Auntie Irene."

"Jeez." Pancho shook his head in disgust, picked up the paper, and turned to page two. Before he started reading he looked up at Susan. "Is Drew going to be around today, do you know? I'd like to see him after court if he's available."

"I'll call him." She turned and started for the door, but then stopped and turned back to Pancho, her craggy face still tight and grim. "Pancho, will Jackson be okay in jail? I mean, some of those *mokes* could eat him for lunch."

Pancho frowned. "Good point. Let me read this, then maybe I'll talk to the warden and see if we need to take some precautionary measures. Last I talked with Jackson he seemed okay. Even though he's a skinny little kid, he looks so damn mean it may the first time in his life it's worked in his favor. But thanks for bringing it up. I should've thought of it sooner."

Pancho read the article. The two black kids were sons of military families. Before this event they had gotten along well with the other kids in school. They had even been on some of the same athletic teams as their assailants.

When he finished the article, he picked up the phone and called OCCC, the O'ahu Community Correctional Center.

***

Drew was waiting in Pancho's office that afternoon when he got back from the arraignment. The big man was reclining on the brown leather couch on the wall across from Pancho's desk. His huge feet stuck out well past the end of the couch. He was reading the paper. When he saw Pancho, he moved to sit up, grimacing. Pancho knew both of Drew's knees were bone on bone, that he would need a total knee replacement in each leg sooner, rather than later.

"Don't get up on my account," said Pancho, but Drew was already past the painful part and sat up on the couch. He smiled.

"Damn things tighten up if I stay in one position for more than five minutes." He tossed the paper aside. "Everything go smoothly at the arraignment?"

"Nothing much to go wrong. Did you read the article about the black kids being beat up at Radford?"

Drew nodded. "Disgusting, but not surprising. When I first moved here, I thought Hawai'i really was a paradise, even when it came to bigotry. But even though it's a hell of a lot better than most places, there's still an awful lot of prejudice and racism. Mostly it's below the surface, which, to me, makes it all the more insidious."

Pancho's six-foot frame leaned back in his desk chair and he interlocked his hands on top of his head. "Yeah. When I first started practicing, most of the court personnel were local Japanese, and a lot of the young *haole* attorneys would complain that they were mean, or standoffish, or whatever.

"Maybe it was because I grew up in a largely Hispanic place and had to learn to get along, but I never had a problem. I just gave everyone the respect they obviously wanted and got along just fine. But I've had any number of *haole* and even black clients complain bitterly to me about what an awful racist place this is and how they couldn't wait to get back to the mainland. It was the white guys who irked me the most. For the first time in their lives, they were the minority. They didn't like being called 'haole,' as if it were some sort of racial epitaph."

Drew chuckled. "It's only a racial epitaph when they put the word 'fucking' in front of *haole*."

Pancho gave a wry, fleeting smile. "The irony is that I know damn well that when they were back home on the mainland, they were the ones who would've been doing the discriminating. At first I took it on myself to lecture them, hoping they'd learn how to get along being the minority and that maybe, just maybe, they wouldn't be the bully when they got back home." Pancho sighed and sat up in his chair. "But then I realized I was wasting my time."

Drew rubbed his left knee. "Unfortunate but true, my friend. Once someone becomes a bigot, it's pretty hard to turn them into someone else. I grew up in Oceanside, CA, where there're a lot of Samoans, so even though some of us are darker than our black brothers, we didn't get a whole lot of that shit. But once we ventured out in the real world, things changed." He laughed through his large nose, crooked from multiple breaks over the years. "Until they found out I was Polynesian. For some reason I've never figured out, we Polynesians are 'exotic.'" He made air quotes with his hands. "So somehow, okay, whereas blacks were just, well, black. Go figure."

"Anyway," said Pancho, "I talked to the warden this morning and they'd already put Jackson in protective custody, which, unfortunately, means that he's kept in a tiny individual cell. It's disgusting. But I don't know what else to do. The warden said there'd already been several death threats against Jackson." Pancho smiled an ironic looking smile. "Seems like even the big bad criminals loved Auntie Irene."

He looked from Drew down at the thin file on his desk. He picked it up. "So, have you solved the case yet, Mr. Private Dick?"

Drew chuckled. "Not quite. I've been trying to talk to the owner of the security company for the shopping center and the secretary keeps putting me off. Do you suppose the flow of information from the prosecutor's office has started yet?"

Pancho shook his head and tossed the file back onto the desk. "All I know is that Jackson's fingerprints were on the purse, which was found right outside the bathroom he was exiting when arrested. I don't even know why he was arrested, since they couldn't have known his fingerprints were on the purse at that time. And, of course, our client can't remember squat."

He frowned and picked the file up again. He opened it and leafed through the police report until he came to a page toward the end. "This is pretty weird, though. Most of the things that would ordinarily be in a woman's purse were found in Auntie Irene's glove compartment. Make-up kit. Tissue. Wallet with photos." Pancho looked up at Drew. "She apparently took out her license and credit cards and put them in the inside zipper of the purse. They were still there when the purse was found."

Drew nodded slightly. "Yeah, I read that, too. I've been meaning to talk to you about it, but I was trying to make sense out of it first. The only thing I can think of is that she emptied her purse to make room for something else." He paused for a moment, rubbed his jaw absently. "But what? And why wouldn't the thief take her credit cards?"

Pancho shrugged and let the file drop to the desk again. "Which raises the question of whether the thief knew she had something worth stealing in her purse that night. Something more important than credit cards."

"So you think this may have been more than just an opportunistic robbery gone wrong?"

"I think," said Pancho, "that it's something we should keep in the back of our minds." He picked up the police report again. "There's a short list here of other things found within a hundred yards of the murder scene. Did you go through that? Anything you think might be important?"

Drew shook his head. "I did, and offhand I don't think there's anything related to the murder there." He took the report from Pancho. "An empty Coke can. A quarter. An old fashioned black plastic men's comb. A squashed McDonald's Quarter Pounder cardboard box. One woman's earring, apparently cheap costume jewelry, which didn't match what Auntie Irene was wearing. And a rubber slipper."

Pancho leaned back in his chair, locking his hands on his head. "The comb and the slipper could be from an assailant."

Drew nodded and tossed the report back onto the desk. "Yeah. A long shot. But there are no prints. There could probably be some DNA on each, but I doubt the cops will be doing a full DNA match run unless and until they have another suspect. Jackson was wearing both slippers, and he probably wouldn't use that kind of comb for his hair, but I'm sure the cops at least checked that out."

The two men sat silent for a while. They could hear the seemingly incessant buzzing of the phones and Susan's ever patient voice through the office wall. Drew finally broke the silence.

"Pancho, you know how the personal injury lawyers sometimes put an ad in the newspaper asking for any witnesses to an accident to come forward? Why don't we try that? Let's put an ad in the *Star-Advertiser* asking for anyone who was in the vicinity of the makai parking area between Longhi's and Nieman Marcus around the relevant timeframe to contact the office."

Pancho thought for a moment. "Can't hurt. We can't afford to run it for long, but it's worth a try. I'll draft something and give it to Susan to call in. We'll run it on and off until just before the trial."

Outside, the late afternoon sun had turned into a huge orange orb, sinking fast into the darkening ocean.

"I'm trying to interview the other two women in Auntie Irene's trio," said Drew. "Maybe they'll know if she had anything of value on her."

Pancho gave a kind of facial shrug. "Who knows? Or maybe they know if someone's been stalking her."

***

A few moments after Drew left, Susan stuck her head in Pancho's office. "I'm leaving now. Anything you need me to do first?" She walked into the room, looking closely at Pancho. "You okay, hon?"

Pancho nodded, but his face was drawn and sad looking. "Just having a selfish moment of feeling sorry for myself," he said. "I've got a case I didn't want and about which many people are going to hate me. I've got a client who's getting death threats and who, despite everything, is pulling at my heart strings like I've never felt on behalf of a client before. This'll be my first murder case since I started having those stupid panic attacks. And I'll be turning away good paying cases so I'll be able to devote most of my time to a court-appointed case that'll pay me ninety dollars an hour in court and sixty out while my fixed overhead is well over a hundred bucks an hour."

Susan walked to Pancho's desk and leaned down, putting both hands on the desk. Her husky voice was soft but determined. "You believe in this kid, Pancho. You're the best attorney in town for him. We're fine financially, and if the trial runs long and we run into trouble I'll take a cut in pay for a while. This is what you do. This is who you are." She grinned at him while taking a step back, patting her hair bun self-consciously. "And this is why you'll probably die a lonely old man."

Pancho laughed out loud, transforming his demeanor. "Ouch! Good one, Suse. But you forget I've got Paula now."

Susan turned and began walking toward the door. She looked back as she walked. "And you damned well better hang on to her is all I'm saying."

When she was gone, Pancho thought about what she'd said. Susan knew him better than anyone, and she was right that this was his kind of case. It was a case he could believe in. He had a client for whom he felt an overwhelming, almost paternalistic, need to protect.

Pancho swiveled around in his chair and looked out the window at the dusky evening. The lights at the Aloha Tower Marketplace below him looked festive but somehow made him feel uncomfortable. Not sad, really, but what? He ran his fingers through his hair, an unconscious habit he usually did when he was pondering something.

Fear. The word came to him in a flash of understanding. What if he couldn't protect Jackson? What if he wasn't up to the enormity of the task ahead?

Nine

Bernard Singer, M.A., Ph.D., M.D., stroked his gray beard thoughtfully, an affectation Pancho noted the first time he retained the neuropsychologist/neurologist on a case six years prior. Singer's untrimmed eyebrows reminded Pancho of former Soviet leader Leonid Brezhnev. Pancho had to work hard not to stare at the mass of hair over each eye, as his brows moved up and down when Singer talked.

"All of the medical tests are negative," Singer was saying. "There is no cardiac or vascular disease that would account for the syncope. Which means that my preliminary diagnosis of stress-induced syncope is most likely correct. I don't think he has any Axis III diagnosable mental illness, but I would definitely say that at the very least, he has Axis II borderline personality disorder, which, I might add, isn't surprising, based on what we know about his upbringing."

Pancho allowed his gaze to wander around Dr. Singer's Kahala office while the doctor talked so that he wouldn't stare at the eyebrows. The office was large and lined with bookshelves. The carpet was a plush tan in keeping with the low lights and overall soothing environment the doctor obviously sought to create. His desk was piled high with papers and open books. There was a couch against the only wall where there were no bookshelves. Above the couch was a window with closed curtains.

Pancho sat in an uncomfortable chair facing the heavy wood desk. Dr. Ginsberg, his family doctor, had recommended that Pancho see a psychologist when he began having panic attacks, but although Pancho used psychologists and psychiatrists often as expert witnesses, he couldn't bring himself to seek treatment from one. He was determined to work through the attacks on his own.

"What does borderline personality disorder mean in terms of Jackson?" asked Pancho.

"Well, it's a classical manifestation in many ways. He sees himself as worthless, even evil. To some extent, it's as if he feels like he doesn't exist at all, or at least that he shouldn't exist at all." Singer interrupted his beard stroking and began absently pulling on a particularly long piece of eyebrow hair. Pancho had to look away.

"With regard to relationships," the doctor continued, "a patient with borderline personality disorder may have hazy relationships, love-hate relationships, which I think is probably how Jackson views his mother. On the one hand, he's sympathetic toward her, not blaming her for wanting to abort him, etc. On the other hand, like most everyone, he desperately wants to be loved, so there is suppressed anger at his mother for not loving him."

"Are these people dangerous?"

Much to Pancho's relief, Singer went back to working on his beard. "Not necessarily. But they can often become enraged with little provocation and exhibit inappropriate anger, often leading to violence. They may also become suicidal, but I didn't note any suicidal ideations with Jackson."

"What about the loss of memory?" asked Pancho.

"Well, it's certainly not unusual to have memory loss just prior to passing out. But Jackson claims to have no memory from the time he walked up the ramp from the park side of the shopping center to go to the restroom. That wouldn't be attributed to the syncope, I don't think. More likely it would be the result of the concussion he suffered when he hit his head on the concrete floor of the bathroom." The doctor paused and stopped playing with his beard. "Of course, we can't rule out the possibility of some sort of significant psychological trauma that might have occurred before he got to the bathroom. That could theoretically account for the subsequent stress induced syncope and could account for the memory loss of the event itself."

"You mean like murdering Auntie Irene?" asked Pancho.

Singer nodded slowly. "That, or witnessing her murder."

***

Two hours later, Pancho sat across from Jackson in the small interview room at O triple C, O'ahu Community Correctional Center.

"Why'd you go an' bother mama, Pancho? You know she don' wanna have nothing to do with me. She don' wanna be reminded of me." Jackson's voice was small and fearful, as if he thought his mother or, thought Pancho, more likely his Aunt Clio, would rush in and give him a beating.

"Two reasons," said Pancho calmly. "One, I thought she had a right to know that you were in trouble. If she didn't care, then fine, but if she cared and wanted to help, then I think she had a right to make that decision. Two, I wanted to find out more about you so that I can help you as best I can."

Pancho watched Jackson as he processed what Pancho had just said. Instead of constantly looking down at his hands as he had done during the first interview, this time Jackson leaned back in his chair and looked up toward the cracked and peeling ceiling. Pancho waited him out, until Jackson finally looked back at Pancho and, in a tentative voice, almost a whisper, he said, "What'd she say?"

"Well, first of all she was shocked that your aunt had told you about the rape and about how your mother wanted an abortion. She never intended for you to know any of that. Which, if you think about it, Jackson, shows that she did care enough about you to try to protect you from all that. She also told me that you'd been a good kid and that she didn't think you could ever hurt anyone."

There were tears welling up in Jackson's eyes. He didn't avert them and he didn't wipe the tears away. He looked at Pancho almost as if he was in a kind of trance. The misting gray eyes, so young and vulnerable looking, contrasted sharply with the ugliness of the snarling face.

"She said that?"

Pancho nodded and leaned forward, holding Jackson's gaze. "Yeah, she did. I think the poor woman really wants to be able to love you, but she just won't allow herself to forget where you came from."

Jackson let tears fall unimpeded for several seconds more before finally swiping at his eyes with his right hand, then once again looking up toward the ceiling.

"I think I knew that," he said softly.

Ten

obby Lopaka lay on his big leather couch in his Waimea study
listening to Gabby Pahinui sing Hi'ilawe. He'd known Gabby in
the old days and, as he listened, he let his mind wander, thinking
about all the guys who were gone now, thinking about the good times.

There used to be impromptu luaus almost every weekend on the Big
Island. They would sit around on the beach, often at Hapuna Beach before
there was any hotel, eating *lau lau* and *opihi* and fresh *poi* and drinking
Primo beer by the gallon. Any one of the several great entertainers like
Gabby would start playing music and Bobby would lie back on the sand
and watch the stars and feel like he was the king of one of the greatest
places on earth.

The door to the study opened and Rigger entered without knocking.
The song was winding down and Rigger respectfully waited for it to
end before turning off the iPod in its docking station. With the music off,
Bobby could hear the wind howling outside. The fog was low, thick, and
wet, and he knew it was cold, colder than most tourists would believe it
could get in Hawai'i.

"I hear Scotty Gouveia found his security guard who had
disappeared," said Rigger.

Bobby pulled himself up to a sitting position, grunting as he did
so. "And?"

"Not much yet. Our guy just let me know that Gouveia finally tracked the guy down. He's still on O'ahu, but he's been hiding out at some place in Ka'a'awa."

"Hiding out? Meaning he's guilty of something?"

Rigger shrugged, non-committal. "Probably. We don't know yet. Gouveia is confronting him even as we speak. Our guy is outside in the yard, so he doesn't know what's going on. He called me on his cell when they found the guy."

"How come Scotty didn't call us when he found him?"

Rigger smiled, a crooked, evil-looking smile. "That's what we're going to find out."

Bobby grunted in acknowledgement and understanding and laid back down on the couch. "Turn Gabby back on when you leave."

***

Scotty Gouveia held the Glock loosely at his side. Marcus Young sat on the tattered and dirty tropical print cloth couch looking up at his boss.

"I neva' do nothing, Scotty. Honest. I was too far back when that black fucka wen go after Auntie. By the time I got to her she was dead already. I got scared 'cause I knew this was super kine important to you, Scotty. Once I ran, which I know was seriously stupid, I figured I couldn't come back 'cause I already looked guilty. I fucked up brah, but I swear I neva' wen kill her."

Scotty looked around the room. It was filthy. The kitchen counter was strewn with frozen dinner boxes and empty cans of beer. The sink was filled with dirty dishes. Newspapers and clothes looked like they'd been randomly thrown about the room. The plate glass window looking out to the rough ocean was caked with salt water and dirt. A new-looking flat screen television hooked up to an Oceanic cable box was tuned to a porn station with the sound off.

"Who's place is this?" asked Scotty.

Marcus looked around, almost as if he wasn't sure where he was. He shrugged. "Just a guy I know. He lent 'em to me for stay awhile."

"Who else is living here?"

"Nobody. Jus' me."

Scotty looked behind him and saw a dinette chair close by. He pulled it to him without taking his eyes off Marcus and sat down. "Now tell me what really happened," he said.

Marcus was a typical looking 'local,' which meant that he was a combination of any number of ethnicities, Japanese, Hawaiian, *haole*, and probably some Portuguese. His hair was jet black and straight, which he wore down to the base of his neck. It looked stringy and unwashed. His round face was well tanned. He was obviously doing his best to keep his Eurasian eyes as wide open and as innocent looking as possible. He wore a dirty white tee shirt that had a Quicksilver logo on the front. His shorts were plain blue knee-length swimming trunks. His dirty bare feet were wide, 'luau feet', from growing up barefoot.

"I wen tol' you already, Scotty. I fucked up and didn't get to Auntie in time. So I panicked and ran."

"Bullshit." Scotty's tone was matter-of-fact, dismissive without argument.

"Honest . . ." Marcus began, but Scotty raised the Glock and fired to the left of Marcus' head, blowing out the dirty window to the beach.

"What the fuck! What're you doing, man?"

"What happened?" asked Scotty again.

When Marcus didn't answer right away, Scotty raised the Glock again and shot the television. Coitus interruptus, he couldn't help thinking.

Scotty's man, whom he'd left outside the small house to stand guard, looked into the broken window and Scotty nodded to him that everything was all right.

Marcus, whom Scotty knew was twenty-four years old, was visibly shaking. His eyes were still wide, but wide with fear instead of innocence. He looked to Scotty like he was about to cry.

"Well?" said Scotty, his voice still conversational. "Are you going to talk to me?"

Marcus was breathing deeply. He wiped at the sweat on his face. "C'mon, Scotty, brah, lemme go. I swear to God I was gonna do exactly what you told me for do, but this little black fucka wen get to her first."

Scotty shot the back of the couch, inches from where Marcus sat. "Bullshit. C'mon, Marcus, you know there are cameras all over the place. I saw you running with the black kid, like you were in it together.

I saw he had the purse and you had the ukulele case. So quit fucking with me, Marcus."

More shots rang out.

Eleven

It was a glorious spring afternoon, with only a few puffs of cloud in the absurdly blue sky. Hawai'i didn't use Daylight Savings Time, and it was finally staying light long enough for Pancho to get some surfing in at the end of the day. He rode his last wave at Queen's break, a languorous three footer, and paddled in. When he was still twenty-five yards from shore, he spotted Drew sitting on the beach, still in his 'work clothes' of green cargo shorts and an old silky aloha shirt.

"Hey, bubba, howzit?" said Pancho as he plopped his old red Velzy surfboard down next to Drew's hulking figure, then sat on top of the board.

"Man, I wish I was still able to surf with you. It looks great out there." Drew's knees had finally forced him to give up surfing, the only sport he'd still been able to do until recently.

Pancho smoothed back his wet long hair. "I know. I miss you out there. It's more fun to share it with someone."

Both men were quiet as they watched a scantily clad young lady walk down to the water's edge and proceed to splash water onto her body. Drew chuckled. "Do you think she knows people are watching her?"

"She'd be devastated if she thought they weren't. She knows she's got a world class *okole*, that's for sure."

"Well then, why's she covering it up with that string?"

When the girl finally waded into the water and dove under, Pancho turned back to Drew. "So, is this a business house call or are you looking for dinner company?"

Drew leaned back onto his elbows. "Both. I brought you some discovery documents that just came in. Susan and I thought you'd want to see them right away." He sat up and brushed sand off his hands, then picked up a manila folder that had been lying next to him. As he handed it to Pancho he said, "It seems they have an eyewitness who identified our guy."

Pancho felt like his heart skipped a beat. He opened the folder and began reading. Drew went back down on his elbows. After several minutes Pancho closed the folder and handed it back to Drew so it wouldn't get wet from his surfboard. "Doesn't look good. I assume you read it?"

Drew nodded, taking the file back. An older man coming out of the shopping center into the parking lot had seen a "slightly built black man" running away from where Auntie Irene's body was found moments later. The black man was holding what looked like a purse. It looked like he was being chased by a man in a short sleeve white shirt and black pants. The ethnicity of the man in the white shirt was not stated.

"Anything to attack?" asked Drew.

"Maybe. I think it's worth filing a Motion to Suppress, but I won't be too optimistic about it."

The sun was sinking fast, a huge pink ball. The beach, which minutes before had been emptying of beachgoers, was now becoming populated with tourists dressed for cocktails and dinner, ready with camera in hand for the nightly sunset show. There was just a breath of wind, but it was enough for the still wet Pancho to shiver himself into action. "Let's get inside and have a beer. Then we can walk into Waikiki for dinner."

Ten minutes later, the surfboard was stowed in its locker in the parking garage of Pancho's condo and Drew was sitting on Pancho's lanai overlooking the ocean with a can of Stella Artois in hand. The sun had set with no hint of a green dot, and the lights of Waikiki to his right were beginning to twinkle invitingly.

Pancho came out of his bedroom, showered and now also wearing cargo shorts. He pulled on a plain blue polo shirt and smoothed his hair. "Tell me what you notice about the photo line-up."

Drew put the beer down on the side table, picked up the folder, and leafed through the pages inside. "Wellll," he drawled out, "all six of the guys are dark skinned. That's good, yes?"

Pancho nodded. "If by 'good' you mean proper procedure, yes. What else?"

"Two of the guys look like dark skinned Polynesians. The rest of the guys are obviously black." He looked up at Pancho. "Good or bad?"

"Good, so long as they're dark enough to fit with the original description by the witness. It keeps the possibility open that the assailant might not have been black, so it was fair to include them. What else?"

"Hmmm. Let's see, all the other black guys look to be older than Jackson."

"Anything else, Mr. Private Investigator?"

Drew studied the photos closely. When he looked up at Pancho again he was smiling. "Facial hair. All but Jackson have some kind of facial hair. And," he continued before Pancho could comment, "all are obviously much bigger than Jackson."

Pancho was nodding in agreement. "Well done. I think we can argue that the line-up was flawed by making Jackson stand out by virtue of being the only clean shaven one in the group. The size is important, too. Even though the witnesses only had the mug shots to work from, it's pretty clear that all five of the other guys were much bigger than Jackson."

Drew closed the file and put it back on the side table. "Still, it's kind of worrisome that an eyewitness identified our guy."

"No shit, Sherlock. Let's go eat."

Twelve

Eleanor Ho'opai was several years younger than her Cousin Auntie Irene, but the years hadn't been as kind to her. Her hair was already completely gray and her light brown face was lined and slack and had a worn look that conflicted with the gentle temperament for which she was famous. She had long ago given up trying to fight her weight. Instead, she wore big *mu'umu'us* which, she joked, had been made for her special by Omar the Tent Maker.

Drew learned nothing from Auntie Hazel, the third cousin in the Auntie Irene trio. Nothing more than what everyone in Hawai'i already presumed about Irene, which was that she was a wonderful, caring, talented person, a perfect ambassador of Hawaiiana. Now he was in Eleanor's wood frame home at Kealakekua Bay, just south of Kona on the Big Island of Hawai'i. He sat rigid on the living room couch, afraid to lean back against the Hawaiian quilt draped over the back and which was so spectacular that he assumed it was an antique. One wall was chock-a-block full of awards and photos. Three ukuleles sat in display stands on a koa wood credenza. Eleanor's bass leaned against the wall.

"Sit back and relax," Eleanor said as she returned to the room carrying a tray with a tea set. "You're not going to hurt anything. Do you like the quilt?"

Drew accepted a cup of tea and nodded. "Very much. Is it an antique?"

Eleanor laughed. "Only if you consider me an antique. I'm proud to say that it's my handiwork. Quilting is a hobby of mine."

Drew complimented her again on the quilt, then nodded toward the large picture window that looked out on Kealakekua Bay, which was a deep, rich blue, just a shade or two darker than the cloudless sky. The Bay was bordered by lush foliage. Drew tried to imagine what the area would have been like when Captain Cook dropped anchor in the Bay in 1779. Probably a lot less lush, he decided.

"And your house is wonderful. What a spot. Has it been in the family long?"

Eleanor beamed. "Yes. I actually grew up here. A lot of the houses around here are still in the family." Her smile faded a notch. "Irene's family home is just a block away."

"I didn't realize that. I thought she lived on O'ahu."

Eleanor put down her cup and poured Drew more tea. "We all grew up on the Big Island. Even Hazel, who never comes back except to play a gig."

"Why's that?"

Drew watched the sparkle leave Eleanor's eyes. She waved a hand dismissively. "I shouldn't have said anything, although it's not exactly a secret."

Drew smiled. "Now you have to tell me. The detective in me is demanding it."

Eleanor looked at him for a few beats, then seemed to make a decision. "Hazel's husband, Danny, was also from here. We all grew up together. They'd been together since junior high school and were very much in love. Danny was a good guy and a loving husband, but he didn't have much in the way of ambition. His idea of a perfect day was to smoke some *pakalolo*, have a few beers, and go fishing. The trio was doing pretty well, so Hazel let Danny do what he wanted. She never pushed him to work. He'd do odd jobs, sell his fish, harvest *opihi*." Eleanor made a face. "Yuck. Sea snails. I think I was the only one in my family that hated them.

"Anyway, what Hazel didn't know was that Danny had also started doing jobs for our cousin, Bobby Lopaka." She paused and looked questioningly at Drew. "Do you know who he is?"

Drew nodded. "Sure. Who doesn't?"

"Well, Danny began growing *pakalolo* for Bobby. A lot of it, up just *mauka* from where we are. Bobby gave Danny some guns to guard the site against poachers."

Drew thought he knew where the story was heading now.

"So one day some tourists were hiking and they decided to follow the trail through the jungle that Danny used to get to his weed. To everyone's bad luck, it happened to be on a day that Danny was there. He heard the couple coming and figured them for poachers." Eleanor stopped and sighed heavily. "Long story short, one of the tourists was shot and killed and Danny is serving a life sentence for murder."

"Jesus," Drew said softly. "What happened to Lopaka?"

Eleanor snorted derisively. "What do you think? Nothing. He tried to give Hazel money, but she refused to take it. She won't have anything to do with that side of the family anymore, and she stays as far away from the Big Island as she can manage."

"What about you and Irene? Did you folks continue to associate with Lopaka guys?"

"Not me so much, although I still go to big family *luaus* and don't make it a point to ignore Bobby if he's there." She nodded to Drew's cup. "More tea?"

"No, thanks."

"I don't blame Bobby so much. Danny made his decisions. No one forced him to grow dope."

"What about Irene? Was she still close to that side of the family?"

Drew thought he detected a slight change to Eleanor's demeanor, but it was subtle and fleeting.

"Irene is, was, probably the closest to Bobby. Their family connections were the strongest. She married the son of one of Bobby's oldest friends, and Bobby was Jimmy's godfather."

"Who's Jimmy?"

Eleanor looked surprised. "I'm sorry, I thought you must've known. Jimmy was Irene's son. Both he and Irene's husband were killed in a horrible car accident on the old Saddle Road." She paused and wiped a strand of gray hair from her face. "Gosh, that must have been fifteen years ago. Irene never got over it."

"But she stayed close to Lopaka?"

Eleanor made a face, as if she didn't know exactly how to describe the relationship between Irene and Bobby Lopaka. "I don't know about close, but I know she went up to Waimea to visit fairly often. She didn't talk about it much, especially after the thing with Hazel's husband."

Drew was listening intently. He wasn't sure if there was any relevance to the question, but he figured that anytime a gangster is injected into a murder investigation, the realm of possible scenarios expands exponentially.

Eleanor seemed to be thinking, and he gave her time, hoping she had more to say. "There was a time," she finally continued, "right after Danny was convicted, that Irene acted like she was on Hazel's side and professed to be angry at Bobby for getting Danny involved. But that didn't last long, and Irene and Bobby became close again. She went up to see him pretty much every week." She absently sipped some tea, then looked out at the bay for a moment.

"I don't know what the relationship between them is now," she finally said. "Was," she corrected. "I mean, Irene and I used to be best friends. We told each other everything. But once she started going up to Waimea every week or so, she kind of clammed up on me, at least about what she and Bobby talked about."

Drew shifted his huge frame on the couch and leaned forward. "How old is Lopaka now? He must be in his eighties."

Eleanor smiled broadly. "He is. If you're wondering if their relationship was sexual in any way, that, I can assure you, was not the case."

"Then what do you think it could have been besides just family friends?"

Eleanor pursed her lips. "That may be all it was."

"But?"

"But Bobby's the kind of guy who just seems to, I don't know, overcome some people. Like he just takes over their lives." She shook her head. "It's hard to describe."

"Meaning Irene may have been into something illegal?"

Eleanor frowned, as if it was inappropriate to be so blunt. "I'm not sure what I meant. I asked her once; not if she was doing something illegal, but if she was doing business with Bobby. She got upset with me and didn't talk to me for several days after that. She wanted me to think

I had insulted her, but I didn't buy that. I'm not sure why, but I didn't. In any case, I never asked her about it again and we eventually settled back into our usual relationship, with the exception of my never talking to her about Bobby again."

Drew leaned back against the beautiful quilt and thought about what Eleanor had said.

"Eleanor, may I ask you something?"

She chuckled good-naturedly. "Seems to me that's what you've been doing since you got here."

Drew smiled. "What I mean is, you know I work for the attorney defending the man accused of killing your cousin. So why are you so willing to talk to me? A lot of people would tell me to get lost."

Once again Drew saw Eleanor's expression change. He could see that she was searching for the right way to answer the question.

"Let me put it this way," she finally said. "If your client did it, I hope he's convicted and put away. But from what I've read, it seems a little too pat to me. I mean, where were the contents of the purse? I read that it was found empty. Where was the ukulele? Why would an accomplice knock your client out so close to the scene of the crime? If he wanted to rip your client off, why not wait until they were both safely away, then do it somewhere less public? And what could Irene have had in her purse that would make one assailant want to rip off the other one? It wasn't like she was rich or carried a lot of cash on her." She paused, but Drew could tell that she wasn't finished and he kept quiet.

"So what I'm saying, Mr. Tulafono, is that I want you to investigate this case. I want you to try to get to the truth of what happened. I know that's what Irene would want, too."

Thirteen

The day was already hot and sticky as Pancho walked to court for the hearing on the Motion to Suppress Photo Line-up he had filed. The wind had shifted from the usual trades to the southerly Kona winds, which were generally light and induced an increase in humidity. He had his linen sport coat slung over his shoulder, but he could still feel the onset of perspiration under his arms. When he got to Ka'ahumanu Hale he saw several pickets at the entrance to the portico. The television crews were there as well. Pancho sighed heavily.

Justice for Hawaiians read one sign. *Malihinis go home,* read another. A *malihini* was a newcomer or stranger to Hawai'i, and there was no question in Pancho's mind that in this context, it was aimed at the fact that Jackson was African-American. His stomach tightened in disgust. He walked quickly through the throng, ignoring the shouted questions by the reporters.

He was already not in a good mood. He'd had a full blown panic attack at his desk that morning. It had been so severe that he began to doubt it was only a panic attack, but was instead an actual heart attack. It began to subside just as he'd made the decision to ask Susan to call an ambulance. The residual scare of the attack and the gut tightening fear that he might have one in public put him in a foul state of mind, and the weather and now the ignorant demonstrators were not helping.

The day before, Pancho received a call from Estelle, Judge Makena's clerk, to say that Judge Hirota was going to hear the Motion. Judge Alan Kingsley was the trial judge assigned to the Jackson Steele case, but pre-trial motions were heard before the motions Judge. That should have been Judge Herman, whom Pancho liked and admired, but according to Estelle, Judge Herman was called away to the mainland for a family emergency. Judge Hirota had agreed to hear Pancho's motion.

So this is how I get repaid for taking this case on, thought Pancho. The mutual animosity between Judge Hirota and him was legendary in the Hawai'i judiciary. They were bitter enemies when the Judge was a prosecutor, and things hadn't changed when he somehow got appointed to the bench. He was arrogant, vindictive, and, in Pancho's opinion, none too smart.

Thirty minutes later, and only ten minutes into the Motion, the Judge sustained yet another weak objection by Harry Chang, the lead prosecutor in State of Hawai'i v. Jackson Steele. The Judge's face was narrow and angular, and his eyes were perpetually flitting around the room, as if looking for someone. "Move on, Mr. McMartin," said Judge Hirota in a voice that sounded more like a hiss. Pancho glanced at Harry Chang, who had retaken his seat and was looking at him with a barely suppressed smile. *Harry's having way too much fun,* thought Pancho, as he turned back to the witness.

"Detective Wong, at the time of his arrest, did the Defendant have any facial hair?"

The detective glanced down at his file for a moment, then looked back up at Pancho. "No, sir."

"Yet all of the men in the photo array except the Defendant had facial hair of some kind, isn't that correct?" The detective looked down again and studied the file, as if the question had taken him by complete surprise.

"Yes sir, that's correct," he said finally.

"So if we were to pick someone in the photo array as standing out by being different in some way from the five others, Mr. Steele would be the one to stand out, is that correct?"

Wong shifted in his seat and again pretended to study the file, then he shrugged. "I guess you could look at it that way if you wanted to."

Pancho turned and picked up his own file from counsel table. "Detective Wong, can you tell the court what else in the array makes Mr. Steele stand out as being different from the others?"

This time Wong looked genuinely perplexed as he stared down at his file. Pancho stared at the top of Wong's head for a full ten seconds before the face reappeared. "I'm not sure what you mean."

"Then let's go through the photos one by one, Detective. How old would you estimate the subject in photo number one to be?"

"Objection, Your Honor." Harry Chang was on his feet. "How would the detective be expected to know the ages of all the men in the photo array?"

Pancho didn't respond to the objection. Even Judge Hirota had to give him this one.

"Overruled. That's part of the detective's job, Mr. Chang. Proceed."

"Thank you, Your Honor." Pancho looked back to Wong. "Detective?"

"Oh, I guess I would say around thirty-five or so."

"And number two? That's the Samoan subject, yes?"

"Yes, he's Samoan. I would say he's about twenty-four or five."

Pancho took Wong through each photo, saving Jackson's for last. "How old is Jackson Steele, Detective?"

"Nineteen."

"So, the closest subject in age to the defendant would be five or six years older?"

Wong glanced up at the Judge, then over at Harry Chang. "That's about right, I guess, but let me add, and I don't mean this in any kind of racist way, it's much harder to tell the age of dark skinned people, so I don't see the age differential as anything significant here."

Pancho noticed that Harry Chang had his face buried in his file.

"One more thing, Detective. How did the eyewitness describe the build of the person he saw running from the murder scene?"

Detective Wong didn't look down at his file this time. "Slightly built."

"So let's take a look at Jackson Steele's mug shot photo that was used in the array. It's pretty easy to tell he is slightly built from that head shot, isn't it?"

Wong took a moment before finally nodding. "Yes, I guess so."

"But once again, let's look at all of the other photos. Every one of those men have large heads and necks, suggesting a much bigger build than Mr. Steele, would you agree with that?"

Out of the corner of his eye, Pancho could see that Harry Chang was rising before the question was finished. "Objection, Your Honor. Calls for speculation."

Pancho sighed and looked to the Judge, waiting a beat before responding. He felt the objection was so weak that the Judge should overrule it without asking for argument from Pancho, but obviously that was not going to be the case, so he rose and addressed the Judge.

"Your Honor, as you correctly pointed out with regard to the age issue, a trained police detective should be able to provide an opinion as to someone's build by studying a head shot. Heck, even lay people should be able to do that."

Judge Hirota sniffed. *He doesn't look pleased, but then,* thought Pancho, *he never does, except maybe when he's sustaining an objection against me.*

"I'll allow the question. Please answer, Detective."

Detective Wong seemed to shrug the question away. "I guess you could say that the other guys look bigger than the defendant, but I wouldn't say that it necessarily jumps out at you."

The Motion went on for another twenty minutes, but Judge Hirota was ready to rule even as the last words came out of Pancho's mouth.

"The Motion to Suppress is denied. I find no evidence that the photo array was unduly suggestive or in any way biased against the defendant in this case. In fact, I applaud the Honolulu Police Department's efforts to make the line-up as fair as possible."

The Judge rattled on for a few more minutes, but Pancho tuned him out and put a hand on Jackson's shoulder. His client had sat through the hearing without having moved a muscle that Pancho could tell. He'd briefed Jackson before court was in session about what would transpire, but he wasn't sure if Jackson comprehended much of what was going on. Pancho squeezed Jackson's shoulder as the Judge finally finished and whisked himself away in a flurry of black robe.

"We lost?" The childlike voice coming out of the ugly sneer never failed to take Pancho by surprise.

"Yeah, we lost. But don't worry about it. I thought it was a long shot. All it means is that when we go to trial the photo line-up can be admitted into evidence. I can still attack the weight of the evidence and will be able to cross examine the eyewitness who picked you out of the lineup." Pancho could see the blank look on Jackson's face.

"But how can someone say I was runnin' from the murder scene when I don't think I was even there?"

"We're going to argue that the person identified the wrong person, that it must have been someone who looked like you."

Jackson nodded slowly. "Okay." He saw the sheriff coming to take him away and he stood. He looked down at Pancho, who was stuffing his papers back in his leather briefcase. "Thank you, Pancho. I know you trying real hard for me."

***

Drew was sitting on the edge of Susan's desk when Pancho walked in from court. One look at him and they both knew he'd lost the Motion to Suppress. Pancho was about to walk through to his office without stopping when Drew reached out and grabbed Pancho's arm.

"Try wait, bossman. You gotta see this." Drew picked up the sheets of paper and held them out to Pancho. "The toxicology report on Auntie Irene just came in."

Pancho took the papers and scanned them, then he tossed his briefcase onto the outer office couch and reread them. Drew and Susan watched him with bemused smiles. When Pancho looked up at them his face showed his surprise.

"Auntie Irene was a heroin addict?"

"That's how we read it," said Susan.

"Track marks and all," said Drew.

"Holy shit," said Pancho.

Fourteen

B obby Lopaka nodded to the weathered looking *paniolo* who had ridden the *mauka* fence line with him that morning and dismounted. Another cowboy took the reins and led his horse away. Bobby turned to his son, who had been leaning against a fence rail, obviously waiting for him. Rigger wasn't looking forward to the conversation he was about to have with his dad. He took Bobby's elbow and led him toward the main house.

"Fucking Scotty killed the guy," Rigger said when they were alone.

"You mean his employee? The one who disappeared after the murder?"

"Yeah, him."

Bobby walked along in silence for a few moments. "Why?"

"He claims he was torturing the guy for information and the guy died." Rigger spit into the dirt. "It's all fucked up."

"Well, did he get any information?"

"Not according to Scotty. He says the guy knew he'd be in deep kim chee once Auntie was murdered, so he ran. Scotty claims he shot both kneecaps and the fucker still never admitted any involvement."

Bobby chuckled. "Scotty did that? I wouldn't have thought he had it in him."

"Yeah, well, it ain't all that funny, Pops. Now that guy is dead, we don't know for sure what he told Scotty and we aren't any closer to finding out who killed Auntie."

The two took off their shoes at the kitchen door and walked inside. The cook was at the stove, stirring something in a large pot, and the father and son nodded to her and walked through to the study.

Bobby sat behind his desk. Rigger threw himself down on the couch. "So," said Bobby, "didn't you have a guy at the scene? One of Gouveia's guys? What'd he say happened?"

"Oh, he confirms Scotty shot the fucker, but he doesn't know if Scotty got any more information out of him than Scotty told us. Scotty had our guy bury him in the hills above Malaekahana."

Bobby toyed with a cigar. "So why is Scotty still walking around? Seems to me you have to find out what he knows."

Rigger frowned. "You want me to have Winston question Scotty? Maybe kill him? I'm not so sure that's a good idea right now. The cops are all over the shopping center thing, and having Scotty disappear at a time like this could lead to all sorts of shit."

Bobby lit the cigar and the room quickly filled with smoke. "Could be right," he mumbled, the cigar still in his mouth.

"For now I think we work with the premise that Scotty is telling the truth. If you think about it, he'd be fucking crazy to lie to us. He knows what Winston would do to him. He has a damn good thing going with the agency. Why would he throw that away for peanuts?"

Bobby cocked his head. He took the cigar out of his mouth. "I'm not so sure he would consider that peanuts, but I get your point. Let's watch him closely, though. I don't like the fact that he didn't turn the guy over to us right away. What'd he think he was doing? Trying to look good to us? Like maybe he wants to be a real bad guy instead of some pissant businessman?" He shook his head from side to side. "Stupid fuck."

Rigger smiled, stood, and walked over to his dad. He leaned over and kissed the top of his head. "I've got to get back to Honolulu. I'll keep you posted, Pops.

Fifteen

A s summer approached, the days got longer and hotter. The Jackson Steele trial was scheduled to begin in a few weeks, and Pancho's anxiety level was increasing exponentially. Drew was working full-time on the case but didn't seem to be making much progress. He'd given Pancho some background information on the eyewitness that Pancho hoped would provide good ammunition for cross-examination, but Drew was running into a dead end on the connection between Auntie Irene and the notorious Bobby Lopaka.

Auntie Irene's heroin addiction had to be related to her relationship with Lopaka, but what, if any, role might it've played in her death? Drew had even tried the direct route of asking for a face to face meeting with Lopaka, but it was refused.

Pancho had just finished a one day misdemeanor trial in district court and was debating whether he should catch up on office work or head out and catch the tail end of a South Shore swell when he heard Drew's unmistakable deep voice in the outer office. A moment later there was a knock on the door, then Drew entered.

"You look like shit, man. What's wrong?" asked Pancho.

Drew eased himself down onto the couch and leaned back. "I feel like I'm bashing my head against the wall is what's up," he said. "Nothing seems to pan out."

Pancho sighed inwardly. No surfing for me this afternoon, he thought. He bent over, opened the bottom right drawer of his desk, and brought out a bottle of Patron tequila and two glasses. After he poured two shots, he got up and took Drew's to him. He couldn't bear to watch the big man get up so soon. They toasted to nothing, and Pancho went back to his desk chair.

"So what's the latest dead end?"

"The surveillance videos from Ala Moana Center," said Drew.

"I thought we got all that through discovery? We didn't see anything besides Auntie Irene leaving the gig. There was a security guard walking behind her. That's it. Wasn't it?"

"Yeah, but remember you and I had talked about getting more videos from different locations? Like near the restrooms where they found Jackson?"

Pancho nodded. "Yeah. We sent out a subpoena for those weeks ago. I'm supposed to meet with our security expert, but I keep putting him off pending receipt of the videos."

"And we haven't received jack. I had Susan call the court reporters and they said the security agency was stalling, something about having a hard time finding the right date. Sounded like bullshit to me. So I went to the main office of Paradise Security Systems and talked to the owner, a guy named Scotty Gouveia."

"And?"

Drew took a sip of Patron. "And he seemed like a nice enough guy, but he said the video files are recorded over after two weeks. So when his people type in the date and time of the file they want to review, nothing comes up. He did say that he reviewed what he thought were all of the relevant video files right after the murder and didn't see anything unusual. He had them burned to DVD. He released the one that showed Auntie Irene and says he had the others filed away, but now they can't find them. He assured me he wanted to cooperate and that we'd get everything we wanted."

Pancho gave Drew a crooked half-smile. "Like right after the trial is over?"

"What I don't understand," said Drew, still serious, "is why the cops aren't all over them. Why didn't the cops get all of the video files for the day of the murder?"

Pancho thought about that, then he picked up the phone and punched in some numbers.

"Harry Chang, please. Pancho McMartin calling." He looked at Drew, smiled, and took a sip of his drink.

"Harry, howzit?"

He listened to Harry complain about how overworked he was.

"Yeah, me too," said Pancho when the rant was over. "Listen, man, don't you guys have all the surveillance videos for Ala Moana Shopping Center on the day of the murder?"

Pancho fiddled with a pen in his left hand and his drink in his right as Harry told him the cops were doing their best to get the tapes.

Finally Pancho said, "Yeah, I'd appreciate that, Harry. *Mahalo.*" He hung up and looked at Drew.

"Harry sounds as frustrated as you are. He says he talked to Detective Wong, and his guys have been all over Gouveia's *okole,* but they're getting the same story. He promised to redouble his efforts and get back to me."

Pancho noticed that Drew was looking at him with a strange look. It wasn't exactly humor, but something akin to it. "What?" asked Pancho. "Why are you looking at me like that?"

Now Drew really did break into a smile. "Because, my dear friend, I haven't finished. After I met with Gouveia and got nowhere, I decided to do a little checking on him. Guess who he bought the security business from?"

Pancho thought for a moment, but then shook his head. "Who?"

"Auntie Irene's cousin and apparent buddy, Bobby Lopaka." Drew didn't say anything for a few moments, then added, "That's how Paradise got the Ala Moana account, not to mention the airport and Blaisdell Arena accounts."

Pancho ran his hand through his hair and scrunched up his face. "Are Gouveia and Lopaka still in bed together?"

"As best I can tell, and I'm sure you can appreciate how lightly I have to tread on this, Gouveia got a sweetheart deal on the business and, in exchange, he pretty much does whatever bidding the Lopaka syndicate wants from him. But there's no formal business relationship there."

Pancho reached into the drawer and pulled out the bottle of Patron. He poured himself another shot, then got up and poured Drew a shot. The late afternoon sun was pounding in through the floor-to-ceiling windows and the room was getting warm. Pancho clicked a button and window shades lowered, providing immediate relief.

"So let's think this through," he said. "Auntie Irene is Lopaka's cousin. She's apparently close to him and her other cousin and trio partner doesn't rule out that she might have been involved in something with Lopaka. Irene is hooked on smack and I think we can assume the Lopaka guys are still heavy in the drug trade. Irene is murdered at the Ala Moana Shopping Center where Lopaka's former security company provides the security." He snapped his fingers. "In fact, just before she's murdered, the one DVD we do have shows a security guard following her out of the gig she'd been working. He was possibly the last man to see her alive."

Pancho pulled the Jackson Steele file to him and rifled through some papers, then he looked up at Drew. "But I don't even see that the cops have identified that guard, let alone interviewed him."

Drew was nodding. "You're right. I already checked. There's nothing. So I asked Gouveia about the guy. He gave me a name." Drew looked down at his notes. "Marcus Young. But he said the guy has disappeared. Hasn't been heard from since the day of the murder."

"What?" Pancho was out of his chair. His face was rapidly turning pink with anger. "Wait, wait, wait. Do you mean to tell me that the guy in the surveillance tape who was following Irene from the party has been missing since the night of the murder and there isn't some kind of warrant out for his arrest? A material witness. Whatever. What the hell's going on here?" Pancho began pacing the room.

Drew gave Pancho a wan smile. "Gouveia said the guy called in a couple of days later and said that he quit and ran away because he felt so bad about what happened to Auntie Irene. He claimed that he stopped following her when she got on the escalator to go down to the mall level where her car was parked, so he doesn't know anything. He won't say where he's living now." Drew paused, but then added, "Gouveia says he told the police about the phone call."

Pancho stopped pacing and picked up the police report, which he scanned for a few minutes. Drew watched him, saying nothing. Finally Pancho looked up at Drew again. "Then why the hell isn't that in the police report?" His voice was hard, angry. "Next thing you're going to tell me that the missing guy is black."

Drew shook his head. "Sorry. It isn't going to be that easy. It was some local dude. I told you I feel like I'm banging my head against a wall. Everything's just so elusive."

"Well, we need to find him. And soon. I can't believe the cops are just accepting the hearsay from Gouveia about some absurd phone call. What the hell's up with this Detective Wong anyway? A guy doesn't just give up a good job and leave town if he doesn't have something to hide."

Just then Susan stuck her head in. "You boys fighting or just loud talking?" She was smiling, and it took some of the wind out of Pancho.

"Sorry. I got a little hot under the collar about something." He looked concerned. "We don't have any clients out there, do we?"

Susan shook her head, still smiling. "No. And I'm out of here. I'll lock the door behind me so you can holler your little *okoles* off." She paused and looked down at Drew, still sitting on the couch. His broad behind had squished the cushions to pancakes. "Or maybe not so little *okole* in your case, big boy. See you tomorrow."

Pancho sat back down in his chair. He looked and felt deflated. "Another Patron?"

Drew shook his head no. "I'm going to try to find friends or neighbors of this Marcus Young and see if I can get a lead on where he might've gone. Do I have permission to hire a mainland PI if I get any kind of lead?"

Pancho waved a hand. "Hell, yeah. Whatever it takes. Let's find the guy and get to the bottom of this. I don't want Jackson going down because the cops won't do their job."

When Drew let himself out, Pancho was pouring himself another shot of Patron.

Sixteen

rew's knees were killing him. He'd been in and out of his car and up and down stairs for two days straight trying to find someone who might know where Marcus Young, the missing security guard, could be. So far, it had been more dead ends. This morning he'd located a former roommate living in a run-down wood frame house in Manoa, near the University. Naturally there was a long concrete and lava rock stairway from the sidewalk to the front porch. Drew was sweating, and his knees felt like they were being stabbed with ice picks by the time he reached the front door. He took a moment to look around and catch his breath.

The house had been white at some point, but the paint was almost all peeled off, leaving exposed wood that looked perpetually damp and rotting. An old easy chair sat on the porch, its cloth covering torn in multiple places so that stuffing was visibly seeping out. There was a slight odor of mildew.

Drew knocked on the door, hoping he was early enough for someone to still be home. He assumed the house was shared by several University of Hawai'i students as the university was only a few blocks away. A slight Asian woman in her early twenties opened the door. She looked tired and irritated at having to answer the door. She wore a tank top and no apparent bra. She had intricate tattoos on both arms, from her shoulders to her elbows.

"Yeah?" She had a long way to look up to Drew's face.

"Hi. I'm looking for a guy named Marcus Young. Do you know him?"

She shook her head and scratched at her arm. "Naw, but I heard of him. He used to live here. I think I'm in his old room. What you looking for him for?"

"I'm a private investigator and I think he may be an important witness in a case I'm working on. I'd like to find him and interview him to find out."

"Witness to what?"

"Murder."

Her eyes widened and she stopped scratching. "Oh wow."

When Drew saw she had nothing more to say, he asked, "So, are any of the guys who lived here when Marcus did around?"

The girl shrugged and began scratching again, but she moved back into the house, opening the door wider as she did so. Drew took it as an invitation to enter. He followed her as she walked across the dank and dirty living room toward the kitchen. She wore tiny short shorts and her legs were thin as rails.

"I think Billy Boy may still be home," she said over her shoulder. "He was pretty wasted last night so I doubt he's up and about yet." She walked into the kitchen and opened the refrigerator door. She peered inside. Drew leaned against a counter full of dirty dishes. They looked like the old plastic cafeteria dishes he used to wash when he was in school. A cockroach skittered across the counter. A bountiful feast for the roaches, thought Drew.

"Anyone besides Billy Boy?"

She closed the refrigerator without having taken anything out. "Candy may've been here then, but I'm not sure." She turned from the fridge and looked up at Drew. "Want me to wake Billy Boy?"

"Would he want to be wakened?"

She shrugged and a smile played at her mouth. "Who cares?" She walked out of the kitchen. Drew stayed where he was, still leaning against the counter. Every so often he could hear little sounds of scurrying cockroaches under the pile of dishes. The smell of old grease, cockroach shit, cigarettes, and stale beer made him slightly nauseous. The florescent light in the kitchen was too bright. Drew would have liked to go back into the living room, but in contrast it was too dark. He closed his eyes and willed away the throbbing pain.

A few moments later he heard voices, one raised in anger, and he assumed it was Billy Boy giving the girl grief for waking him. A minute after that, a man who looked to be in his mid-twenties literally staggered into the kitchen, his right arm up to shield his eyes. He wore only striped boxer shorts. He was 'local'—dark skinned, squat, Samoan style tats around his biceps, long jet black hair, and eyes that were only part Asian.

"What the fuck?"

Drew chuckled. "Nice meeting you, too. You must be Billy Boy."

Billy Boy opened the fridge and stared inside, just as the Asian woman had done. Drew assumed there was nothing inside that wasn't either rotten or alcoholic, because eventually Billy Boy slammed the door shut just as his roommate had done.

"I'm looking for Marcus Young," said Drew.

Billy Boy's eyes had adjusted to the light and he took his arm down. He went to the sink and pushed aside some dirty dishes so he could get his mouth under the faucet to drink, then he wiped his mouth with his forearm and looked at Drew. "Jesus you're a big motherfucker. Did you play football? You that Samoan dude who used to play for San Diego? Drew, yeah?"

"That's me."

Billy Boy smiled for the first time. He looked younger when he smiled. "Sweet. I used to watch you when I was little." His gaze swung down to Drew's huge knees, exposed below his cargo shorts. "Your knees are all fucked up, yeah?"

Drew nodded, and Billy Boy went under the faucet for another drink of water.

"Yeah, Marcus used to live here," said Billy Boy after he had once again wiped his mouth with his arm. "But he hooked up with some babe from UH and moved out about six months ago."

"Do you know where he went?"

Billy Boy made a face which conveyed that Marcus could have gone anywhere. "Don't know. The girlfriend was living with her parents at Mayor Wright housing in Kalihi, so I doubt he would have gone there."

"Do you remember her name?"

"Just the first. Amy. She was pretty cute. Part Korean I think." He grinned. "Those fucking Koreans get one serious temper, though."

"Do you know if Marcus had any close friends or family who might know where he is?"

Billy Boy's face turned serious. "Why you like find him, anyway? He do something wrong?"

Drew kept his face neutral. "I don't think so. But he may have been a witness to a murder, so it's important that I find him."

Billy Boy's face seemed to light up with excitement. "You mean that murder at Ala Moana? Auntie Irene? Whoa!" He pushed some pans aside and pulled himself up so he was sitting on the counter. "Yeah, man, now that I think about it, he was working at Ala Moana as one security guard, yeah? Shoots, that's cool. You think Marcus did it?"

"Why would you say that? Was Marcus violent?"

Billy Boy started scraping some hardened food off a plate with his fingernails. "Nah. I was just wondering. If he was there and now he's gonzo, maybe he's the killer."

Drew shook his head, more to himself than to convey anything to Billy Boy. The guy sounded excited about Marcus being the possible murderer. He watched Billy Boy focus on the plate for a moment, scratch, scratch, scrape.

"So, Billy Boy," Drew tried again. "Any ideas where I might find Marcus or someone who might know where he is?"

"I'm guessing his work don't know where he stay?"

"You guess correctly. I wouldn't be here bothering you so early if I could have just found him through work." Drew realized his tone had gotten a little sarcastic, which Billy Boy picked up on.

"Hey, brah, no need get li' dat. I'm just trying for help."

Was it Drew's imagination or was Billy Boy's Pidgin getting thicker as they talked? Drew raised the palms of his hands in apology. "Sorry, man, but I've been at this for days now, my knees are killing me, and I don't seem to be any closer to finding Marcus than I was when I started. So I'm just a little frustrated is all."

"No worries," said Billy Boy brightly. His moods seemed to change by the minute. "Try go to Mayor Wright and find some Korean couple with a daughter named Amy. If that don't work, try go out to Ka'a'awa and find one guy everyone calls Booger. He and Marcus used to surf together. They were pretty tight at one time. Maybe they still are."

Drew pushed himself away from the counter, preparing to leave. "The girl who woke you said there was a roommate by the name of Candy who might've been here when Marcus was here. Do you think she might know anything more?"

Billy Boy shook his head. "Nah. Candy hardly knew him. She's a stripper and works at night, so she and Marcus never wen' have much for do with each other."

As Drew slowly and painfully made his way back down the stairway to the sidewalk, he greedily sucked in the fresh air.

***

Drew skipped trying to find a Korean couple with a daughter named Amy in Mayor Wright housing. The housing project was too big and, with only two story buildings, too spread out to undertake such a search. Besides, his knees were in full rebellion mode. He would have to get some drugs out of his orthopedist if he was going to start canvasing a low income housing project.

Instead, he drove straight to the other side of the island, to the small oceanside community known as Ka'a'awa. He pulled into the 7-Eleven across from the beach park and hit pay dirt within minutes. One of the customers overheard Drew ask the clerk about someone named Booger and came over to the counter. He was a middle aged man who looked mostly Hawaiian. He wore a dirty red bathing suit and a tattered and sweat-stained tee shirt. His rheumy eyes were red, which contrasted with the dark, leathery, face.

"Yeah, I know da guy Booger. But he no stay. His house wen get all shot up."

Drew felt his pulse quicken. "When was that?"

The man looked up, like the answer would be written on the ceiling. "Oh, shoots. Week, maybe more."

"Was someone shot there, do you know?"

The man was shaking his head before Drew had finished the question. "Don't know. I think there was one guy staying there for a few days before it wen happen, but no more nothing after. Booger hasn't been around since."

Drew got the location of the house out of the man, but not much else. He paid for the beer the man was holding and left to find Booger's house.

As it turned out, Drew could have walked to the house, even with his bad knees. It was a small, single frame wood house on the ocean. Drew pulled into the driveway and parked on the sparse lawn. He knocked on the front door and called out. When there was no answer he walked around to the back. The strong ocean breeze struck him the moment he turned the corner. The reef was several hundred yards out, where good sized swells were breaking. The trade winds were strong enough to cause white caps inside the reef.

Drew immediately saw that the plate glass windows in the living room were broken. On inspection he saw a bullet hole in one of the wood posts on the lanai. Glass crunched under foot as he peered into the house. It was sparsely furnished with a tattered cloth couch and a dinette set. One of the dinette chairs had been pulled up by the couch. A flat screen television looked like it had been shot.

Drew tried the lanai door and found it was unlocked. He walked in, calling out just to be safe. The small kitchen reminded him of Billy Boy's house. It was filled with dirty dishes and all sorts of trash. Drew wondered if transients had been living in the place since the shooting. He wandered through the two bedrooms and one bathroom, but saw nothing out of the ordinary. He looked for bloodstains amid all the stains on the couch, floor, and walls, but there was nothing he could definitively identify as blood. Other than confirming that the place had been shot up, the house told him nothing.

Disappointed, he decided to leave through the garage, which had a door into the kitchen. He opened the garage door for light and looked around. There was a green kayak leaning against one wall. He was surprised it hadn't been stolen. There was an old push style lawn mower next to the kayak. A small workbench was empty except for a couple of empty beer cans and some balled up papers.

He unfolded and looked at the papers, just some receipts for work done on a 2000 Mazda. He looked to see if there was a license plate number, but there was nothing. It was a generic receipt from the kind of booklet one could buy in any stationery store. Drew tossed the papers back on the workbench and was about to leave when he noticed a small white rectangular card encased in plastic. He picked it up. It was a bicycle registration. The name read: Davis P. Bogarty.

"Bogarty," Drew said aloud, then, also aloud, "Booger."

Seventeen

Two weeks before the trial of State of Hawai'i vs. Jackson Steele was scheduled to start, two hikers found the badly decomposed body of Marcus Young. Rigger called his dad to let him know in case he hadn't seen it on the news yet.

"Where'd they find him?"

"Just off some ranch road up mauka from Malaekahana."

"So," said Bobby, "at least we know Gouveia wasn't lying about the little shit being dead. But what we don't know is whether the rest of the story is true, or if Gouveia is playing us."

"I'm keeping an eye on Gouveia, but he'd be completely *lolo* to try to burn us. My problem is that now I don't see how we can know for sure whether that *popolo* kid was really the killer, or if there's someone out there who got away with murder."

Rigger heard his dad cough on the other end of the line. The old man had a bad cold and sounded miserable.

"Well," rasped Bobby when he finally got his cough under control, "if you believe Gouveia and believe he got everything he could get out of his employee, the little *popolo* going on trial is guilty. But if that's the case, where's the shit?"

"Gouveia should have left it to us to question the guy," said Rigger. "But it's still possible there was an accomplice that the security guard didn't see."

"Mmm." More coughing.

"Pop, you better take it easy. You sound like shit. Go back to bed."

***

After Pancho heard the news story about the hikers finding the body of Marcus Young, he called Drew and asked him to come by the condo. Paula, who was an investment counselor with Morgan Stanley, was supposed to wine and dine some mutual fund managers that night and Pancho had begged off. He told Drew they could go to dinner at Michel's, virtually next door, so that Drew wouldn't have to walk far. Now the two sat on Pancho's lanai. The summer sun was low on the horizon, an enormous orange ball against a backdrop of fading pale blue. A few tourist dinner cruises were in position to watch the nightly spectacle. One lone outrigger from the Outrigger Canoe Club was heading in to shore.

Pancho poured them each a shot of Patron over ice. "Okay," he said, "what do you make of it?"

Drew shook his head. "Man, I'm seriously confused. I mean, think about what we have so far. One of Hawaii's most loved entertainers, someone presumably beyond reproach, turns out to be a heroin addict. She's related to and buddy-buddy with the man reputed to be Hawaii's number one gangster. She has a gig at Ala Moana where the security company was at one time owned by the same said gangster. Whether there are still any connections between the company and Lopaka we don't know. But we can see from the security video that when Irene is leaving the gig, she's followed by one of the security guards, Marcus Young.

"We don't seem to be getting any other videos anytime soon, so we don't know what else will show up, but Marcus Young disappears and now turns up dead. Our guy is passed out in the bathroom, but his fingerprints are all over Irene's purse, which was tossed into the trash just outside the bathroom." Drew paused, obviously thinking. "Oh yeah, and Marcus Young's buddy, some dude named Booger, is also missing."

Drew took a sip of his tequila and nodded at Pancho. "Did I miss anything?"

"Just the eyewitness who supposedly saw Jackson running away from the murder scene, possibly being chased by someone who could have been Young."

Drew smiled wanly. "Oh yeah, how could I forget?"

"What it tells me," Pancho said, "is that there's a whole lot of stuff going on here that we don't understand, which points to other people being involved. It sure as heck isn't a coincidence the security guard disappeared, then gets murdered." He ran his hand through his hair. "And I'll bet you a hundred bucks that Lopaka is right in the middle of whatever's going on."

***

Scotty Gouveia's normally brown, pock-marked face was red. Spittle flew from his mouth as he yelled at his right hand man, Tiny Tanaka. "You assured me that no one would find the fucking body." His voice took on a mocking, imitative tone. "'That fucka's so well buried they won't find him until the end of the next ice age.' Isn't that what you said? Well that was the shortest fucking ice age I've ever heard of."

Tiny stood stoically in front of Scotty's desk in the small office. "Boss, I swear, he was well buried. But I think the feral pigs probably dug him up. Then it was just bad luck for the hikers to come along. They weren't even supposed to be there. That's private property."

Scotty snorted in disgust. "You took the body up there in your pick-up?"

Tiny nodded.

"Well, you better go and wash it down again. Go over it with a fine tooth comb. No blood. No hairs. No fibers. No fucking mud from the ranch road. Got it?"

Tiny nodded again. When Scotty didn't say anything further, he turned and left the office.

Scotty pulled at a nose hair. He had long suspected that Tiny worked for the Lopakas, which was why he'd kept Tiny at a distance while Scotty was interrogating Marcus. Making Tiny dump the body made him an accomplice to murder, which, reasoned Scotty, on the one hand would serve to keep Tiny's mouth shut, while on the other hand, made Tiny a witness the prosecution could turn against Scotty if they ever got on to him. *A fine fucking mess I got myself into*, thought Scotty.

Eighteen

Pancho took a seat in Harry Chang's cramped office on Bishop Street. The walls were stacked high with banker's boxes labeled with the case names. Unboxed files took up almost every remaining square inch of the office. Harry's diplomas and Bar admission certificate hung crookedly in cheap fake wood frames behind his desk.

Harry himself looked pale and exhausted. Pancho thought he looked even bigger and rounder than the last time he'd seen him. Although Pancho never used it, he could see how Harry got tagged with his 'behind-the-back' nickname, Pillsbury Dough Boy.

"Jeez, Harry, you look worse than I feel." Pancho pushed a file on Harry's desk aside so he could put his Styrofoam cup of coffee down.

Harry expelled a large breath and rubbed his eyes. "Man, this shit is killing me, Pancho. You don't need an associate by any chance?"

Pancho smiled. "What, the famous Harry Chang going over to the dark side? That'll be the day."

"Yeah, probably." He put his hands on his belly, and Pancho couldn't help thinking that he looked like a modern day, overworked Chinese Buddha.

"So what, Pancho? We gonna deal this one? As far as I can tell you don't have much to work with."

Pancho's expression turned serious. He leaned forward in his chair. "Harry, I don't have much to work with because the cops are fucking with me—I suspect with you, too."

Harry's face remained impassive, a trial attorney's face. "What do you mean by that?"

"C'mon, Harry. Where's the evidence we should have by now? We have a week to trial and we still don't have all the security videos. And what's going on with the investigation into Marcus Young's death? Don't tell me it's just a coincidence that doesn't have anything to do with this case. And what about Auntie Irene's drug habit? Just another coincidence?"

Harry raised his hands in a conciliatory gesture. He kept his voice calm. "No one's fucking with you, Pancho. The owner of the security company is trying to find the DVD's he burned, but he assures us there's nothing on them."

Pancho looked out the one dirty window trying to gather himself. "And you buy that, Harry? Seriously?"

Harry shrugged good naturedly and replied in mock Pidgin English. "I neva' get one real choice, eh?" Then, more serious, he said, "What d'you want me to do, raid the place?"

"Sure, why not? Withholding evidence is a crime, last I checked. And what about the Marcus Young case? And the heroin angle?"

"Pancho, chill out, man. The police tell me they're investigating the case. They apparently have few clues so far. If anything turns up that connects that case to yours, you'll be the second to know, right after me. Regarding the heroin addiction, as far as we can tell, all that does is besmirch Auntie Irene's reputation. From what we can tell it has nothing to do with her murder." He put his hands back on his belly. "Why don't we deal the case, Pancho? Take some stress off both of us." It didn't escape Pancho's attention that this was the second time Harry had mentioned a deal.

"You making an offer?"

Harry shook his head. "No authority right now, but if you want to talk about it, I can see what Ron would be willing to do." Ron Shigemura was the chief prosecutor, Harry's boss.

Pancho chuckled. "You know I don't negotiate against myself, Harry. If you want to come to me with an authorized offer, I'll take it to my client." He picked up his coffee cup. "Until then, I'd appreciate you getting on someone to get the rest of those security videos and find out why the security guard who may've been the last person to see Auntie Irene alive, disappeared immediately after the murder, then showed up dead." He stood. "I think any jury is going to want the answer to that before they convict some poor schmuck who was in the wrong place at the wrong time."

"Yeah, with his fingerprints on the dead woman's purse," Harry shot back.

"Get some rest, Harry. We both have some long days ahead."

Nineteen

Five days before the trial of Jackson Steele was to begin, Pancho walked into the office and saw Susan pick up the Honolulu *Star-Advertiser* from her desk and hold it out to him.

"Front page," she said. He took the paper and missed-call slips and headed into his office.

It took Pancho only a couple of seconds after settling into his chair to see what Susan wanted him to read. He felt a tightening in his throat as he read the headline:

RACIAL TENSIONS FLAIR
AS STEELE TRIAL NEARS

He read the article quickly. A black kid at Roosevelt High School, born and raised in Honolulu, was set upon by a gang of thugs as he walked home from school. He was badly beaten, and though he surely knew at least some of his assailants, he steadfastly denied that he could identify any of them. At Mililani Middle School, two black kids were severely beaten. The doctors said one would have permanent neurological damage to his left ear.

Civic and religious leaders spoke out against the racially motivated violence. An op-ed piece in the *Star-Advertiser* called for "a return to the spirit of aloha." A fringe Hawaiian group issued a statement that, while condemning the violence, said all of the non-Hawaiians who were now living on stolen land should immediately leave and refrain from further degrading the *pono* of the sacred *aina*, referring to the moral sanctity of the land.

***

.

Pancho received his first death threat the Friday before trial was to begin. The usually unflappable Susan burst into his office holding a piece of paper. Her whole body was shaking and she began to cry. Pancho jumped up and ran to her.

"What's wrong, Suse? You okay?"

She couldn't answer. She was hyperventilating. She held the paper out to Pancho. He took it and read it. "To the scumbag lawyer with the Mexican name. You and your little nigger client will die a slow and painful death. The way Auntie Irene had her head bashed in. You better watch out."

Pancho placed the letter on his desk and took Susan into his arms. The sturdy, motherly figure he knew so well felt frail. The chopstick she used to hold her hair bun in place poked against his chin. He held her until she got herself under control, then he sat her down on the couch and got her a glass of water.

"What's going on, Pancho? This isn't what Hawaii's supposed to be. Maybe it's still that way on the mainland in some places, but . . ." She looked up at him, wiping at her tears which made her look old and tired. "Do you think it's for real? Should you call the police?"

Pancho sat next to her and put his arm around her. She leaned into him. "I doubt it's anything more than bluster," he said. "If someone wanted to kick my ass they'd probably just do it and not write about it. But I'll report it anyway." He paused, thinking how to say what was on his mind without causing Susan more worry. In the end he just decided to say it. "In the meantime, I want you to lock the front office door while we're here. No one gets in that we don't already know or has an appointment. Okay?"

She nodded, and he thought she was probably so scared she didn't realize yet that she was at risk, too.

***

The rest of the afternoon passed with nothing more exciting than one crank caller who told Susan that if her "fucking *haole* boss got that little black bastard off, there will be hell to pay." She thanked him for his "kind words" and hung up.

Drew came by not long before Susan was ready to leave for the weekend. She asked if he'd heard about the letter and he said he had. She reached out, grabbed his hand and pulled him close to her desk, motioning for him to bend down so she could whisper in his ear.

"Keep an eye on him, Drew. Don't you let anything happen to our Pancho." Her voice was stern and cracked with fear and intensity.

Drew squeezed her hand gently. "Don't you worry, Suse. Nothing's going to happen to our boy." What he didn't tell her was that Pancho had called him to come in and make sure no one followed Susan to her car. Once she was away from the office they figured she would be anonymously okay.

***

Pancho hadn't intended to say anything to Paula about the death threat, but good old Susan had already called her and told her to keep an eye out. Now they were in bed in Pancho's condo. Pancho had his left arm around her and she rested her head on his chest.

"I'm scared for you, Pancho. Maybe you should have Drew hire a bodyguard to stick with you until the trial is over."

Pancho gently rubbed Paula's bare back. Her lightly tanned skin was smooth and soft. He stared through the sliding glass doors that looked out on the ocean. The small waves that made it past the reef to break on shore made a soothing whooshing sound. The sky was brilliant with stars.

"I'll be fine." Pancho's tone was light without being dismissive. "People who send trash like that are cowards. But don't worry, I'll take precautions and keep an eye out for weirdoes coming at me." Paula didn't respond, but he could feel her shudder. He knew she was trying to be strong, but he put himself in her place and thought about how he'd feel if she'd been threatened.

"Back when my parents were in school here," said Paula into his chest, "the whole Hawaiian movement was just starting. Most were legitimate and peaceful and were trying to grapple with some of the issues Native Americans on the mainland had already confronted. But some of the teenagers used it as an excuse for their delinquent behavior. There were a bunch of loose knit gangs who called themselves the Primo Warriors. They were mostly high school kids on drugs. They'd go around terrorizing *haoles* when they had the chance and thought they could get away with it. At some of the schools, there were 'beat up *haole* days.'"

Paula lifted her head to look at Pancho. "Hawaii's never been the perfect paradise some people make it out to be, but it was sure better than most other places. But now we have crystal meth and other drugs that make people act crazier than ever." She moved her body so she could bury her head in Pancho's neck. When she spoke again her voice was muffled and soft. "Just be careful, my love. I don't want to lose you."

Twenty

J udge Kingsley's courtroom was virtually identical to all of the other courtrooms in the Circuit Court. The walls, from waist high, were paneled with beautiful local koa, a reddish acacia wood that is endemic to Hawai'i. There were no windows and no pictures. On one side behind the bench was an American flag and on the other was the Hawaiian flag. The koa-paneled jury box held fourteen seats, two for alternates.

Pancho sat at the counsel table reserved for the defense. His briefcase sat unopened on the table. Behind him the wood railing with a swinging gate separated the court from the spectator section. It was eerily quiet. Pancho had long ago developed a habit of coming early to the first day of every trial to sit alone in the courtroom. He let his gaze wander and allowed his mind to drift. This was sacred ground to Pancho. This courtroom and the thousands of others across the United States were an integral part of a judicial system that was Pancho's veritable religion. This was where regular citizens came to decide right and wrong and pass judgment on their fellow man. This was, to Pancho, an essential part of the machinery that made America function.

He closed his eyes and tried to empty his mind, to get ready for battle, but instead of nothingness he saw Jackson's face. It wasn't the mean, ugly face he'd seen when he first met Jackson. Now all he saw was the young, scared, vulnerable boy who had placed his life in Pancho's hands.

He gave up on his meditation and opened his eyes. He looked down at his clasped hands on the table. They were tan in contrast to the white dress shirt cuffs that stuck out from the dark blue linen blazer. He picked his right hand up and held it out in front of him, palm down. There was a barely discernible tremor of nerves.

Pancho smiled to himself. *I look a hell of a lot better from the outside than I do from the inside*, he thought. His stomach was in a knot and his throat was dry. Never before had he wanted to help a client more than he did now. Never before had he invested so much of himself in a case. Never before had he started a trial afraid of how his own body would handle the stress. It wasn't a good feeling.

The previous afternoon Pancho had gone to visit Jackson in jail. He wasn't planning on putting Jackson on the witness stand, so he didn't have any real prep work for them to do other than to explain what was going to happen, so it took Pancho by surprise when, toward the end of their session, Jackson said he needed to say something.

"I think I remember something." Jackson's voice was soft, almost apologetic sounding.

"What's that?" asked Pancho.

"Well, I think I remember a moped coming right at me when I got to the top of the parking ramp. There was two guys on it. The one driving was black looking, like me, an' the other was a local guy. I was scared they was going to hit me. But just as they got to me the one guy, the black one, throwed this thing at me, which I caught—you know, automatic like. It was the purse."

Pancho studied Jackson for a moment. "When did you remember this?"

Jackson averted his eyes. "'Bout a week or so ago."

"How come you're waiting until now to tell me?" Pancho was trying hard to keep the frustration out of his voice.

"'Cause I was scared you wouldn't believe me."

"Why not?"

"Well, don't it seem kind of funny that I remember it just before we gotta go to trial? I mean, I don't know if I'd believe me if I was you."

Pancho took a deep breath, then let it out. "So do you remember what you did next? After you caught the purse?"

Jackson nodded. "Yeah. I ran. I knew I wasn't s'posed to have no purse on me, so I ran toward the bathroom. When I got there I throwed the purse away, fast as I could. Then I went into the bathroom and must have passed out, 'cause that's all I remember."

Pancho sat silent for a few moments, processing what Jackson had just told him. It did make sense, he thought. The doctor had told him that it was possible the memory lapse from the concussion could remedy itself and that he might remember things before the fall. It would explain the fingerprints on the purse and why nothing from the purse was ever found in the area. The excitement and fear of the moment may have been what triggered the syncope episode just then.

Pancho thought about how he would use this new information. He'd have to put Jackson on the stand, but he knew a good attorney like Harry Chang would make mincemeat of someone as childishly honest as Jackson. It would take about two seconds for Harry to get Jackson to admit he wasn't sure about his memory, or even to admit he wasn't sure that he didn't murder Auntie Irene.

Pancho heard the front door to the courtroom open and he turned to see Harry Chang enter, lugging his large trial briefcase and sweating profusely. A moment later the door to the Judge's chambers opened and Judge Kingsley's law clerk, Lester, entered with some files. The spectacle was about to begin.

***

Jackson, still in the shackles he was required to wear during transport, was brought in by two sheriffs. He was wearing a plain gray sport coat over a subdued aloha shirt and blue slacks. Pancho had purchased those items for him with great care. The jury would know Jackson was homeless, so Pancho didn't want him looking too sharp, but by the same token, he wanted him to look as respectful and respectable as possible. When he was at the defense table next to Pancho, one of the sheriffs removed the shackles. Pancho put his hand on Jackson's shoulder and gave him a reassuring squeeze. A few short months ago Pancho would have thought that the smile he got from Jackson was grotesque. Now it pulled at his heartstrings and he smiled back.

Jackson glanced back toward the spectator section where people were filing in and taking seats. He leaned toward Pancho. "All them people come to watch me?" he whispered.

"No. They're the jury pool. Certain of them will be called to take a seat in the jury box, over there. Then the prosecutor and I will be allowed to ask them questions to see if we want them on the jury. Once we have twelve jurors and two alternates, the trial will start. Then whoever you see sitting back there will be here to watch the trial."

When the jury box was full, the process called *voir dire* began. The attorneys for each side posed questions to the jury as a whole and, more often, to individual jurors. Pancho often asked what magazines someone read or what their favorite television show was. The purpose was to learn as much as possible about a potential juror so Pancho could make a decision on whether to keep them or use a peremptory challenge to knock them off. Rarely a juror would display blatant bias one way or the other such that the Judge would excuse the juror 'for cause,' so each side was allowed twelve peremptory challenges, for which they did not have to state any reason.

Harry's courtroom style was formal, even a little stilted. At 5'5" and overweight, he was not an imposing figure. He was in his late thirties. His hair was jet black and his round, Chinese-American face was soft, even kind looking, but Pancho learned a long time ago not to underestimate Harry. He was as formidable an adversary as there was.

The good thing about Harry, thought Pancho, was that Harry knew himself and had adapted his style to his personality. He didn't try to be theatrical or play the 'local boy' card many local attorneys tried to play when they came up against a *haole* like Pancho. Juries were not dumb and were more than capable of seeing through an act.

Pancho used *voir dire* not just as a tool to learn about the jurors, but as an opportunity to sell himself to the jury and educate them about the case. The more they liked and trusted him, the greater chance he had of convincing them of Jackson's innocence.

Pancho memorized the jurors' names as he filled them into his jury chart. When he stood to ask questions he did not use the podium and held no notes. He kept a respectable distance from the jury so as not to intimidate them, yet not so far away as to seem distant. He knew some of the issues in this case could be dicey. He focused first on a middle aged *haole* man in the second row, juror number ten, whom he knew owned a small construction company.

"Mr. Wilcox, I see from your information that your business office is in Iwilei, is that correct?"

"Yes sir, that is. Right on Iwilei Road in fact." The man looked around a little, as if uneasy because he was first to be questioned by Pancho. He had short cropped graying hair and a hard jaw line.

"I know there are a lot of homeless people who live on the streets in that area, and a lot more who go for meals at the Institute for Human Services. I'm wondering what you think when you drive by these people."

Mr. Wilcox seemed to sit up straighter in his chair. "I guess I wonder why they don't go out and get themselves jobs like the rest of us."

"Do you assume there are jobs out there for all of the homeless people?"

"Oh, I know there's probably some of them who can't work for whatever reason, but by and large I think that if someone wants to work, they can. Most of those guys I see on the street look like they're on drugs or drunk out of their mind, in the middle of the day."

Pancho nodded, as if he were weighing Mr. Wilcox's words carefully. "So if one of those homeless people were to be charged with a crime, would you assume the person was guilty?"

Now it was Wilcox's turn to nod. "Heck yes I would." He held up his hand as if to ward off another question before he finished. "But let me assure you that I'm a fair man, and if you can prove to me the guy wasn't guilty, then I'd have no trouble finding him not guilty." He leaned back in his chair, a satisfied look on his face.

"Mr. Wilcox, right now my client, Jackson Steele, is innocent under the law. It's not up to me to prove to you that he is not guilty, it's up to the prosecution to prove to you that he is guilty. Guilty beyond any reasonable doubt." Pancho paused and panned across the jury before turning back to Wilcox. "Now that you understand the law, do you think you can accept the fact that Jackson Steele sits before you as an innocent man?"

Pancho could see Wilcox's jaw clench and unclench. He looked from side to side at his fellow jurors, then, when he once again faced Pancho, he nodded.

"Yessir, if that's the law I'll go along with it."

Pancho stole a glance at Judge Kingsley, who was as impassive as ever. He then turned to juror number two, an attractive young Asian woman, and asked her some questions about her work.

After some fairly innocuous banter with a couple more potential jurors Pancho returned to one of the sensitive issues. "Now, ladies and gentlemen, can I have a show of hands from any of you who saw some of the news stories after this terrible murder where African-Americans, usually kids, were being beat up or bullied because my client, a black man, has been accused of killing Auntie Irene Kamaka?" About half of the jury raised their hands.

"Can I have the assurance from all of you that the color of my client's skin will have no bearing on your determination of guilt or innocence?" Most everyone nodded in the affirmative. Pancho looked at the few who hadn't and each one quickly nodded or muttered 'yes.'

"And as I have explained the concept of reasonable doubt to you, can I have the assurance from each of you, a contract, if you will, that unless the State proves Jackson Steele's guilt beyond any reasonable doubt, you will find Mr. Steele not guilty?"

The nods and muttered agreements came faster this time. Pancho couldn't help a quick glance at Mr. Wilcox before adding, "And as Judge Kingsley will instruct you, it's not up to the defense to prove that Jackson Steele is innocent; it's up to the State to prove that he's guilty, guilty beyond any reasonable doubt."

Pancho asked the Judge to excuse Mr. Wilcox for cause. Judge Kingsley then spent a few minutes asking Wilcox some questions. Although Wilcox repeatedly said he would follow the law if that's what he had to do, it was clear to everyone that as far as he was concerned, Jackson wouldn't be sitting in court on trial for murder if he wasn't guilty. The Judge finally excused Wilcox.

Pancho then bumped a former police officer and a retired teacher from Texas using peremptory challenges. Harry knocked off the lone dark-skinned man, a Samoan. He also used "preempts" on a UH professor of sociology and a law student. The jury of eight men and four women was, as far as Pancho was concerned, mediocre at best for his team. Harry seemed positively elated.

Judge Kingsley, a portly, prematurely balding man with a face badly scarred from teenage acne, pronounced that it was too late in the day to start the opening statements. Trial would commence promptly at nine the following morning. Pancho said goodbye to Jackson, then collapsed back into his chair. *Voir dire* was his least favorite part of any trial, but to dance around issues like race and homelessness made it all the more stressful.

"You look like I feel," said Harry as he sat next to Pancho.

"Hey, Harry. Looks like you got a pretty good jury."

Harry grunted. "Maybe. You never know."

Pancho looked at Harry. Although they were friendly combatants, it was unusual for Harry to come over and sit by Pancho after court. "Something on your mind?"

Harry gave Pancho a grim smile. "What? You no like *da kine* small talk? Okay, let's deal this case. I can do manslaughter and stand silent on sentencing."

Pancho raised his eyebrows in surprise. "That's an official offer?"

Harry nodded. "Yeah." He glanced around the courtroom. "This part is off the record, Pancho. Between you and me. If Frank Nip were still head detective in homicide I'd have no doubt that we'd be sitting here starting the trial of not one, but two defendants, with an air-tight case. As it is, Detective Wong has run a shoddy investigation. Our case is okay, but nowhere near what it should be. We have your guy's fingerprints and an eyewitness who saw him running from the scene of the murder, being chased by someone, probably the security guard. Not bad, but not what I would have liked. So I went to Ron and got him to give me authorization to deal."

Pancho ran his right hand through his hair, thinking about the offer and what it meant. Harry gave him time to think.

"It's not a bad offer, Harry, and I appreciate your candor. I'll take it to my client." He paused, deciding whether or not to say more. "The only problem I have with it is that I really think my client is not guilty."

"What?" Harry's voice rose an octave. "Oh, come on, Pancho. I'm trying to be open and honest with you and this is how you respond? Your guy is guilty as hell and we both know it. I just don't have the tightest case because of some lazy cops, and it's a testament and compliment to your trial skills that I acknowledge that you should be able to capitalize on that. So don't play games with me. Jeez." Harry looked away in apparent disgust and started to rise.

"Calm down, man. I said I appreciate the offer and I said I'd take it to my client, and I will. But I'm being totally honest with you about thinking Jackson is innocent. It makes it harder for me to sell a deal that could put him away for twenty years."

Harry was on his feet by the time Pancho was through talking and he looked down at Pancho, his face still showing his anger. "Yeah, well, I guess that's why you do what you do. But I've never known you to be so gullible before. Let me know as soon as you can." He turned and walked out of court, lugging his trial briefcase as if it weighed two hundred pounds.

Pancho sat still, alone in the courtroom just as he'd started the day, until Lester, the Judge's law clerk, stuck his head in and asked if Pancho still needed the courtroom. He wanted to lock up.

"I'm out of here. Thanks, Lester. See you tomorrow." Pancho rose slowly. He felt tired. He packed up his briefcase and checked his watch before heading out. It was still early. He debated going straight home to catch an hour or two of surf. Another summer swell was hitting the South Shore. He knew it would help clear his head and energize him, but then he realized he had to go back to the office to get his keys. With an audible sigh he steeled himself for the onslaught of reporters he knew would still be waiting for him outside the courthouse.

Twenty-One

Susan followed Pancho into his office and waited for him to toss his briefcase onto the couch and sit at his desk. She handed him a pile of pink 'while you were out' slips.

"You look awful, Pancho," she said.

Pancho's eyes crinkled in amusement. "Thanks, mom."

"I'm serious. You need to go home and get some rest. You know what Dr. Ginsberg said. There's only one call I think you should return before you leave. The rest can wait." She watched while he leafed through the pink slips. When he looked back up at her she could see he was looking at the one she meant.

"Did you talk to this guy? Do you think he's for real?" Pancho's demeanor had changed in a flash. His face looked energized and excited.

"I did and yes, I think he's for real. At least he was convincing to me. Give him a call. I'll come back in when I see you're off the phone and you can bark some orders at me."

Pancho watched Susan walk out of the office. He didn't know if it was his imagination, but she seemed more stooped and walked with less spring in her step than he ever remembered. This case is taking its toll on all of us, he thought; then he looked back down at the slip and punched in the phone number.

"Mr. Hasegawa? This is Pancho McMartin."

***

Twenty minutes later Pancho was still writing up his notes from his conversation with Mr. Hasegawa when Drew burst into the office. He looked so excited that Susan followed him in.

"I found Booger," said Drew. "And he's willing to talk."

Drew lowered his sizeable frame into one of Pancho's client chairs and Susan did the same.

"When you said 'he's willing to talk,' I assume that means he has something to say?" asked Pancho.

Drew grinned. "Plenty. He knew Marcus Young as well as anyone and he knows why Marcus was murdered — tortured, then murdered, I should say."

Pancho raised his eyebrows at that. "Okay, fill me in and I'll add his name to the witness list. I have to add another witness anyway. A witness called in response to our ad and the news stories about the trial. He sounds credible and he has some good stuff, too."

Drew held up a hand. His grin had disappeared. "There's a slight problem with Booger. He'll talk, but he won't testify. He's in hiding and he's scared shitless. Part of the deal is that we keep him anonymous and we hire someone to protect him while the trial is going on."

Pancho put down the pen he'd been holding and sat back in his chair, a puzzled expression on his face. "And so Booger is going to help us how, exactly?"

"He's going to feed us all sorts of information which you should be able to use at trial," said Drew.

Pancho ran his hand through his hair and shook his head slightly. "Unbelievable," he muttered. "Okay, let's have it."

Twenty-Two

O pening statements in a criminal trial are supposed to be limited to a general overview of the case and usually a summary of what each side believed the evidence will show. Argument was not allowed, although many attorneys, Pancho included, often walked the line and even crossed over if they thought they could get away with it.

Harry Chang's approach was almost always straightforward. Of course, as Pancho loved to point out, he had the full resources of the State of Hawai'i at his fingertips and, more often than not, a guilty-as-hell defendant, but as Harry had acknowledged the day before when offering Pancho the deal, he didn't have a whole lot of evidence stacked up in the Jackson Steele case. Consequently, his opening statement was even briefer than usual.

"Ladies and gentlemen," he said in closing, "it is the State's position that there was a second man involved in the robbery and brutal murder of Auntie Irene, and until we find him and bring him to justice, we will only know what we have to work with here today." He paused and ran his eyes across the jury box, a rare moment of drama coming from Harry. "Yes, there are some holes in this case. We don't know who the defendant's accomplice is and we don't know where the stolen goods are. But what we do know and have to work with is compelling as far as this defendant, Jackson Steele, is concerned. An eyewitness saw him running from the murder scene with someone running behind him.

"Auntie Irene's purse was found, mostly emptied and tossed into the trash just outside the bathroom where Jackson Steele's accomplice turned against him and knocked him out. Jackson Steele himself claims that he can't remember anything, including whether he had participated in a robbery and murder. Finally, of course, there is the matter of Jackson Steele's fingerprints all over the purse stolen from Auntie Irene. We believe, based on that compelling evidence, you must find Jackson Steele guilty of murder in the second degree. Thank you."

Pancho told Harry before trial that he hadn't had a chance to talk to Jackson about the deal yet, but that he'd discovered some new information that would probably cause him to recommend against any deal. Harry wasn't happy, but Pancho had timed his entrance into court such that there would be little or no time to engage in any kind of substantive discussion with Harry. He promised to talk to Jackson at the first break.

Judge Kingsley looked at Pancho. "Mr. McMartin, are you ready to proceed with your opening?" The defense had a choice of making the opening statement immediately following the prosecutor's or waiting until the close of the State's case, but it was rare for defense attorneys to wait. Pancho actually considered deferring his opening in this situation as it would give him time to assimilate Mr. Hasegawa's and Booger's information and allow him to give more than his standard 'reasonable doubt' opening. In the end, however, he decided it wasn't worth putting off. Even if he couldn't give the jury a hint of the fireworks to come, at the very least he wanted them thinking about all the holes in the State's case and how important it was to be constantly evaluating the evidence in terms of reasonable doubt.

After talking in detail about the definition of reasonable doubt, Pancho got to the heart of his short opening.

"Ladies and gentlemen, some of what Mr. Chang told you is absolutely correct. There are holes in the chain of events surrounding the terrible murder of Auntie Irene—holes that are so large you could drive a Mack truck through. Mr. Chang recounted the minimal evidence that the State has against Mr. Steele, fingerprints on a purse found in the trash and a so-called eyewitness to . . ." Pancho paused as if thinking of something. "To what exactly? Not to the murder. No, what the prosecution witness will say is that he saw two people running from the direction of where the murder took place. He identified the black person in front as my client, something we will vehemently dispute.

"The holes in Mr. Chang's case are huge. We have heard about a mysterious accomplice who betrayed Mr. Steele and knocked him out, taking all the stolen property. But Mr. Chang isn't going to give you that accomplice. He can't. He can't even give you the security guard whom the video records will show had followed Auntie Irene following her gig. He can't do that because the evidence will show that the guard in question was murdered—murdered after apparently being tortured." Pancho paused again, hoping the implications of the torture and murder of the security guard would take hold in the minds of the jury.

"Ladies and gentlemen, as I've said before, I don't have to prove Jackson Steele's innocence. He sits before you right now as an innocent man. He is, by law, presumed innocent. Only if the twelve of you find that these huge holes Mr. Chang has brought to your attention are not troubling, only if the twelve of you find that you have no doubt as to my client's guilt, only if you can find Jackson Steele guilty beyond any reasonable doubt, will the shroud of innocence be lifted. I respectfully suggest that the evidence will not only highlight the gaping holes which Mr. Chang has so fairly pointed out, but will force you to conclude that Jackson Steele was not the perpetrator of this terrible crime."

Both openings had taken less than forty-five minutes. Pancho could tell from the Judge's face that he was pleased with the unusual brevity of the attorneys.

"Mr. Chang, you may call your first witness," Judge Kingsley intoned.

Harry stood. "Thank you, Your Honor. The State calls Sergeant William Aki."

Pancho watched Sgt. Aki stride confidently to the witness stand. Pancho knew him as a journeyman officer who was competent and confident. He was one of the first responders to the murder scene, and Harry had him describe the location and the hideous sight of a beaten Auntie Irene.

"Her face was badly beaten and bloody. She'd clearly been hit repeatedly with a hard object, probably before being dragged to the secluded and partially hidden hallway next to the parking lot, about halfway between Neiman Marcus and the entry hall next to the Longhi's and Morton's elevator. After multiple blows to the head, she appears to have fallen and struck her head on the asphalt." He paused and looked at the jury. His voice cracked as he concluded, "I didn't even recognize her as Auntie Irene at the time. Her face was so destroyed."

Harry then asked Sgt. Aki to identify several photos of the body and scene. Pancho had tried to keep the photos of the dead Auntie Irene from being admitted into evidence as being too inflammatory for the jury to see, but Judge Kingsley only disallowed a close-up shot of her beaten-in face. "The rest," ruled the Judge, "while disturbing, have sufficient probative value to be admissible and relevant to issues such as the location of the body and the fact that the purse and ukulele case were missing."

Pancho could do nothing but watch impassively as the jurors passed the photos to each other to view. Several of the women on the jury were surreptitiously but clearly weeping. The courtroom was stunningly silent as everyone watched the jurors.

When the photos had been viewed, Harry continued with his examination of Sgt. Aki. "While you were at the scene, did you have occasion to determine if there were any witnesses to the robbery and murder?"

"Yes, well, we immediately instructed some patrol officers to fan out around that part of the shopping center to stop people and ask if they had seen anything. One of the officers, William Jones, found a gentleman who had seen two men running in a direction away from what turned out to be the murder scene. He didn't witness the assault and eventual murder itself and didn't know why the men were running, until he was questioned by Officer Jones."

Pancho jumped to his feet. "Objection, Your Honor! What the purported witness said to Officer Jones is hearsay and further calls for speculation as to what the witness knew or didn't know."

"Sustained. Rephrase or move on, Mr. Chang."

Harry nodded and looked down at his notes. "We will have both Officer Jones and the witness testify, so there's no reason to rephrase. I'll move on." He directed his attention back to Sgt. Aki. "Now, Sergeant, did you or the other officers at the scene find any other witnesses?"

"No. I was told by Officer Jones that one of the perpetrators may be African-American. In the meantime, another officer had searched the trash bins in the vicinity and located an empty purse. I was aware that we were potentially looking for an African-American male, and I was aware that a purse had been found and where it had been found. Shortly after being apprised of these things, the defendant, Jackson Steele, walked out of the bathroom next to the trash bin where the purse had been found. Of course, I noted that he was an African-American male. I saw that Mr. Jackson seemed groggy and was holding some paper towels to the top of his head. I asked if he was all right and he said he had fallen and hit his head. I saw he was bleeding and instructed an officer to call an ambulance. While we were waiting for the ambulance I asked Mr. Steele what he'd been doing before he fell and hit his head."

"What was his response?" asked Harry.

"He said that he didn't know. He couldn't remember."

"Did you ask him anything else?"

Sgt. Aki nodded. "Yes, I asked if he had just participated in a robbery."

"What was his response?"

"He kind of shrugged and said he didn't know. He said again that he couldn't remember what had happened, which, of course, was troubling."

"What did you say or do next?" asked Harry.

"Well, I informed him that there had been a murder not far from where we were and that I was going to send an officer to the hospital with him while we investigated further. Then he was sent off to Queens for treatment for his head."

"Was Mr. Steele under arrest at that time?"

"I had him placed in custody pending treatment and possible charges, so yes, that would be the same as being detained. While at Queen's he was fingerprinted, and as soon as it was determined that his prints matched those on Ms. Kamaka's purse, Detective Wong came to me and told me to go to Queens and arrest Mr. Steele for the robbery and murder of Irene Kamaka."

"Did you do so?"

"Yes, sir. That was accomplished without incident."

"Thank you, Sergeant. I have nothing further." Harry sat down and all eyes turned to Pancho.

"Mr. McMartin."

Pancho stood, picking up his yellow legal pad as he did so. "Thank you, Your Honor." He turned to the witness. "Sergeant Aki, good to see you again." The Sergeant smiled and nodded pleasantly.

"Your testimony was pretty straightforward, so I have just a few things to cover," said Pancho. "First of all, just to confirm, at the scene of the murder itself, you did not see any purse or any other personal items belonging to the decedent, is that correct?"

Sgt. Aki, nodded. "That's correct. We searched a one hundred yard range around the murder scene. We found various discarded or lost items, all of which are itemized in the police report, but none of which appears to have belonged to Ms. Kamaka."

"But is it also correct that in addition to the purse, Auntie Irene also was thought to have her ukulele, in a case, with her?"

"That's also correct. According to the shopping center surveillance tape, Ms. Kamaka was seen leaving the restaurant where she and her cousins had performed carrying both her purse and her ukulele case."

"Has the ukulele or its case ever been found?"

"No, sir, it has not."

"Do you find that at all strange, Sergeant, when the perpetrators obviously want to rid themselves of incriminating evidence such as the purse, yet they retain the ukulele?"

"Objection," said Harry, somewhat mildly. "Calls for speculation."

"Sustained."

Pancho nodded amiably. He had made his point.

"Sergeant Aki, have you viewed the surveillance video in question?"

"No, sir, I have not. The homicide detectives took over the case once we had secured the scene and searched the area for evidence and witnesses."

Pancho nodded, as if to himself. "Okay. Let me ask you this. When my client, Jackson Steele, came out of the bathroom holding a paper towel to his bleeding head, did he try to run when he saw you or any other police officers?"

"No, sir, he did not. Like I said, he was kind of groggy."

"But you say he explained that he had fallen and hit his head, is that correct?"

"Yes it is."

"Did you have any reason to doubt that explanation?"

Sergeant Aki gave a half shrug. "Not really. Certainly not at the time."

"What was Mr. Steele wearing when he came out of the bathroom?"

"A plain white, although dirty, tee shirt and dark colored cargo shorts. He had rubber slippers on his feet."

"Was there any blood on his clothes?"

"Yes, there was blood on the back of the tee shirt."

"Was that from his bleeding head injury?" asked Pancho.

"I presume so."

"So my client's clothes were not splattered with blood as one would expect to see if he had just beaten a woman to death?"

"Objection!"

"Sustained."

Pancho gave a half nod to Judge Kingsley. "Let me rephrase. Sergeant Aki, did you observe any blood on Mr. Steele's clothing other than on the back of his tee shirt?"

"No, sir, I did not."

"Or on his body?"

"No, sir, I did not, although that would be harder to see."

"So correct me if I'm wrong, Sergeant, but it sounds like the only reason you took my client into custody was because you had a witness who claims to have seen a black man running from the direction of where the murder occurred and my client, who had just suffered a head injury, couldn't remember what he had been doing before the injury, is that correct?"

Sergeant Aki seemed to ponder the question before answering. Finally he nodded. "Well, yes and no. I mean, the purse had already been found right next to the bathroom where he was. So that also entered into my determination."

Stupid question, good answer, thought Pancho. He moved on quickly. "Were any of the contents of the purse found at or in the vicinity of the shopping center?"

Sgt. Aki frowned. "Well, when we searched Ms. Kamaka's car, we found items which a woman would ordinarily have in a purse, but they were in her glove compartment. Other than that, in the purse itself her driver's license and some credit cards were found in a zipper compartment."

Pancho glanced at the jury and noted that they appeared to be paying attention. He turned back to Sgt. Aki. "Other than the items in the glove compartment and the license and credit cards still in the purse, were any other items that might have been in Ms. Kamaka's purse found anywhere around the shopping center?"

Sgt. Aki shook his head. "No, sir." He paused. "Of course, there were the items we found lying on the ground at the Center within a hundred yards of the murder scene. I mentioned those a few minutes ago. But none of those items appear to have any relationship to this murder."

"Did Mr. Steele have any items belonging to Ms. Kamaka on his person when you took him into custody?"

"No."

"Do you have any ideas or opinions as to why Ms. Kamaka would have taken items normally kept in her purse out and put them instead in her glove compartment?"

Harry half rose, his hands on the arms of his chair. "Objection, Your Honor. Assumes facts not in evidence. We don't know what items Ms. Kamaka normally kept in her purse versus in her glove compartment." He paused for half a second, then added, "It also calls for speculation as to what she may have been thinking."

Pancho smiled and nodded at Harry. "I withdraw the question, Your Honor." He felt confident that the jury would be wondering what was in Auntie Irene's purse if her make-up and other things were in her car. Now all he had to do was come up with some ideas as to what could have been in the singer's purse.

"Did Mr. Steele have any implements on his person that could have been the murder weapon?"

"No."

Pancho decided there was nothing more he needed to get out of this witness. "Thank you, Sergeant. No further questions."

"Redirect, Mr. Chang?" asked Judge Kingsley.

Harry half stood. "Nothing further, Your Honor."

The Judge excused Sergeant Aki, then recessed court for lunch. Pancho knew that the medical examiner would be the first witness after lunch. That's when the fireworks would begin.

Twenty-Three

Pancho watched Jackson consume the deli turkey sandwich as he explained the deal Harry Chang had offered.

"Manslaughter carries a maximum prison term of twenty years," Pancho said. "So for now I'm inclined to recommend that you reject their offer. I think we may be making some good progress with Drew's investigation. But I want to caution you that it's still a long shot to get a not guilty verdict, and if you go down for Murder Two, it'll probably mean life in prison."

Jackson concentrated on his sandwich. Pancho took a bite of his own, assuming that Jackson was thinking it over. Minutes passed. They were in a small conference room reserved for counsel and their clients. A sheriff stood guard outside. When Jackson swallowed the last of his sandwich he deliberately folded the wrapping paper and napkin into one and set it aside, then looked directly at Pancho.

"Pancho, I know you believe in me. I know you doing everything you can to help me. I trust you. I ain't ever trusted anyone before, 'specially a white man, so I want you to know that. I gonna do what you say. I knows I could go to prison. If that happens, then I guess I'll know that Aunt Clio was right after all, that it was God's will for me to pay for what happened to my mama."

It was a long speech for Jackson, and Pancho was moved. He closed his eyes for a moment and ran his hand through his hair. *This is getting harder and harder,* he thought. *I can't let this boy go to prison.*

"I don't know if Mr. Chang will keep the deal on the table for long," Pancho finally said, "but I don't think it's the right deal for us now. Let's keep going forward."

Jackson nodded, then looked back down at his clasped hands.

***

Pancho was not surprised that Dr. Padma Dasari, the chief medical examiner for the City and County of Honolulu would not be testifying. One of her assistants, Dr. Melvin Yee, was taking the stand. There was little doubt as to the cause of Auntie Irene Kamaka's death and therefore no need for the first string. At least, thought Pancho, that's what the prosecution was obviously thinking.

Dr. Yee was a pale, stooped man in his late fifties who looked more like he was in his late sixties. His thinning hair was white, turning to yellow. His pallor was almost gray, *probably not much different from the corpses he worked on,* thought Pancho. The doctor's small eyes seemed to dart everywhere at once. He wasn't known for his courtroom demeanor, but Pancho figured Harry was going to try to get him on and off the stand as soon as possible.

"The decedent suffered repeated severe blunt force trauma to the head," said Dr. Yee in response to Harry's examination. "The injuries included fracture of the left mandible, or jaw bone, the nasal bone, the left zygomatic bone, and the left maxilla. In addition, the left temporal portion of the skull suffered a depressed fracture, which caused cerebral hemorrhage and would be considered the cause of death." Dr. Yee used a pointer and a chart showing the bones in a human face to indicate the areas of injury.

"Was there evidence of trauma to any other parts of Ms. Kamaka's body?" asked Harry.

Dr. Yee looked down at his notes before responding. "Yes, there were bruises and contusions all along the left side of her body, including arm and leg. Those were consistent with the decedent having been dragged along the asphalt to where she was ultimately left."

Harry asked a few more follow-up questions before giving up the witness. Pancho was out of his seat even before Judge Kingsley formally turned the witness over to him.

"Dr. Yee, I call your attention to the toxicology report which is part of State's Exhibit Nine."

"Your Honor, may we approach?" Harry was on his feet.

Pancho and Harry and the court reporter sidled up to the Judge's bench at the farthest point from the jury. They spoke in whispers.

"Your Honor, I believe I know where Mr. McMartin is going with this testimony and I want to object in advance so that the jury isn't prejudiced by something that should not be admissible."

The Judge frowned and pulled out the exhibit in question. "And that is?"

"Your Honor, I think we should maybe adjourn to your chambers for this discussion," said Pancho. "I commend the prosecutor's office and the police for keeping the lid on the contents of the toxicology report, but I'm afraid it contains relevant information which will be damaging to the reputation of Auntie Irene Kamaka."

Judge Kingsley had been reading while listening to Pancho, and Pancho could literally see the Judge's eyes go wide. Judge Kingsley looked up at the two attorneys. "By all means we should take this up in chambers. I'm going to excuse the jury for the day, then we'll resume the bench conference in my chambers."

Fifteen minutes later the attorneys, the court reporter, and the Judge's law clerk were seated in Judge Kingsley's office. A table extended from the front of the Judge's large desk, and the two attorneys sat across from each other at the table. The court reporter sat closest to the Judge. Lester, the law clerk, sat in the corner, taking notes. The room was not overly spacious, but was comfortable and warmly furnished with family photos, awards and, of course, the wall of diplomas and bar admissions.

"So, am I reading this correctly? Auntie Irene was addicted to heroin?"

Harry Chang nodded solemnly. "That does appear to be the case, Your Honor. But I don't see what conceivable relevance it has to her assault, robbery, and murder at the hands of thugs. All Mr. McMartin will accomplish by bringing this out will be to besmirch the reputation of one of Hawaii's most beloved entertainers."

The Judge gave a slight nod, but Pancho couldn't tell if it was simply an acknowledgment or a nod of agreement.

"And why," said the Judge, "did you not file a Motion *in Limine* on this subject prior to the commencement of trial?"

Pancho had been about to ask the same thing. A Motion *in Limine* is generally a pre-trial motion used to limit or even exclude evidence that is objectionable. By hearing the motion before trial, everyone knows whether the evidence will or will not be allowed.

Harry Chang took a deep breath before responding. "I apologize for that, Your Honor. Frankly I was hoping Mr. McMartin wouldn't go there and that we wouldn't need to hold a hearing which would have the same character assassination result as if we allowed it in evidence."

Pancho waited for Judge Kingsley to turn to him and invite him to respond. Pancho spoke slowly and deliberately, without any of the drama and passion he reserved for the courtroom. "Your Honor, believe me when I say I was as saddened as anyone else when I read this. But I'm afraid I have no choice but to bring it out. The fact that Auntie Irene was a heroin addict is relevant on so many counts it's almost ridiculous to try to enumerate. Was she held up by another junkie who knew her? Was she holding any heroin or other drugs that someone would be willing to assault her for? This evidence brings in a whole new realm of potential scenarios, which I'm obligated to pursue."

He paused, then said, "And frankly, Your Honor, while I can understand Mr. Chang's hopefulness, I can only suggest that it was extremely misplaced. He should have known I would have to use this information, and he should have filed the proper pre-trial motion to contest it."

"But Your Honor," interjected Harry, now in an obvious plaintive, almost whining, tone, "there isn't one shred of supporting facts to justify the kind of rank speculation cited by Mr. McMartin. And yes, I've apologized for not filing a Motion *in Limine* pre-trial, but again, this is a bombshell which I, apparently naively," a quick glare at Pancho, "had hoped to avoid. Are we going to ruin a person's reputation and further traumatize her family just so Mr. McMartin can take the jury to a 'what-if' fest?"

Judge Kingsley leaned back in his chair and clasped his hands on top of his head. Pancho looked across the table at Harry, who looked angry and worried. Pancho gave him a small shrug and a "gotta do what I gotta do" half smile, but Harry just shook his head and looked away.

"I don't know how I would have ruled at a pre-trial motion on this, but that clearly would have been the proper vehicle for addressing this issue," the Judge finally said. "And I do understand the prosecution's concerns that this information is tantamount to character assassination without probative value to the question of guilt or innocence of the defendant." He sighed, unclasped his hands, and put them on his desk. "But I don't see that I have a choice but to allow this line of questioning." The Judge looked at Pancho and narrowed his eyes, an ominous looking gesture from a judge to a trial attorney. "But Mr. McMartin, I'll expect that you'll handle this matter appropriately. I will not allow wild speculation."

Pancho held the Judge's look for a couple of beats before responding. "I'm not completely sure what you mean when you say I should handle this matter appropriately, Your Honor. I mean, what speculation could I engage in that's any worse than the State's wild accusation that my client was assaulted and robbed by his own accomplice?"

There was dead silence in the chambers. After a few beats Pancho decided he had better wade back into the breach.

"Your Honor, I apologize. Of course I'll do my best to deal with this issue as appropriately as humanly possible. I think you'll find, however, that as this case proceeds, this issue will become more and more relevant."

"Just what's that supposed to mean?" Harry's tone was now openly hostile.

Pancho shrugged. "Just what I said. For now I'll simply ask the doctor to tell the jury what the toxicology report says and what it means. I won't address the issue further until or unless it becomes clearly relevant." He turned his head to the Judge. "Will that be acceptable and appropriate?"

Judge Kingsley and Pancho's eyes locked until the Judge suddenly smiled and looked to the court reporter. "Motion denied. We're now off the record." He turned to Pancho, still smiling. "Don't push me too hard, Pancho."

Twenty-Four

"**M**rs. Steele?"

"Yes."

"This is Pancho McMartin from Hawai'i."

Silence. Then, she said, "Did they execute the boy?"

Pancho held the phone away from his mouth and swore to himself in disbelief. "No ma'am," he said after he composed himself. "We've just started the trial. And anyway, we don't have the death penalty here in Hawai'i. I'm calling because I'd like you to reconsider your position and come and testify on behalf of Jackson."

"And say what, Mr. McMartin? That I didn't want to have him in the first place?"

"You don't have to say that, but it would help the jury understand him some if they could see his mother and hear what his life was like growing up. Maybe you can explain about his fainting spells. You could say how gentle he'd always been."

The line went silent for so long that Pancho was about to give up and hang up when she spoke again. "You just don't get it, do you, Mister? As that boy growed up he looked more and more like the man who done raped me. By the time I asked him to leave the house it was like I was looking in the face of that man." The venom in her voice was palpable. She paused, and when she spoke again her voice had gone so soft Pancho had to strain to hear her.

"It was like I had to meet my rapist over and over. The monster what killed my parents was living right there in my house, and I had to feed him his meals and wash his clothes. They should never have made me birth that child, but I did, and I did my duty, and now I don't have to look in that face no more. So I'm sorry, Mr. McMartin. I knows you got to do your job, but that boy is on his own now."

Pancho heard the line disconnect and slowly hung up his phone. He swiveled around in his chair and stared out his floor to ceiling windows at paradise.

***

Pancho was still staring out the window when Susan knocked, then entered his office. When he swiveled around, his face held such raw sadness that she instinctively went to him. She put a hand on his shoulder.

"You all right, Pancho? You look like you just heard someone died."

He closed his eyes and sighed. "I just got off the phone with Jackson's mother. She won't have anything to do with him. She says he looks exactly like his father, the man who raped her and killed her parents in front of her." He expelled a large breath. "I guess I understand her feelings, but Goddammit, Susan, it's her son."

"There's nothing you can do about it, Pancho. It is what it is. Don't let it get to you."

"Ah, but it just never fails to amaze me how horrible people can be. The preacher forcing her to have a child she doesn't want and won't love. The aunt telling Jackson he's evil and must pay for the sins of his monster of a father."

Susan chuckled throatily beside him. "For crying out loud Pancho, you represent murderers and thieves and you're surprised at how horrible people can be?"

Pancho gave a small grunt. "Yeah, stupid I guess."

Susan chuckled again. "No, not really. It's just you being you."

Susan patted Pancho's shoulder as a parting gesture, then walked back to the side of the desk. She picked up a CD. "I take it you haven't noticed this yet."

He took it from her and looked at the label. "Another surveillance video surfaces finally?"

Susan nodded. "I looked at it while you were in court. It isn't good."

Pancho shook his head and sighed. "What now?"

"It shows Jackson running into the camera's view with the purse, which he throws into the trash. Then he goes into the bathroom. He looks nervous and guilty."

"Great."

"I'll get out of your way now so you can go back to your sulking. If you need anything, holler."

Twenty-Five

"We're back on the record. Doctor Yee, you are still under oath. You may proceed, Mr. McMartin."

"Thank you, Your Honor." Pancho rose, smoothing his gray linen sport coat as he did so. He wore his 'uniform' of blue jeans and cowboy boots. His starched dress shirt was blue today and his tie was a pastel pink. He felt overwhelmingly tired, and his tan and handsome face was tight and strained. His usually penetrating eyes seemed sad and distant.

"Now, Dr. Yee, yesterday I had asked you to look at the toxicology section of the Autopsy Report, State's Exhibit Nine. Do you have that in front of you now?"

"Yes sir, I do."

"Were there any substances found in Irene Kamaka's body which were unexpected?"

Dr. Yee swallowed, then picked up the report. He nodded. "I assume you're referring to the fact that the metabolite of heroin, 6-0-acetylmorphine, and morphine-3-0-glucuronid were found in both the blood and urine."

There was a noticeable gasp, almost in unison, from the spectators, then it was bedlam as Judge Kingsley tried to restore order. When things had calmed down Pancho nodded to the doctor.

"Doctor, you mentioned both heroin and morphine, were both of these substances found in Ms. Kamaka's body?"

"They're basically one and the same," Dr. Yee said stiffly. "Heroin metabolizes into morphine almost immediately upon entering the bloodstream. The concentration in the blood of morphine, the catabolite of heroin, was 0.03 mg/l. This corresponds to the lower limit of morphine levels measured in current heroin users." Dr. Yee swallowed again. He picked up a glass of water and drank.

"Doctor Yee, were you able to determine if Ms. Kamaka was a recurrent user of heroin or whether this was a one-time anomaly?"

"The autopsy found numerous traces of punctures by injection needles of various age on both upper limbs and the lower limbs. Traces of an infected but healing needle puncture were found inside the right elbow." Yee stopped, and his eyes darted first to Harry, then to Pancho. "Ms. Kamaka was a heroin addict."

Once again the spectator section erupted. Pancho could hear several shouts of "No." He closed his eyes and let the noise slowly abate. When it was quiet again, he opened his eyes and saw that the Judge, Dr. Yee and the jury were all looking at him. He nodded to the doctor. "Thank you, Doctor. I have nothing further." He walked slowly back to his table and sat down. The courtroom was stunningly silent.

"Mr. Chang, please call your next witness."

Harry stood. "The State calls Detective Bryson Wong."

The bailiff left the courtroom to call Detective Wong. During the wait the courtroom remained eerily quiet. The shock of Auntie Irene's heroin addiction had not worn off.

Bryson Wong was a big, burly man with a thick neck and full head of salt and pepper hair. His dark, Chinese eyes looked intense and hard. He held his mouth in a gruff-looking down-turn. Harry took him through the preliminaries quickly, then had him describe the photo lineup which he'd overseen.

"Detective Wong, is the man the witness identified from the photo lineup in the courtroom today?"

"Yes he is. It's the defendant, Jackson Steele."

"And on the basis of finding Mr. Steele's fingerprints on the purse and the photo identification by an eyewitness you charged Mr. Steele with murder?"

"Yes sir, we did."

"And was there any further evidence against Mr. Steele discovered after his arrest and charge?"

"Yes, one of the video surveillance films shows Mr. Steele clearly running with the purse, which he then put into the trash can where it was later found."

Harry looked to Judge Kingsley. "Your Honor, we will be putting the owner of the security firm on the stand to authenticate the video." He turned to Pancho. "That is, unless Mr. McMartin wants to stipulate that it's authentic and that it shows his client as described."

Pancho rose. "No, Your Honor, we will not do so." Harry looked surprised. Judge Kingsley just nodded.

When it was Pancho's turn to cross-examine Detective Wong, he walked to the easel he had set up that morning and turned over a large blown-up photograph of a dark skinned man, then he turned to the detective.

"Detective Wong, is this photo the one you used in the photo line-up at which my client was identified by the eyewitness?"

"Yes, I believe it is."

"Can you describe this man to us?"

"You mean the man in the photo?"

"Yes, him." Pancho pointed to the easel.

"Well, he's an African-American man who looks to be in his thirties. He has a small beard, I guess what we would call a goatee."

Even though Wong had already been through this with Pancho at the Motion to Suppress, Wong stopped there.

"What size would you say this man is, based on the photo?"

Wong made a pretense of studying the photo in detail. Finally he sat back in his chair and looked at Pancho. "I would guess that he's a fairly big man."

Pancho smiled. "Fairly big." He looked at the jury, then back at Detective Wong. "By 'fairly big', would you mean over two hundred pounds?"

Once again the detective studied the photo, then nodded. "Yes, I think that would be accurate."

"How much did Mr. Steele weigh when he was arrested?"

Wong consulted his notes. "A hundred and thirty."

"How old is Mr. Steele?"

"Nineteen."

"And Detective, tell us if Mr. Steele had any facial hair at the time of his arrest."

"No, he did not."

Pancho scratched his head. "So Detective Wong, the only thing this man had in common with my client was that he's black, is that correct?"

"Objection. Vague and ambiguous, argumentative."

Pancho smiled and nodded at Harry before turning to Judge Kingsley. He didn't wait for the Judge to rule. "I'll rephrase, Your Honor." He turned his attention back to Wong, pleased to have been given the opportunity to hammer his point. "Detective, Mr. Steele is nineteen and the man in the photo is in his thirties. Correct?"

"Yes."

"Mr. Steele has no facial hair and the man in the photo has a beard, correct?"

"Yes." Wong threw a glance toward Harry. He looked none too happy.

"And Mr. Steele weighs one thirty while the man in the photo is over seventy pounds heavier, correct?"

"Yes."

"Are you able to point to any other common identifying feature as between my client and this man other than the fact that both men are black?"

Wong again studied the photo. "No, sir, I don't see anything off hand."

Pancho then took Wong through each of the other photos. By the time he was done, it was clear to all that if the eyewitness was looking to identify a slightly built, clean shaven young man, the only choice would have been Jackson. The problem, as he explained it to Drew and Susan back at the office at the end of the day, was that there was still a surveillance video showing Jackson running with the dead woman's purse. The only way he'd be able to explain that away would be to put Jackson on the stand to testify about having the purse tossed to him by two men on a scooter.

***

Although the photo line-up had been something of a disaster for Harry Chang, he still had to put the eyewitness on the stand to say that he saw Jackson Steele running away from the direction of where the murder had occurred. Pancho could tell Harry wasn't looking forward to the experience.

Pancho wasted no time when it was his turn. "Now Mr. Englehart, when did you move to Hawai'i?"

"Objection. Your honor, what conceivable relevance could the timing of Mr. Englehart's move to Hawai'i be?" Harry Chang glanced at Pancho, and Pancho saw a fleeting smile, meant only for him. Pancho knew Harry was trying to signal his client to be careful. Pancho assumed Harry had tried his best to brief the witness on how to handle the questions Harry knew damned well Pancho would ask.

"Your Honor—" but Judge Kingsley interrupted. It was obvious to Pancho that he knew the game Harry was trying to play, and he didn't need to hear argument on the objection.

"I'll allow it. Objection overruled. But please keep it moving in a relevant direction, Mr. McMartin."

"Thank you, Your Honor." He turned back to the witness. "Do you recall the question, Mr. Englehart?"

Englehart nodded. "Sure do. My wife Effie and I moved here three months ago."

"From where?"

"Montana." Englehart looked up at the Judge, whom he thought to be an ally. "We was plum tired of the cold."

"What town?"

"Oh, we wasn't from no town. We were ranchers. Lived out in the middle of nowhere. It would get colder'n a witch's tit." Englehart caught himself and put his hand to his mouth. He looked at the Judge again. "Sorry about that, Your Honor."

Judge smiled affably and nodded. "It's best if you just answer the question, Mr. Englehart."

"I sure will, Your Honor."

"Mr. Englehart, how many black people that you know of lived within fifty miles of your house?"

Englehart shrugged and shook his head. "There weren't none that I know of." He paused for a second and, before Pancho could get his follow up question out, he added, "but there's plenty of them on television nowadays."

Pancho could hear some snickering from the spectator section behind him. The Judge didn't look happy. A little folksiness might have been charming, but the Judge's expression told Pancho that enough was enough. "Just answer the question, sir."

"How about Samoans, Mr. Englehart? How many do you know of who lived anywhere near you in Montana?"

"Shoot, Mister, I don't know if there are any of them people in all of Montana." Then he added, "But there probably are, somewhere."

"Mr. Englehart, can you tell the difference between a Samoan and a Tongan and a Hawaiian?"

The elderly *haole* witness rubbed his chin and looked out at the gallery, as if he were looking for some to compare. Finally he shook his head. "Not yet. But I'm sure we'll be learning to tell the difference after a while. We want to learn all about Hawaiian culture and stuff."

"And Mr. Englehart, if—"

"But I know a black man when I see one, and I saw a black man that night." He looked at Harry Chang, clearly pleased with himself. Harry Chang stared down at the legal pad in front of him.

"I'm sure you do, Mr. Englehart. And did this black man you saw have any facial hair?"

Englehart's brow furled in apparent thought. He rubbed his hand across his mouth and chin. "Don't think so."

"How about size? Was the black man you saw big or small?"

"Oh he was small. Kind of wiry. Couldn't have weighed more'n one fifty wet."

"Mr. Englehart, you were shown photos of a number of dark skinned people and were asked if you could identify the person you saw running, do you remember that?"

Englehart nodded amiably. "Oh yeah. That Detective Wong showed me a bunch of photos and asked me to pick out the guy I saw that night. I picked out your client right away."

Pancho heard someone in the spectator section snicker, obviously thinking that Pancho had just screwed up.

"Why did you pick out my client, Mr. Englehart?"

Englehart gave Pancho a broad smile. "Why, he was the only one who was small enough to be the guy I saw. It had to be him."

Several spectators openly laughed, and Judge Kingsley called for quiet. Pancho glanced at Harry, who was still staring intently at his legal pad.

"Mr. Englehart, can you describe the man you say you saw running behind the black man?"

"You mean the guy chasing your client?"

Pancho smiled, as if indulging a child. "Well, sir, let's talk about that for a minute before we get into the description. Can you tell the jury how you know the second fellow was chasing the first one as opposed to running with, but behind him?"

Englehart frowned and wrinkled his nose in thought. "Well," he finally said, slowly, "I guess you could make an argument that he wasn't chasing your client, but it sure looked that way to me."

Although the litigation wisdom was that an attorney shouldn't ask a question to which he doesn't know the answer, that wasn't always possible in criminal cases. Pancho had no chance to question or depose Mr. Englehart before trial, so he was flying blind, but Pancho's gut and Englehart's prior testimony told him that Mr. Englehart would continue to step on his crank, so he asked a question he rarely asked in court. "Why?"

Englehart looked genuinely surprised at the question. "Why because some black guy was running away from something with a woman's purse. Something had to be wrong with that picture, and the guy behind him must have been chasing the son-of-a-bitch down."

Pancho smiled and nodded. "And that's because the guy doing the chasing wasn't also black?"

Englehart nodded. "Yeah, sure, I hear those people tend to stick together."

Despite the audible snickering from the gallery, Pancho continued to nod amiably. "And so what did the fellow chasing the black guy look like?"

Englehart seemed to shrug. "Not sure. I just know he wasn't black like your client. I mean, once I saw that, I kind of stopped looking at him and focused on your client."

"And what, if anything, was the non-black guy holding or carrying?"

Englehart seemed to think about it for a few seconds before shrugging again. "Don't know. Didn't notice if he was or wasn't carrying anything."

"What was he wearing?"

"White shirt was all I can recall. Short sleeves."

"Is there anything else you can tell us about this fellow giving chase?"

Englehart shook his head. "No, sir. I guess maybe I should have joined him and helped out, but frankly I'm getting a little old for that kind of thing."

This time there was outright laughter in the courtroom. Englehart looked around with a smile.

"No further questions of this witness, Your Honor."

Twenty-Six

It was a hot but perfect cloudless day on the Big Island. The summits of both Mauna Kea and Mauna Loa volcanoes were fully visible. The rolling emerald green pastureland of the Lopaka ranch in Waimea looked like it could be in Wyoming or Montana. Even the vog, the volcanic smog, coming from the continuously erupting Kilauea volcano, had taken a day off. It was the kind of day that Bobby would normally have gone for a ride with one of his *paniolos*. Instead, he was cloistered in his study with Rigger.

"So where's that sleazebag lawyer going with the heroin angle?" Bobby said. "Why the fuck did he have to ruin Irene's reputation like that?" He picked up his glass of Bourbon and took a sip.

Rigger watched his father closely. He knew his moods and knew how angry Bobby was, but he wasn't sure exactly what he was angry at. Rigger knew Bobby loved Irene like a daughter and was protective of her, so it could certainly be the taint on her reputation that had him so worked up, but Rigger suspected there was more to it than that.

"Pops. Was Auntie Irene really a heroin addict? Did you know that?"

Bobby stared hard at his son for a moment before dropping his eyes to his cut crystal glass of Bourbon. He nodded. Rigger shifted in his seat. He kept his voice even.

"Did she get the stuff from you?"

Bobby looked out the window at the pastoral scene, then back at Rigger. "When Irene's husband and son were killed, she lost it completely. Nothing we tried could get her out of her depression. You know how I hate shrinks, but I even got her to go to one down in Kona town. But she'd just withdrawn into herself. She wouldn't even play music with her cousins." He stopped and sipped his drink.

"I thought she was going to kill herself. I don't know if you remember, but I had her move in here for a while. Eventually I gave her a small snort of heroin to try to ease her pain. Long story short, it was the only thing she responded to. She slowly started to come out of her shell. But by then she was using regularly." Bobby held out his hands in a 'what could I do?' attitude. "So I made sure she got *manini kine* doses. Small. I would only give her enough for a week at a time. Just enough to let her cope and start enjoying life again. She's been on the stuff since."

Rigger nodded in ambiguous acknowledgment. The fact that his father had been secretly supplying Auntie Irene with heroin for years now was only marginally surprising. What was more surprising was that his father had kept it from Rigger. "So, are you thinking that this could come back at you in any way?" he asked.

Bobby shrugged. "Don't see how it can. As far as I know, Nappy and I were the only ones who knew she was using. But that sleazebag's investigator has been sniffing around, so I can't just stick my head in the sand."

Rigger didn't know exactly what that meant, but he didn't pursue it. "I hear Scotty Gouveia will be testifying tomorrow," he said.

Bobby rolled his eyes. "And what?"

"Shouldn't be any surprises. I'm told he's just expected to verify the surveillance videos. On and off in no time."

***

Harry Chang looked even more disheveled than usual, like he'd dressed in the dark. He wore a stained and frayed gray blazer over blue pants and brown scuffed shoes. His white shirt was rumpled and his forest green tie was loosely knotted. He hadn't bothered to smooth down his black hair that had blown in the wind on the walk to court.

"Mr. Gouveia, what do you do for a living?"

"I own Paradise Security Systems, which provides security guards and security systems to businesses around the State."

"Does your firm have the security contract with Ala Moana Shopping Center?"

"Yes, it does."

"Does that include both security guards and surveillance monitoring?"

Gouveia appeared to be poised and comfortable. His jet black hair was combed and seemed to have been spritzed with hair spray. He was freshly shaven. There were pock marks on the brown, rugged looking face. He smoothed his Reyn's aloha shirt and smiled at Harry.

"That's correct."

"So there are video cameras located at various locations around the center?"

"Yes, there are. Two hundred, in fact."

"I will show you State's Exhibits Twenty-six and seven and ask if you can identify them." Harry handed Gouveia two CD cases that had been marked for identification.

"Yes sir. Exhibit Twenty-six is from the camera at the mall level just outside of the Asian Seafood Restaurant where Auntie Irene Kamaka had performed. The date of the CD is February twelfth. The time covered on the CD is 8:15 to 8:45 P.M."

"And the next exhibit?"

"Exhibit Twenty-seven is from the camera just *makai* of the Longhi's and Morton's elevator, at the entrance to the Center. The date is the same as Exhibit Twenty-six. The time period covered is 8:45 to 9:15."

Harry glanced at the jury and smiled. "Just for the record, when you say *makai* of the Center, you mean the ocean side?"

"Yes."

"And are these videos kept in the normal course of business?"

"Yes, the video files from the various cameras are retained for one to two weeks, after which time they're recorded over unless there's some need to permanently save them."

"So these two CD's of video from the date of the murder were saved from being recorded over?"

Gouveia blinked a couple of times and nodded. "Yes, they were the only videos I could find that were relevant to the murder."

Harry turned to Judge Kingsley. "With the Court's permission I'd like to move these two exhibits into evidence and play these them for the jury."

The Judge turned to Pancho. "Mr. McMartin?"

Pancho stood. "I'd like to *voir dire* Mr. Gouveia."

Harry Chang looked surprised. Judge Kingsley nodded. "Proceed."

Pancho looked squarely at Scotty Gouveia. "You testified that there are two hundred surveillance cameras on the Ala Moana premises, is that correct?"

"Yes, it is."

"But out of all those cameras, you report that only two had video feed relevant to the murder of Irene Kamaka?"

"Yes sir. The day after the murder I personally called up the videos from the cameras along the *makai* side of the Center within the hour before and after the estimated time of the murder."

"Who asked you to do that?"

Gouveia smiled. "No one. I viewed it as part of my job."

Pancho nodded. "How do you call up the video files?"

"They're all digitized, so I just type in the date and time and the camera location and I can view the video. If that video is not saved to something, like a CD, within two weeks or so, then it's recorded over and would be lost forever."

"Correct me if I'm wrong, Mr. Gouveia, but isn't the industry standard for retention of surveillance video six to eight weeks and not one to two weeks?"

Gouveia coughed into his hand before answering. He seemed surprised that Pancho would know that detail. "There are some in the industry who advocate longer retention times such as six to eight weeks. But with a large property like the Ala Moana Center, that just isn't economically and practically feasible. Usually we know if a video is needed within our retention timeframe."

"Okay. So tell me, Mr. Gouveia, how many cameras would provide coverage, with a margin for error, for that section of the Center?"

Gouveia was nodding as if he was expecting the question. "About ten."

"And you viewed video from all ten cameras for the timeframe in question?"

"Yes."

"Is it your testimony that those videos did not show any people in any of the scenes you viewed?"

Gouveia scowled. He shook his head. "No, sir. I didn't say that. There were probably people in about ninety percent of the videos I viewed. Just none that *seemed* relevant to the murder of Auntie Irene."

Pancho ran his hand through his hair. He looked perplexed. "When you say none that seemed relevant to the murder of Auntie Irene, is that by way of your own personal assessment of what is or is not relevant?"

Gouveia's forehead scrunched up in thought. He paused a beat before answering. "Well, yeah, I guess you could say that. But I *am* trained in security and I think I'm able to tell if someone is an innocent shopper versus a thug running away from a murder scene with a purse." There was some mild chuckling in the spectator section behind Pancho. He ignored it.

"Don't you think it would have been prudent to retain all of the videos for the place and time in question—at least until the police had a chance to review them?"

Gouveia smiled broadly. "Oh, but they did. Or at least I gave them the opportunity to. Detective Wong came by the office and I showed him the two CD's that I'd burned and he asked me about the other videos from other cameras, and I told him what I'd seen. When I asked if he wanted to go through all the video files on his own he said 'no, I trust you'."

Pancho's face registered surprise. He turned and looked at Harry Chang, whose face remained impassive, then he turned back to Gouveia. "Do you mean to tell me that other than these two CD's the police didn't review any other surveillance videos for the night of the murder?"

Gouveia nodded amiably. "That's correct."

"Are you sure?"

"Objection; asked and answered." Clearly Harry wanted to move off the topic as fast as possible.

Pancho looked up at the Judge. "Sorry, Your Honor, but I'm sure you can understand how shocked I am at this testimony. I just want to make sure that Mr. Gouveia is correct as to the police procedure."

Judge Kingsley gave Pancho a half smile. "I think you have everything you need, Mr. McMartin. Do you have anything further on *voir dire?*"

Pancho shook his head. "No, Your Honor. And I'd like to note my objection to Exhibits Twenty-six and Twenty-seven on the basis that they are incomplete and selective pieces of the surveillance films from the date of the murder. Apparently all of the other video which may have exonerated my client has been destroyed without even having been reviewed by the authorities."

Judge Kingsley waved Harry Chang down. "I'll allow the exhibits into evidence. Your arguments as to what may be missing will go to the weight of the evidence. You may proceed, Mr. Chang."

Harry thanked the Judge and arranged for the two videos to be played for the jury. Gouveia remained on the stand.

"Mr. Gouveia," said Harry, once the videos were shown, "in Exhibit Twenty-six we see two people, one of whom is Irene Kamaka. Do you know who the man behind her is?"

Gouveia nodded. "Yes, he's Marcus Young, one of my security guards."

"Is he in uniform? White shirt and black pants?"

"Yes sir. You can kind of make out our company patch on his left sleeve."

"What time does the video show when Auntie Irene first appears?"

"Eight-seventeen."

"Do you know why he happened to be there at that time?"

Pancho rose. "Objection. Calls for speculation."

Judge Kingsley nodded curtly. "Sustained. Rephrase, Mr. Chang."

"Mr. Gouveia, was Marcus Young assigned to patrol the area of the shopping center where this camera was located?"

"Yes he was." Gouveia paused and looked at Harry as if he expected a follow up question, but before Harry could say anything, Gouveia added, "And in fact I had specifically asked him to keep an eye on Auntie Irene and her cousins when they were *pau* with their gig to make sure they got safely back to their cars."

"Why did you do that? Was there a specific threat that concerned you?"

Gouveia's response was swift and firm. "Oh no, not at all. I just knew they wouldn't be getting through until fairly late and wanted to make sure they were fine."

Harry Chang nodded absently. "Did you talk to Marcus Young after it was reported that Ms. Kamaka had been murdered?"

"Not until a couple of days later. Marcus didn't report in that night and didn't show up for work the next day. I was obviously concerned, what with the chain of events and all, but before I called the police he called me. He said that when he heard Irene had been murdered he panicked and ran because he felt responsible. He hadn't walked her to her car like I'd instructed him. Instead, he left her at the escalator. He figured he'd be fired, maybe even blamed. So, in his words, 'like an idiot' he ran."

Gouveia's calm and confident demeanor had undergone a transformation, and Pancho was watching him closely. His eyes had become active, darting around the courtroom. There was perspiration evident on his forehead. He coughed repeatedly.

"How long had Marcus Young been working for you?" asked Harry.

"About five years."

"Any problems with him until that night?"

"No, none whatsoever. He was a great employee. Seemed like a real nice kid. Reliable. That's why I asked him to keep an eye on the aunties." Gouveia wiped his forehead with his bare hand.

"Mr. Gouveia, Marcus Young was found murdered some weeks after Ms. Kamaka's death, is that correct?"

"Yes. Poor kid. We were all devastated to hear the news."

"Had you seen or talked to Marcus other than the one phone call since the murder of Ms. Kamaka?"

"No. I kinda thought he'd left town." Gouveia's nose wrinkled up, like he had just smelled something bad. "I mean, he gave up a pretty good job."

Harry Chang looked at the jury, then at the Judge, then back at Gouveia. Pancho could see he was struggling with the line of questioning. "Is there anything at all that you can think of, Mr. Gouveia, which would link Marcus Young's murder to that of Irene Kamaka?"

Gouveia acted surprised at the question. "Why no. Of course not. What would there be?"

Harry shrugged. "I have no idea, sir; I'm just asking if you could think of any."

"No." Gouveia looked up at the Judge. "I have no idea why the poor kid was murdered, but I can tell you that it didn't have anything to do with the robbery and murder of Auntie Irene." Pancho started to rise to object, but then he decided to let it go and sat back down.

"I have no further questions." Harry Chang looked to Pancho to be happy to be done.

"Mr. Gouveia," said Pancho slowly, as he rose. "Why are you able to tell us that Marcus Young's death had nothing to do with the murder of Irene Kamaka?"

Gouveia seemed taken aback. "What do you mean? I just know. How could there be?"

Pancho held his hands out in a kind of 'you tell me' gesture. "Well, forgive me, sir, but when the security guard assigned to protect Auntie Irene disappears after her murder, then turns up murdered, there's a lot of room to speculate."

There was a silent beat before Harry jumped to his feet. "Objection, Your Honor. Is there a question there? Or is Mr. McMartin just making a speech?"

"Sustained. Ask a question or move on, Mr. McMartin."

Pancho smiled and nodded. "Mr. Gouveia, what time does the video, Exhibit Twenty-seven, show when my client, Mr. Jackson, appears on screen?"

Gouveia looked down at his file before answering. "Eight forty-one."

Pancho frowned. "So more than twenty-four minutes passed between the time Auntie Irene left the gig at the upstairs restaurant and the time Mr. Jackson appears on the surveillance video, is that correct?"

"Yes."

"And it's your testimony that despite having two hundred cameras at the Center, these are the only two video files which you deemed to be relevant?"

Gouveia nodded slowly. "Yes sir, that's correct. I saw nothing unusual in any of the other videos I reviewed."

Pancho looked down at his notes for a moment. "Why did you say you assigned Marcus Young to keep an eye on Auntie Irene and her cousins?"

Gouveia sniffed before answering. "No particular reason other than I admire them so much and knew they'd be *pau* with their gig at about the time most of the Center was shutting down. I wanted Marcus to make sure they got to their cars safely."

"Had there been many incidents of mugging at Ala Moana Shopping Center lately?"

Gouveia was shaking his head before the question was finished. "Oh no. Not at all. I was just being careful is all."

"Mr. Gouveia, is it your testimony that you did not talk to Marcus Young after Auntie Irene's murder except for the one time he called in to explain why he left?"

"Yes. That's correct."

"And you never saw Marcus Young again?"

Gouveia's eyes became active again. He seemed to look everywhere at once before settling back on Pancho. "Yes. That's correct."

Pancho nodded, as if to himself. He walked back to his table and picked up a yellow legal pad. He pretended to read. What he was really doing was thinking furiously. Drew had supplied him with some ammunition via Booger to go after Gouveia, but to Pancho it felt like he'd be stepping into possible quicksand with no way out. He could either wing it and go after Gouveia, or he could ask the Court to require that Gouveia be subject to being recalled to testify. He decided he needed to hear Booger's story in full and in person before going after Gouveia.

Pancho looked up to Judge Kingsley. "I have no further questions at this time, Your Honor, but I request that the witness be subject to recall."

The Judge looked to Harry Chang, who did not look happy, but made no move to object. "So ordered." He then dismissed Scotty Gouveia after explaining to him that he may be required to testify again at a later date.

"Mr. Chang? Your next witness."

"Your Honor, the State rests."

Twenty-Seven

Judge Kingsley gave everyone the afternoon off. Pancho had until the next morning to decide on whether or not he was going to present a case, but for the moment, he leaned back in the passenger seat of Drew's black Thunderbird convertible and stared up at the powder blue sky. There were only a few wispy clouds. As Kamehameha Highway ran through some of the last remaining pineapple fields in Hawai'i, the ocean came into view, a deep blue contrast to the sky. They took the Hale'iwa bypass road, then reconnected with Kamehameha Highway, the ocean on their left.

This was the North Shore, the famed surfing area. Although still part of the City and County of Honolulu, it was a different world. Some locals still called it 'the country,' although it was becoming more and more built up and populated every year. As they rounded Waimea Bay, Pancho smiled to himself as he watched all the young bucks brave the jump into the Bay from the huge rock sticking out of the water on the left side of the Bay. The surf at Waimea didn't break unless the waves were over twenty feet. Today the Bay was flat, blue, and enticing.

At Pupukea Road they turned right and headed mauka, up the mountain to the residential community of Pupukea. The homes ranged from modest, single wall construction to large mansions. The word on the street was that there were more than a few retired drug dealers living in the area. Drew pulled in at a one story stucco house with a yard that needed attention. The grass was brown and full of weeds. The lone plumeria tree in the front yard looked tired and lean. There were desiccated plumeria flowers lying on the ground.

"Whose house is this?" asked Pancho.

"A friend of my partner. The guy's off on some extended trip. My partner is supposed to look after the place," Drew said, and chuckled, "but that obviously doesn't involve watering the yard."

A Samoan man almost as large as Drew opened the door before they had a chance to knock. Keani Sefo was something of a local legend. Born and raised in Honolulu, he was a football star at BYU before being drafted by the San Diego Chargers, where he spent his entire fifteen year career in the NFL as one of the most productive tight ends in the franchise history. Drew and Keani were close friends, and when Drew was forced to retire a few years after Keani, it was a natural fit for Drew to move to Hawai'i and work for Keani at his growing private detective firm. Pancho had known Keani for years, and although Pancho liked him, the two hadn't hit it off in the same way Drew and he had.

Pancho and Drew followed Keani into the living room where a tan and lean, almost skinny *haole* man of about twenty sat on a floral print couch watching television. He had stringy, dirty blond hair and a wisp of a moustache. He was not wearing a shirt, just baggy swim trunks. He had the tan of someone who spent most of his days at the beach. He clicked off the television and stood to face the three men. Pancho saw that his eyes were light blue.

"Pancho McMartin, this is Davis Bogarty, Booger to everyone who knows him." Keani clapped Booger on the back. Pancho saw the gesture as an unconscious assertion of Keani's trust in the kid.

"Howzit?" Pancho said. He transferred the briefcase he was holding to his left hand and shook Booger's hand, which was rough and calloused.

"I'm okay," said Booger, letting himself plop back down on the couch. "A little freaked out by all of this." His voice was deeper than Pancho expected.

"From what I hear, I don't blame you." Pancho sat in a matching print easy chair. Drew and Keani pulled up chairs from the open plan dining area and sat as well. Pancho opened his soft leather briefcase and pulled out a yellow legal pad and pen. "Why don't you tell me everything you know about Marcus Young, then what he told you and we can see where things stand and how we can help make sure you're safe?"

Booger sniffed and let out a small sigh. He rubbed his nose with the back of his right hand. "Shoots, I'm not sure where to begin. I've known Marcus since we were kids. We both grew up in Aina Haina and went to Kalani High School together. We used to surf and hang out a lot."

"Did you keep in touch after high school?" asked Pancho.

"Yeah, pretty much. You know how it is. Sometimes we wouldn't see each other for six months or so, then we'd run into each other at the beach or at a party or whatever and we'd start hanging again."

"What did Marcus do?" Pancho held up a hand. "I mean before he went to work for Paradise Security."

Booger looked toward the ceiling, squinting as he did so, as if that would help him remember. "All sorts of shit. He worked construction for a while, but even though the pay was good, he didn't like it much. He tried being a waiter; I think he worked at Zippy's for a while, but he got fired from that for sassing some customers. He had a bunch of fast food jobs. In between, and sometimes during, he would deal a little dope." Booger looked around at the three men watching and listening to him. "This isn't being recorded or anything, is it?"

Pancho smiled and shook his head. "No. We're just trying to find out what you know. Don't worry about saying anything."

Booger nodded and looked relieved. He scratched his scalp before continuing. "Anyway, I thought it was pretty funny when he got the job at the security company."

"Why's that?" asked Drew.

"'Cause being a security guard's kind of like being a cop, isn't it? I mean, I just couldn't envision Marcus being a cop, even a rent-a-cop." He paused and absently rubbed his left arm. "But shoots, he lasted a long time there. Over five years I think."

"What kind of work were you doing during all this time?" asked Pancho.

Booger shrugged. "Roofing. I've been with Occidental Roofing since I graduated. Did pretty good. I bought that house in Ka'a'awa on the ocean." He curled up his mouth in disgust. "Course that's all shot up and trashed right now. Fuckers."

"Tell us about that. What was Marcus doing there and who shot up the place?"

Booger sighed loudly this time. "I was spending a lot of time at my girlfriend's house at Sunset Beach, so my house was sitting empty for days and sometimes weeks on end. So when Marcus called me and said he needed a place for hang out for a few days where people wouldn't know to look for him, I offered to let him stay at the house."

"Did he tell you why he needed to hide out?" asked Pancho.

"Not right away. And he didn't say 'hide out,' just that he didn't want anyone bothering him for a few days. But when I went to meet him at the house and give him the keys I could see he was all out of sorts. Nervous and shit. So I got a six pack from the 7-Eleven and we sat on the lanai drinking and talking story. Eventually he told me all about Scotty Gouveia, he's the owner of the security company, and Auntie Irene and what happened. It was a total fuck job if you ask me."

Pancho sat forward. "Tell us, as exactly as you can recall, what he said."

Booger looked upwards again. After a few moments he took a deep breath and expelled it slowly. "Marcus had gotten pretty tight with Gouveia. I guess the turnover of security guards is pretty common, so Marcus had become kinda senior. Anyway, this Gouveia dude called Marcus into his office one day and closed the door behind him. Real secretive like. He told Marcus that he was in some deep shit with some Vegas guys for gambling debts. Marcus knew Gouveia took off for Vegas a lot, but he hadn't known how big a gambler he was. So Gouveia asked Marcus if he'd like to make some side money."

Booger chuckled. "Marcus may not have been the smartest dude, but he wasn't a complete dummy. He knew that whatever was about to be proposed was going to be illegal, which didn't bother him any. So Gouveia proceeds to tell Marcus that Auntie Irene was playing a gig with her group at Ala Moana Center and that she'd be carrying a lot of money and some other stuff of value. Gouveia didn't tell Marcus what the other 'stuff' was." Booger made quote signs with his fingers. "But Marcus figured it was drugs of some kind."

"Did Marcus say what he thought when he heard Auntie Irene might be carrying drugs and cash?"

Booger shrugged. "Nah. He didn't say."

"Okay, go on."

"Anyway, Gouveia tells Marcus that he wants Marcus to rob Auntie Irene. Just snatch her purse and ukulele and run like hell. No one was supposed to get hurt. Marcus said he figured that if Auntie Irene was carrying something illegal, like drugs, she couldn't very well report to the cops that she'd been robbed, so it would be kind of a perfect crime."

Drew shifted in his chair, grimacing in pain as he did so, then he asked, "Did Gouveia tell Marcus where the cash Auntie Irene was carrying came from?"

Booger shook his head. "Nah. According to Marcus, all he said was that she'd have money and other valuable 'stuff' on her, and if Marcus could make the snatch, Gouveia would give Marcus ten grand."

Drew emitted a low whistle and asked, "How much did Gouveia say she'd have on her?"

"Don't know," said Booger. "But obviously it had to be a lot."

The room was silent for a few minutes. There was a lot to ponder. Finally, Pancho asked, "So what went wrong? How did Auntie Irene end up dead?"

Booger shook his head in what Pancho took for either disgust or disbelief. "This part I don't know for sure. I think Marcus may have been fucking with me about this. What he claimed was that he didn't trust his boss, Gouveia. Marcus knew there were cameras all over the shopping center, so he enlisted some guy he knew, some black kid, to do the actual snatch. But the kid wasn't supposed to hurt her. Marcus was following along at a distance when he saw the black kid run out from the shadows and start beating on Auntie Irene. The kid grabbed her purse and ran.

"Marcus said he went to Auntie first, to see if she was all right, but when he saw she was passed out and bleeding heavily, he started chasing the black kid. But he was too far behind him and lost sight of him. Instead of going back and calling the cops and helping her, Marcus panicked and figured Gouveia would never believe him that someone else had mugged her. So he ran." Booger shook his head again. "Fucking idiot."

Again there was silence in the room.

"What did he say about the ukulele case?" Drew finally asked. "The eyewitness only saw the black guy running with a purse." He looked at Booger.

Booger raised both his palms. "He didn't say shit about it. Of course, I didn't know about any eyewitness at the time, so I figured either Marcus tried to do the snatch, but the old lady fought back and things got out of hand, or else he really did have an accomplice." He looked at Pancho. "Sorry, I don't know if your client was involved or not."

Pancho looked up from the notes he was taking and nodded distractedly. So far, it seemed like they still hadn't exonerated Jackson. They had just added another layer to the mystery. "So what happened at your house?" Pancho asked.

"Fuck if I know," said Booger. "Someone must've found Marcus and tortured him to try to find out where the stuff he was supposed to have stolen was. Seems like it must have been Gouveia if Marcus was telling me the truth." He paused for a moment. "Or the guys who the scag belonged to found out about him and found him first."

"Any idea from Marcus if he knew who belonged to the money and whatever else there was?" asked Pancho.

Booger stood and stretched. "Naw. Shoots, he didn't even know what he was stealing besides money." He turned and started toward the sliding glass lanai door. "I'm gonna jump into the pool and cool off for a minute."

Pancho, Drew, and Keani sat silent while Booger walked out. In a moment they heard a splash as he dove into the pool. Pancho was first to speak.

"So, what've we learned?"

Drew cleared his throat and slowly, obviously painfully, stood. "Don't mind me," he said. "I have to stretch my legs a little." He put both hands on the back of his chair and did some stretching. "So we know Gouveia was willing to rip someone off, presumably Lopaka, for money and possibly drugs. Pretty ballsy thing to do. Guy could get himself seriously killed acting like that."

"He must have been in some kind of financial jam to take a chance like that," said Keani.

"Yeah," agreed Drew. "I'll do some digging to see what I can come up with."

"In the meantime," said Pancho, "we're still stuck with a slightly built black kid being the assailant." He looked at Drew and Keani and smiled grimly. "We need to find another slightly built black kid."

"You're positive it wasn't your client?" asked Keani.

Pancho's face looked as intense as his response sounded. "Absolutely. There's no way Jackson beat Auntie Irene to death."

Booger ambled back into the room, still toweling himself dry. He folded the towel and set it on the couch, then sat on it. He looked at the three men watching him. "So, what you think?"

Pancho leaned toward him, putting his elbows on his knees. "Booger, do you have any idea who the black kid might be? Any thoughts at all?"

"You mean besides your client?" His tone was light, as if he thought he was being funny.

"I know it wasn't my client, so yes, someone else."

Booger shook his head. "I don't know any black friends of Marcus."

"Any ideas on who might know?" asked Drew.

Booger thought about it. He ran his hands through his still wet hair, then rubbed his hands on the towel he was sitting on. He smiled. "Shit, of course. Try Amy, his girlfriend . . . or ex-girlfriend. She might know."

Drew nodded. "Is she the Korean girl?"

"Yeah, Amy Park. Her parents live in Mayor Wright housing."

Drew turned to Pancho. "She's the one Marcus' ex-roommate told me about."

Booger laughed. "Billy Boy? Did you meet Billy Boy? Piece of work, isn't he?"

Pancho ignored the distraction. "Booger, what if I need you to testify? What if it's the only way to save my client? Will you do it?"

Booger's smile faded immediately and he looked at Keani. He was clearly scared. "No fucking way. That was the deal, wasn't it, man? I'd tell you everything I know, but in exchange you wouldn't try to make me testify. That was the deal." He was still looking at Keani, with whom he'd made the deal.

Keani nodded. "That's the deal. Pancho was just checking."

Booger folded his arms over his bare chest. "'Cause that's the way it is, man. No fucking way I'm going to ruin my life or get killed. Sorry, man." He looked to Pancho. "But I'm not gonna testify and that's final."

Pancho nodded slightly, but said nothing further.

Twenty-Eight

Paula eyed Pancho over her martini. As usual he sipped a Patron on the rocks. "You actually look halfway decent for going into day five of a murder trial."

Pancho had been lost in thought, staring down at his drink, but now he looked up and forced a smile. "Well, I had the afternoon off and had a lovely drive to the country with Drew and now I'm sitting with the woman I love looking out at one of the most beautiful views on the planet." He gestured toward the floor to ceiling window situated next to their dining table. They were in Sarrento's Restaurant at the top of the Ilikai. The view out the window was all of Waikiki and Diamond Head beyond. The sun was setting out of their view, but it cast a soft pink glow on the scene below.

"Dare I ask how the trial's going?"

Pancho shrugged. "About as good as I can expect at this point. Harry got everything in he wanted. I poked some pretty good holes in their eyewitness and the line-up. But so far, that's all I've done, poke holes. Things are moving fast, and I'm scared I'm going to run out of trial before I find the key to the case." He sipped his drink and picked up the menu.

"Tomorrow's Friday. Is the Judge going to go all day?"

"I think he wants to take another afternoon off for motions. He's supposed to start another trial next week, but I haven't been able to give him a good timeframe for when I'll rest."

Susan nodded in understanding. "So that guy Drew found definitely won't testify?"

"Nah. The poor bugga's scared out of his mind. Don't blame him either." Pancho's mouth turned down, and he gave a small shake of his head. "It's pretty frustrating."

They sat in silence for a few moments, both looking out at the sparkling lights of the hotels reflected on the calm water. Since the death threat, Pancho had insisted that Paula sleep at her own place. Their time together became all the more precious.

Pancho looked back at Paula's profile and felt a tightening in his gut; a good kind of tightening, the feeling of overwhelming love. "Let's go to Maui for the weekend when the trial's over," he said.

Paula turned from the window and smiled at him. "Sounds wonderful."

***

The next morning Pancho made his pro forma Motion for Judgment of Acquittal before the jury was reseated. There was no doubt the motion would be denied as the Judge would have to rule there was insufficient evidence upon which a jury could convict Jackson Steele to grant such a motion, but it was a matter of routine for the defense to make the motion at the close of the prosecution's case. When Judge Kingsley promptly denied the motion, the jury was brought in and the Judge instructed Pancho to proceed with his case.

Pancho called William McDowell, his security consultant, as his first witness. He'd wrestled with the order of his witnesses for several days. The main thing was to finish strong, and once he had made the decision to put Jackson on the stand, the probability was that he would be the final witness. The unknown factor was Scotty Gouveia. If Drew could come up with enough ammunition to blow Gouveia out of the water and get him to admit that Marcus Young was supposed to rob Auntie Irene at Gouveia's instructions, then Gouveia could very well be the final witness; but without Booger's testimony, Pancho was still at a loss as to how to break Gouveia.

Pancho took McDowell through his qualifications, which were substantial. He had literally written the book on standards for commercial video surveillance. McDowell, a scholarly looking man with a pinched face and a white Van Dyke beard, confirmed there were two hundred cameras spread around Ala Moana Center, which was quite adequate. He explained how Paradise Security had converted to a digitized system several years ago, which was also state of the art. According to McDowell, the industry standard was that the camera files should be retained for six to eight weeks.

"Why is that?" asked Pancho.

"Well, the need for a particular surveillance video may not manifest itself until several weeks after an incident," said McDowell. "For instance, if someone falls on site they may not retain counsel to pursue litigation until they later determine that their injuries are severe enough to hire an attorney, then, of course, the attorney may not note his appearance with the insurance company until some time later. So unless the security company in this hypothetical case knew about the fall, and its insurance company ordered it to sequester the video file, the video of the fall and thus possible evidence of causation could be lost forever. The six to eight weeks creates a buffer to allow any relevant parties to determine a need to save a particular video."

"Mr. Gouveia testified that they only save the videos for two weeks."

"Yes, so I understand," McDowell broke in, not waiting for a question. "I would take issue with that as being unduly and unnecessarily short."

"Mr. Gouveia also testified that out of the ten cameras which would have possibly captured video of Auntie Irene and her assailants, he was only able to identify two videos of any relevancy. Does that sound logical to you?"

McDowell was shaking his head of stark white hair before Pancho had finished. "No, sir. Not at all. These cameras are constantly recording, or at least they should be. As a subject moves from one area of coverage to the next, she should show up in the respective videos."

"Does this mean that some videos have been withheld?"

"Objection," said Harry, half standing. "The question asks for a state of mind of which he could have no knowledge." Judge Kingsley nodded in agreement.

"Sustained. Rephrase, Mr. McMartin."

"Mr. McDowell, what would the possible explanations be for not having all of the video files on which Auntie Irene and/or her assailants would be seen?" Pancho glanced over at Harry Chang, who made no move to further object.

McDowell gave a grim smile. "They were withheld or simply went missing for some other reason."

"Thank you, sir. Now, given that there were only ten cameras that might have captured Auntie Irene's assailants and less than one hour of relevant timeframe, what would your opinion be as to the proper protocol for dealing with the videos from those cameras during the timeframe in question?"

"That's easy and pretty darn logical," said McDowell. "I, and any well trained security consultant, would have immediately segregated and preserved all of the videos, regardless of perceived content. It's ridiculous to suggest that the police didn't need to review those videos just because the owner of the security firm didn't think there was anything of value on them."

Pancho had noticed Harry Chang rising slowly, tentatively, as McDowell was answering the question. "Objection, Your Honor. Move to strike the answer. Mr. McDowell was not qualified as a law enforcement specialist and he therefore can't render an expert opinion as to what the police should or should not have done."

Judge Kingsely looked at Pancho. A small smile played at his mouth. "Do you want to fix that, Mr. McMartin?"

Pancho nodded. "Yes, thank you, Your Honor. Let me rephrase. Mr. McDowell, putting aside what the police should or should not have done, do you have an opinion as to what the security firm should have done with those videos?"

"Yes I do. The company should have retained and preserved them."

"Thank you. I have no further questions." Pancho sat down and looked at Harry, who was staring down at his notes. In a moment he looked up and rose.

"Isn't that what Mr. Gouveia did?"

McDowell looked confused. "I'm sorry. What's the question?"

"The question, Mr. McDowell, is whether or not Mr. Gouveia did exactly what you recommended he do when he offered to have

Detective Wong review the videos? Was there something more he should have done?"

McDowell glanced at Pancho before answering. "Well, he certainly did the right thing by offering the videos to Detective Wong, but I think he should have turned them over en masse, without any editorial comment, which obviously affected the Detective's decision as to whether or not to view the files." He paused, then added quickly, before Harry could ask another question. "I'll leave it to other experts to determine whether Detective Wong did the right thing by taking Mr. Gouveia's word for the content and importance of the videos."

Pancho could see the corners of Harry's mouth turn down in anger at the unsolicited comment. "But Mr. McDowell," Harry said, then paused. "Strike that." Harry looked up to the Judge. "I have no further questions of this witness." He glanced at Pancho and sat down.

Pancho looked at the clock on the wall. It was only 10:15. Things were moving too fast. He needed to buy time for Drew to do his thing. If they couldn't find Marcus' girlfriend, Amy Park, and if she couldn't tell them who the black guy with Marcus was, then the jury would be left with Jackson being the only logical suspect.

"Mr. McMartin?" Judge Kingsley's voice was inquisitive. "Are you ready to call your next witness?"

"Yes, Your Honor. The defense calls Jiro Hasegawa."

The clerk left the court to call the witness and came back followed by a squat, sturdy-looking Japanese man. His head was completely shaved. Pancho noticed he was bowlegged as he walked to the witness stand. When Hasegawa sat and faced the courtroom he smiled and nodded to the jury, then to the Judge, then to Harry Chang. He looked at Pancho last, the slight smile never leaving his lips.

Pancho took Mr. Hasegawa easily through the preliminaries. Despite his very Japanese name and appearance, Hasegawa had no trace of an accent. His dark eyes sparkled, and when he answered a question, he would often look at the jury.

"Mr. Hasegawa, how did you first have occasion to meet me?" asked Pancho.

"I answered an ad in the *Star-Advertiser* that you had placed in which you asked for anyone who was at Ala Moana Shopping Center on

February twelfth between the hours of 8:00 and 9:30 p.m. to contact you. I recalled that my wife and I had been there on that day, so I called you and first spoke with your nice secretary, Susan, I think it is. She arranged for you to call me back."

"Is there any particular reason why you're sure you were at Ala Moana on that date?"

"Yes sir. The next day, February thirteenth, is my sister's birthday and I hadn't gotten her a birthday present yet." Mr. Hasegawa looked to the jury and gave a sheepish smile. "We were having her and her husband over for dinner for her birthday, so I needed to get off my *okole* and get out and get her a present." Several of the jurors smiled back at him.

"And the timeframe?"

"Since we had to go out anyway, I suggested to my wife that we go out to dinner. So we did our shopping, then went to Longhi's. I know we got there a little before 8:00. We were all *pau* a little before 9:00, maybe around 8:45."

"What did you do when you were through with dinner?"

"We walked to our car, which was parked on the *makai* side of the parking lot, straight out from Longhi's." He looked at the jury. "Lots of room over that side at night."

"Did you see anything unusual on the walk to your car?"

Hasegawa shook his head. "No, not really. I noticed two guys messing around with their moped, or by their moped, but I didn't pay any attention to them."

"At that time did you notice anything out of the ordinary with regard to those two men?"

"No. Sorry. They were in the shadows, by the pillars where the restaurant valet is, so it was too dark to see anything clearly. I assumed they were just getting ready to leave."

"So what happened next?"

"We got into the car and, just as I turned on the headlights and put the car in gear, the moped zoomed out in front of me and took off toward the Ala Moana Park ramp." Hasegawa looked up at the Judge. "I had to slam on the brakes to avoid hitting them."

"Were you able to see the riders of the moped at that point?"

"Yes. Clearly. They literally passed within a few yards of the front of our car. There were two men. The driver was dark skinned. He was thin and looked young. His hair was short. He was wearing shorts and some kind of tee shirt, but there was an obvious bulge in front, like he had put a package under his shirt at his belly so he could drive the moped. The other man was also pretty young looking. He was kind of *haole* looking, but I think he was *hapa*, you know, mixed. So I would say he was a local kid. He had fairly long dark hair. He was wearing long dark pants and a short sleeved white shirt. I could see a patch of some kind on his leftt arm, so I assumed he was a security guard who had just gotten off duty."

"Was he holding anything?"

Hasegawa nodded. "Yes, he had something fairly large in his right hand, but it was on the side away from us and he was holding it down by his side, so I couldn't see what it was. I assumed it was some kind of purchase."

Pancho glanced down at his legal pad, then back up at the witness. "Mr. Hasegawa, were you able to tell if the dark skinned man was African-American or Polynesian or of some other specific ethnic group?"

Hasegawa was shaking his head before Pancho had finished. "Sorry. No, sir. I couldn't definitely say what the race of the fellow was other than that he was dark. It would be easy to say he was African-American, but I don't think it would be fair to do so, since I can't be sure."

Pancho looked at the jury, then back at the witness. "Mr. Hasegawa, can you tell the jury whether or not you believe that the defendant, Jackson Steele," Pancho extended his arm toward Jackson, "is the dark skinned man you saw on the moped that night?"

Mr. Hasegawa looked directly at Jackson and shook his head. "No, Mr. McMartin, the man I saw on the moped was definitely not your client."

Pancho smiled. "And you say they drove off in the direction of the Ala Moana Park ramp?"

"Yes sir."

"Did you go that direction as well?"

"No. I wanted to take the Atkinson exit, so I headed Diamond Head direction, toward Macy's."

Pancho nodded his silent thanks to Mr. Hasegawa. "I have no further questions, Your Honor."

Harry Chang practically jumped to his feet. "Mr. Hasegawa, you testified that you could not identify the dark skinned man on the moped as African-American, yet you state with certainty that it was not the defendant. How can you justify that testimony?" His tone was harsh and accusing.

Pancho suppressed a smile, although on one level he felt bad for Harry, who had just walked into the trap Pancho laid for him. Pancho knew that if Harry had the time to think about it before being forced to take the witness, he would have figured it out. Why hadn't Pancho asked the obvious follow up question, which was why Mr. Hasegawa could be so sure it wasn't Jackson? Pancho hadn't asked the question because he wanted Harry to ask it.

Mr. Hasegawa retained his good natured demeanor despite the harsh tone from Harry. "I know it wasn't the defendant because as my headlights hit them full on, I could see the left side of the moped driver's face quite clearly, Mr. Chang. Mr. Steele here has a visible scar on his right cheek. The moped rider had no such scar." Harry started to say something, but Mr. Hasegawa held up his hand. "Please let me finish, sir. Also, the moped driver had a fairly prominent nose, at least compared to Mr. Steele. If you look at Mr. Steele from the side, you can barely see a protrusion of nose."

Pancho could see that Harry Chang now knew he had walked into a trap, and he was fuming. There was absolute silence in the courtroom while Harry tried to figure out where to go next.

"But you say that the moped rider was wearing a light colored tee shirt?"

"Yes sir."

"Which may have been white, or at least a dirty white?"

"Yes."

"And dark colored shorts?"

"Yes."

"And rubber slippers?"

"I couldn't tell if they were rubber slippers, but he was wearing sandals of some kind."

"The moped driver's hair was cut short, like the defendant's?"

Mr. Hasegawa cocked his head to the side. "I would say that the moped driver's hair was smoother, not so, I don't know, clumpy, as Mr. Steele's."

Harry took a deep breath and reviewed his notes. "Mr. Hasegawa . . ." Harry's tone was once again accusatory. "You testified that you couldn't see what the passenger was carrying because it was on his right side, away from you, correct?"

"Yes, that's correct."

"Yet you also just testified that you were able to definitively see that the dark skinned driver of the moped did not have a scar on his right cheek." Harry paused, obviously hoping it was a dramatic pause.

"How is it that you were able to see the driver's right cheek so clearly, yet not see what the passenger was holding in his right hand?"

Mr. Hasegawa retained his calm demeanor despite Harry's aggressive tone. "Because when they came into view in my headlights I was facing them virtually head on. I looked right into the face of the driver and, although it was brief, I could clearly see his right cheek and his prominent nose. But I couldn't see, even from the head on vantage point, what the passenger was holding in his right hand other than that it was fairly large."

Pancho could see Harry's jaw flex.

"Mr. Hasegawa," said Harry, the exasperation now evident in his voice, "just so we're clear here, you did not see these two moped riders assault anyone?"

"Correct."

"You did not see the two moped riders running from any direction?"

"Correct."

"You did not see anyone chasing or calling after the moped riders?"

"Correct."

Harry paused, obviously thinking. "And so you saw absolutely nothing which would connect these two moped riders with the assault and murder of Auntie Irene, isn't that correct?"

Pancho was elated to see that Mr. Hasegawa didn't miss a beat. "That's correct, Mr. Chang."

"I have no further questions." Harry glared at Pancho as he sat down, his back to the jury.

Pancho ignored Harry and looked at the wall clock. It was 11:10. The Judge had told the attorneys that court would go until 1:00. He would use the afternoon for motions on other cases. Pancho looked from the clock to the Judge, expecting to be told to call the next witness. Instead, he saw that the Judge was conferring with his law clerk. The courtroom sat silent, waiting.

When Judge Kingsley finally looked out over the court, his face was taut with tension. "We're going to recess for the weekend. The jury is excused until nine o'clock Monday morning." The Judge's voice was as strained as his appearance. He faced the jury. "I apologize for sounding like a broken record, but I'm compelled to once again remind you to avoid any media coverage. You are not to discuss the case with anyone else, including your family members, tempting as that may be, and do not allow others to discuss the case with you. When you're all back here together again on Monday morning, remember that you are also prohibited from discussing the case among yourselves. Thank you and have a nice weekend."

The courtroom, including Judge Kingsley, stood while the jury filed out of the box. When they were gone, the Judge, still standing, said, "Will counsel please come to my chambers? Court is adjourned." He left in a swirl of black robe.

Something has happened, thought Pancho. He looked at Harry, who just shrugged, clearly still angry about the cross-examination trap he'd walked into. Pancho patted Jackson on the shoulder and told him he would stop by to see him later that day or the next, then he and Harry used the clerk's door to go to his chambers.

Judge Kingsley had his robe off and was hunched over his desk. He wore a short sleeved white shirt and tie, which was a faded floral pattern. Lester, the law clerk, sat in his usual corner spot. When the Judge looked up at the attorneys, his face was still drawn and his lips were pursed in anger.

"My office received a call about ten minutes ago. Gladys took the call. She's pretty shook up." Pancho knew Gladys had been Judge Kingsley's secretary for almost his entire career. When he'd been appointed to the bench, she followed him into public service.

"Basically the caller threatened all of us, and by that I mean me, my staff, and both of you."

Pancho could see that the Judge was pretty shaken up himself. "Did Gladys write down everything the caller said?" he asked.

Judge Kingsley nodded and handed a piece of note paper to Pancho. Pancho read it aloud.

> *"Ma'am, you need to know that just because you work for a judge you are not above the law of the people. It is important for you to tell Judge Kingsley and the rest of your staff and the attorneys that if that black boy gets off the hook for murdering Auntie Irene, the people will seek their own justice and will kill the Judge, all of you who work for him, and both of the attorneys. Please convey to them that if the boy is convicted, no action will be taken to harm any of you. Thank you for listening."*

The room was silent until Harry asked, "Did Gladys say he was really that formal?"

Judge Kingsley nodded. "Yeah. That made it all the more frightening for her. She said he spoke slowly and politely."

"Did she try to engage him at all?" asked Pancho.

"No. Well, I mean, she started to ask who he was when he finished his statement, but he'd already hung up."

More silence. Pancho handed the paper to Harry, who read it silently.

"What are you going to do?" Pancho finally asked.

Judge Kingsley expelled what seemed to be a huge amount of air. "I've called the Sheriff and they'll be arranging security protection for me and each member of my staff. They've also agreed to provide each of you with a security detail if you want it."

Pancho immediately shook his head. "I'll pass. I've got Drew to keep an eye on me. We already keep the office door locked, and Susan has been instructed not to let anyone in who's not known and expected."

Harry rubbed the back of his neck. "I don't know. I suppose I'm fine right up until the verdict. Then, if I lose, I suppose we're all at risk."

"What about the jury?" Pancho said. "They're the ones who decide the case. If we've been threatened, doesn't it make sense that they have been or will be?"

Judge Kingsley nodded his agreement. "My initial reaction was to meet with each one on Monday morning to see if any of them had been threatened. If so, I would sequester them. But now I'm wondering if I should contact each of them right away and instruct them to report any threatening calls or letters to me immediately."

The room was once again silent as everyone pondered the situation. Pancho ran his hand through his hair and loosened his tie, then he leaned forward, putting both elbows on the table. "I think what Harry said is right. We're all probably fine until the verdict. Then it'll just be a question of what the verdict is and what whoever this is really intends to do about it." He made eye contact with the Judge, then Harry, then back to the Judge.

"My two cents would be not to say anything to the jurors this weekend. Let them be and assume they'll come forward if they're threatened in any way. We don't need a bunch of freaked out jurors." Pancho paused, looking as if he had more to say, but then leaned back in his chair.

Judge Kingsley looked to Harry. "You got two cents to add, Harry?"

Harry nodded slightly. "I agree with Pancho."

The Judge, who had been hunched over his desk during the entire conversation, sighed and leaned back. He finally gave a slight nod. "I guess I agree as well. For now we'll say nothing to the jury. If I detect anything odd on Monday when I meet with each one individually, I'll sequester them. If any juror comes forward during the weekend with reports of any disturbing contact, I'll arrange for them to be immediately sequestered." He locked his hands together on top of his head and sighed again. "What a mess." He looked at his law clerk, who'd been taking notes. "You okay, Lester?"

Lester, who was fresh out of law school and looked to Pancho to be about twenty-five, nodded, although his voice broke just a touch when he said, "I'm fine, Judge."

"Okay then, I guess that's all we can do." The Judge directed his gaze to Pancho. "I assume you've arranged for your client to be in protective care?"

Pancho nodded. "They've had him in a private cell from day one. He's okay."

"Then you're out of here for today. I've got some motions to take care of." Judge Kingsley gave a weak smile. "Try to have a fine weekend."

Twenty-Nine

Pancho felt tired and depressed as he trudged back to his office from court. The day was as dreary as he felt. The trade winds had stopped, and the insidious vog from the Big Island had wasted no time in creeping its way up the island chain. The hot haze felt harsh on his skin. The big leather trial briefcase seemed heavier than he knew it was. He longed for a refreshing swim in the ocean.

"Hey, Pancho, try wait."

Pancho turned to Harry Chang's voice. Despite his mood, Pancho chuckled to himself at the Princeton Law School graduate's use of Pidgin. He watched Harry, obese and out of shape, huff and puff his way toward him.

"Hey, Harry. Pretty weird shit, yeah?"

Harry had reached Pancho and set down his own big briefcase. He bent over, hands on his knees, catching his breath. After a few moments he stood and wiped sweat off his face with his hand, which he then wiped onto his pants. He nodded. "I thought that after the heroin disclosure people would back off a little. But this is crazy." He wiped at his brow again. "I mean, it's not like we have a lot of experience with this racist stuff here, but doesn't it seem kind of weird to you that whoever this is would threaten the whole court?"

Pancho smiled ruefully. "You mean as opposed to just threatening me?"

Harry looked impassive for just a moment before breaking into his own half smile. "Yeah, li' dat." He picked up his briefcase and the two began strolling slowing down Queen Street.

"So," Harry said, "don't you think the best thing for everybody is to deal this frigging case? I don't want anyone getting hurt."

Pancho walked on for half a block before saying anything. He'd been going over that very thing in his own mind since he walked out of court, but the thought of pleading Jackson to anything that would keep him in jail actually made him nauseous. If he knew anything at all, it was that Jackson Steele was not guilty of murder or assault or robbery. He was guilty of being a psychologically abused black kid with bad looks and no support system.

Pancho stopped walking and put a hand on Harry's shoulder, causing him to stop as well. "I know what you're saying, Harry, and believe me when I say I've been grappling with this. I know you believe Jackson is guilty, and that's fine. That's part of what makes you such a good prosecutor. But it's important for you to know that I believe with every fiber of my being that Jackson is not guilty."

"Why's it important for me to know that?" Harry's tone was slightly sarcastic. "It's never been important to you before."

Pancho looked away, down the street back toward the court. He audibly exhaled. "Because there's no way I would put people's lives at risk if I had a guilty client whom I could convince to take a deal." He looked back at Harry, making and holding eye contact. "The irony is that I could convince Jackson to take a deal. He trusts me. I think I'm the only one in the world he trusts. And so he'd plead guilty to something he didn't do if I told him it was the right thing to do."

"Then do it," Harry said harshly. "The kid's a homeless vagrant. If he isn't guilty of this, he's probably guilty of something else."

Pancho began walking again. Harry followed. They said nothing until they got to Alakea Street, where they would part ways.

"You're a fair man, Harry. I'm disappointed you said that. But we're both under a lot of stress and I'll forget it. See you Monday." Pancho turned to walk to his office, leaving Harry standing at the corner watching him go.

***

Pancho saw through the glass front door of his office that Susan was on the phone, so he let himself in with his key. As he paused at her desk to pick up his pink message slips, she looked up at him and gave him a half-hearted smile. He smiled back, but he noticed that her well-lined face looked even more worn. Her normally sparkling eyes were quiet and dull. Her hair bun was sloppy and the chopstick which held it in place was hanging limply, barely doing its job.

Pancho sauntered into his office, feeling guilty at the toll this case was taking on people he cared about. He tossed the briefcase to the side of his desk. It made a loud thud and fell to its side. Pancho ignored it and sat heavily in his chair. He tossed the pink slips onto his desk, as carelessly as he'd tossed the briefcase. He leaned back in the chair and locked his hands on top of his head and closed his eyes, letting his mind drift. *I should go see Jackson. Should I tell Susan about the death threat? I need to find Drew.*

"You okay, boss?"

He hadn't heard Susan enter his office. He opened his eyes and sat up. His hands went to the arms of his chair. He had made a decision. "Have a seat for a minute, Suse." He gestured toward a client chair.

Susan sat. She wore a black pant suit with a white blouse. She crossed her legs and looked at him expectantly. "Something up?" she asked.

"We had another death threat today."

Susan's eyes widened and she unconsciously sat up a little. "Where? At court?"

Pancho nodded. "Yeah. The caller talked to Gladys. Scared the shit out of her. He pretty much threatened to kill all of us if Jackson is acquitted."

Susan coughed; a former smoker's cough. Pancho knew she tended to cough when she was excited or under stress. When she recovered, she asked, "Even the staff?"

"Yeah. That's what had poor Gladys so freaked out. No one's ever so much as snarled in her direction before. Now some asshole's saying he's going to kill everyone in the office plus Harry and me if Jackson gets off."

"Jesus." Susan's voice was soft.

"The caller said nothing about Harry's staff or my staff, but we all have to be diligent. It could be just one more scumbag making threats, but nowadays you never know. The Judge is using the Sheriff's Office to provide security for himself and his staff. Harry and I declined. We have Drew. And I think Harry's analysis is correct that even if it's serious, nothing's going to happen until we have a verdict." Pancho paused and looked at Susan. "You look a little stressed and tired. Did anything happen here this morning? Any threats or weirdness?"

Susan shook her head. "Not really. Some of our less polite clients have made comments like 'why is Pancho helping Auntie Irene's murderer when he should be working on my case.' Things like that. But no overt threats and no overly racist stuff. It's just been busy is all. I'm fine."

Pancho studied her for a moment. "Okay. As soon as Drew gets here he'll walk you to your car. Take the rest of the day off and relax over the weekend. I don't have anything to do other than prepare my witnesses. If I need something I'll call you and you can do it from home."

Susan rose slowly. "Thanks, Pancho. You're going to keep Drew by your side until this is over I hope?"

Pancho nodded. "We'll be attached at the hip." He watched her walk from the office. Of course he and Drew wouldn't be attached at the hip. Drew needed to find Amy Park to see if she knew any black guy whom Marcus Young hung out with.

Thirty

Pancho saw a new set forming, but he didn't lie down on his board yet. He'd noticed a pattern that it was usually the third or fourth wave in the sets which were the biggest, so he let the first two go by. It had the added benefit of clearing out many of the other surfers. He could see that the third wave would be good, and now he lay on his belly and began paddling evenly. As the wave approached, he increased his paddling rate so that by the time the wave began to lift him, he was at the wave's speed; then he was on the wave, his big classic Velzy shooting down the face as he stood, left foot forward. He made a sweeping right turn at the base of the wave's face and rode it back up, about halfway. It was a good wave, and there was only one other rider on it, well ahead of him. He had a better position, and when he felt he was getting too far ahead of the break, he put the pressure on his right foot to turn back into the wave. Just as he approached the whitewater of the breaking wave, he turned back to the right and again rode it halfway up the face.

As the wave began to lose steam he walked forward on the board until his left toes were hanging over the nose. His board's speed increased for a few fine moments, then he knew the wave was spent and he moved back, went down to his belly, let the wave break, and the whitewater pushed him toward shore.

He was tired. Five rides and he was exhausted from paddling back out. Too much work and not enough play he chided himself. As the last of the wave died into memory, he lazily paddled, in no hurry to get out of the water. The air was still hazy with vog and the sky was a white gray that sucked the blue out of the ocean, but the southerly Kona winds were barely a whisper, and the steely ocean was calm except for the sets of perfectly formed waves. The water felt good against the heavy heat of the day.

Earlier, Drew had told Pancho that he had a lead on Amy Park and wanted to head back out while it was still light. Even the big man didn't want to go knocking on doors at the Mayor Wright housing projects in the dark of night.

"Besides," he added, a tight smile on his ruggedly handsome Polynesian face, "the doc only gave me a limited supply of Vicodin for my knees and I want to take advantage of them while I can."

So Pancho had locked up, turned on the voice mail, and headed home. The moment he opened the sliding glass door to his lanai, he saw the surf was up to a respectable four feet or so, and he made the instant decision to head out. Now, as he finally reached the shallows, he slipped off his board and dunked his head under water to get his long hair out of his face. Although his right hand rested on top of the board, a small wave pushed the board forward, causing the sharp skeg, the fin, to hit him in the leg. He swore softly at the fleeting pain, tucked the board under his right arm, and walked out of the ocean. He felt better than he had in days. It was then that it hit him. Scag. The word exploded in his brain. Scag. Booger had used the word 'scag.'

The phone was ringing when he opened the door to his condo. His feet were still wet, so he walked gingerly across the limestone tiles in the entry and grabbed the phone off the kitchen counter. He could see from the caller ID that it was Drew.

"Big boy. Tell me what scag is."

"What?"

"Scag. Booger used it when he was talking to us. What is it?

There was silence on the line for several seconds. Finally, he said, "As far as I know, it's a street name for heroin. You're sure he used that word?"

"Positive. Remember when he said that Marcus must have been found by whoever the money and the scag belonged to? Why would he say that? He claimed he didn't know what else Auntie Irene had on her."

Another short silence. "Maybe he just meant drugs. We were all assuming the other stuff of value was drugs. Plus, since we know she was a heroin user, maybe he just assumed it was heroin."

"Mmmm. Maybe. But I think we should have another talk with the kid." Pancho paused, coming down off the initial excitement he felt at the revelation. He was probably grasping at straws again. He lightened the mood. "By the way, you missed some totally excellent surf."

"Oh fine. Rub it in. What a dickwad."

"Sorry. I couldn't resist. So, you called me, what's up?"

"Well, while you were out having a grand old time, your tireless private investigator, despite severe and virtually crippling pain, was out pounding the pavement searching for leads."

"Blah, blah, blah. So, you found her? Amy?"

"Found her parents. Nice people. Kind of old country. Very polite. The apartment smelled like kim chee. Amy doesn't live with them. Hasn't for quite some time. They'd met Marcus a few times. Liked him well enough; at least that's what they said. They didn't like the fact that their daughter was living with him, but there wasn't much they could do about it. When Marcus was found murdered, Amy was devastated, but she refused to come home. She's still living in the apartment she shared with Marcus. It was under her name."

Pancho had been drying himself off as he listened. Now, with the phone tucked under his ear, he took the towel and mopped up the water he had dripped onto the hallway floor. "So where is it?" he asked.

"Makiki. But she's at work. She's a waitress at that new place in Ward Center. I called and was told her shift ends at eight, so I plan to be there then. Want to come along?"

Pancho thought for a moment. He didn't have any plans. He wanted to keep Paula out of his zone of danger as much as possible, or at least as much as he would be able to stand being apart from her. "Sure. Want to pick me up or should I meet you somewhere?"

"I'll pick you up at six-thirty and you can buy me dinner before we ambush and waterboard her."

***

Amy Park was an attractive, diminutive woman in her early twenties. She had streaks of red and purple in her shoulder-length, otherwise black hair. Her ears, nose, and bottom lip were pierced. She wore a uniform of black shirt and a light blue man's tie and black slacks, but it was obvious that, despite the masculine look, she had a dynamite figure. Drew had approached her alone as she left work. Although his hugeness could be imposing, especially to a five foot woman, Drew somehow had developed a knack for approaching people in a non-threatening manner.

Having talked Amy into talking to them, the three now sat at a secluded table in the bar area of a nearby restaurant. She ordered a glass of chardonnay and both Pancho and Drew ordered Patron.

"We're sorry about your loss," said Pancho once they had their drinks. "We understand you and Marcus had been living together."

Amy gave a slight nod and stared into her drink. When she spoke, her voice was small, childlike even, although the content was hard, rough, and defiant. "I still don't know what happened. The cops won't tell me shit."

"Do you know what Marcus was into? Had he been involved in anything illegal?" asked Drew.

She shook her head. "Not that I know of. He'd been working at the security firm for about five years. It was good, steady work. Then, after the murder at the shopping center, he called and said he had to take off for a week or so. He said he fucked up by not protecting Auntie Irene and was going to have to quit." She looked up at Drew, then at Pancho. Her face was hard and angry. "The shithead wouldn't even tell me where he was. He sounded scared — different than the cocky dude I fell in love with."

Drew asked, "Who was he hanging around with before all this went down? Who were his closest buds?"

She sipped her wine and thought about it. She gave a slight nod toward Drew. "You told me you already know about Booger, although they hadn't been hanging that much lately. There were a couple of security guards at work he'd go out and have a drink with sometimes if they all got off at the same time."

"Any dark skinned guys, black or Polynesian or whatever?" asked Pancho.

Amy looked hard at him. "Why?"

Pancho kept a neutral expression and shrugged. "Just exploring all alternatives. We have a witness who said he thought he saw someone who might have been Marcus on a moped with a dark skinned man."

"Who wasn't your client?" she asked.

Pancho nodded. "According to the witness, it definitely wasn't my client." He paused. His stomach felt like it had a knot in it. "Why? Is there any indication that Marcus knew Jackson Steele?"

"Naw," Amy answered right away, and Pancho relaxed. Amy sighed and leaned back in her chair. She picked up her glass, but didn't drink. "There was this dude everyone called Rash who Marcus had been hanging with on and off for about a month before all this shit happened. I think he was Indian or something like that. He was dark skinned. From a distance I can see someone thinking he was black."

Drew and Pancho both sat forward in their seats, unconsciously excited. "Big guy?" Drew asked.

She shook her head. "Naw. Skinny little fucker."

"Long hair, short hair?"

"Short last time I saw him. The first time I met him, as I said about a month before, he had long hair which he wore in a pony tail. But the last time I saw him, which was a couple of days before the murder, he'd cut it all off and it was super short."

"Did he say why he had cut it?" Pancho asked.

"Yeah. He said it was too fucking hot and he got sick of it."

"Do you know if he had a job?" Pancho again.

Amy didn't answer right away. She sipped her wine and looked at Pancho with a hard expression. "You think Rash might be the murderer instead of your client, right?"

Pancho tilted his head, a kind of nod. "We think it's a real possibility."

Amy expelled some air and set her glass on the table. "Shit, man. That's heavy. You think Marcus was in on it, too? I mean, I know I'm prejudiced, but I can't see him as a murderer."

The three let that statement hang over the table for a moment before Drew spoke, choosing his words carefully. "Can you see Marcus being involved in something illegal that wasn't violent?"

Amy laughed and in her little girl voice said, "Fuck yeah. Marcus wasn't some angel. He'd done some shit, and it wouldn't have surprised me if he was involved in something illegal. I just don't think he'd get involved in anything that involved hurting someone, especially a woman."

Drew obviously felt there was no need to continue to try to be diplomatic, so he put it on the table. "We think Marcus was hired to do a simple purse snatch on Auntie Irene, then Marcus hired Rash to do it with him. No one was supposed to get hurt, but we think Rash went all violent on her and killed her. So the whole thing went wrong, and Marcus and Rash had to go into hiding. Apparently separately. We think whoever hired Marcus didn't know about Rash. They tracked down Marcus at Booger's place in Ka'a'awa and tortured him, presumably trying to find out where the loot was, or whatever it was that they stole."

Again there was silence, almost for a full minute. Finally Amy seemed to nod to herself. "I guess it makes sense. Marcus was doing great at the security guard firm, but he was always about the easy money. And I can see that prick Rash going all commando violent like. I told Marcus that Rash had anger issues. There was always this barely suppressed rage about him. He made me seriously uncomfortable."

"So," said Pancho, "do you have any ideas as to where we might find Rash?"

Amy snorted. "Like he'd be hanging around any of his usual haunts if he'd done what you say? I seriously doubt it."

Drew stepped in. "We know that, of course, but detective work has to start somewhere, and we don't know anything about this guy. We don't even have a real name." He paused and looked at Amy with an abashed look on his face. "I guess I didn't even ask you if you knew his name."

She smiled, letting him off the hook. "You didn't, but I don't. I just know Rash. The last I knew he did some construction, just laborer type shit. I don't think the dude had any real skills. I think he also drove taxi part-time for Charley's."

"Do you know where he lived?"

She shook her head. "Only that I think he lived out Pearl City side."

Pancho pointed to Amy's glass. "Another wine?"

"How much longer we gonna be?" she asked.

"Not much. We just need to pick your brain a little to see if there might be anything at all you know about Rash that can help us find him."

"Then I'll pass. Ask away. I'm supposed to go out with some friends tonight and I'd like to get home."

"Okay," said Pancho. "Any common friends you can think of? Any place where Marcus and Rash would go to hang out?"

Amy scrunched up her petite face. "I don't know. You might try this guy Sammy Lee. He knew both Booger and Marcus. He was in construction, too. I think he may have been the one who introduced Rash to Marcus. Other than that, I don't think I can help. I think they may have all gone to some Korean bars to drink and do whatever they do, but Marcus sure as shit never told me anything specific." She chuckled, almost to herself. "He knew that if I ever caught him fucking around with some Korean bar maid I'd cut his dick off."

Pancho allowed her a half smile, indulging her. He turned to Drew. "Anything else?"

Drew shook his head, but then changed his mind and turned back to Amy. "Did you go through Marcus' things after he died? Did you find any phone directory or cell phone that might have phone numbers on it?"

Amy looked suddenly tired, impatient with the conversation. "There wasn't much, besides a couple of uniforms for work and shorts and tee shirts for after work. He must have had his cell phone with him. And he probably used it as his directory. There wasn't anything in the apartment that would help you find Rash."

"Okay," said Pancho, sensing her loss of interest. "Thanks for everything, Amy. Would you mind if Drew took your number down and if he gave you his so that you could contact each other if anything comes up?"

Amy shrugged her consent. They exchanged information, then she was gone. Pancho ordered another Patron for each of them and they sat in silence, trying to process what they had learned.

After the waitress brought their drinks and they had each taken a sip, Drew said, "So, tell me what you're thinking about Booger. You think he knows more than he's telling us?"

Pancho nodded. "Or at least I'm wondering about it. I'm thinking he let slip that he knew that the other stuff of value was heroin, which he could only have gotten from Marcus."

"Unless, as I said before, he was making assumptions." Drew paused and sipped. "And why would he ask us for protection if he knew shit he wasn't going to tell us?"

"He's scared. He had three choices. Four, actually. One, he could have gone to the cops with what he knows. Two, he could have gone to Gouveia or to Lopaka with what he knows. Three, he could have done nothing and hope his name never comes up, which is kind of hard considering Marcus was staying in his house. Or four, once you had found him anyway, he could ask us for protection in exchange for just enough information."

Drew nodded thoughtfully. "And we were the least scary scenario. But why not come completely clean with us?"

Pancho took another sip of his tequila. "I've been wondering about that. What if Marcus had given Booger some of the money and heroin for safekeeping in exchange for a small percentage? What if Booger now has all of Marcus' share?"

Thirty-One

Bobby Lopaka, his son, Rigger, and the two lieutenants, Nappy and Buddy, were sitting in Bobby's den discussing the monthly income from their drug trade, of which Rigger and his son, Winston, were in charge, when the song *Lahaina Luna* began emanating from Nappy's jean pocket. Nappy smiled sheepishly and pulled out his phone. It was the Makaha Sons' version of the song, which he'd installed as his ring tone. He looked at the caller ID and got up.

"Excuse me, guys. I should take this. Family." Without waiting for an answer, he touched the screen, then held the phone to his ear. "Hold on." Then he walked out of the room, using the door that opened directly onto the backyard.

"What the fuck do you want, Scotty? You shouldn't be calling me." Nappy's tone was raw and harsh.

"Ah, Nappy, don't be li' dat. You know the shit that went down wasn't my fault. Things just got out of hand is all."

Nappy emitted a low, visceral growl. "Not your fault? Not your fucking fault? I betrayed my lifelong best friend and my boss, a dangerous man, I might add, to try to save your ass and what do you do? You get Irene killed, you lose all the shit you were supposed to steal, and you've put our lives in jeopardy. Am I forgetting anything, shit-for-brains?"

Scotty Gouveia was silent. After a moment Nappy spoke again. His voice had become soft, menacing. "I helped you because my sister's *hanai* daughter was stupid enough to marry your sorry ass. But understand this, Scotty, and understand it good. I don't care if we're related by adoption and marriage. That was a one-time deal. I'm done with you."

"But Nappy, they're gonna kill me, or at least fuck me up real bad. Can't you at least loan me ten grand so I can get them off my back and buy some time to find the shit Marcus' friend stole?"

Nappy's laugh was cruel. "Loan you ten grand? What the fuck, Scotty? Didn't you hear anything I just said? I'm done with you. Run for your life. Kill yourself. Rob a bank. I don't give a shit what you do. Just don't bother me." He punched the 'end conversation' display and took a few deep breaths of the high country air before walking back into the meeting with his closest friends in the world; friends he had betrayed in the name of family.

Thirty-Two

O n Sunday afternoon Pancho sat alone in his office. He had finished prepping Dr. Singer an hour earlier and was sitting at his desk, sometimes making notes, but mostly feeling sorry for himself. He rubbed his chest with his right hand for a moment until he realized what he was doing and stopped. His case was going nowhere. He was reasonably sure he knew what had happened, but without Booger willing to testify, he had no way to prove it. It was ludicrous to think he could break Scotty Gouveia on the stand without some kind of real leverage to do so. Pancho knew that if Scotty were to admit what he had done, he'd be signing his own death warrant.

The building didn't run the air conditioner on Sundays and it was getting increasingly warm in the office, even with his floor-to-ceiling blinds closed. Pancho decided to head home, maybe go for a swim and clear his head. He was standing at his desk, stuffing files into his briefcase when he heard a key in the front door lock. A moment later Drew shuffled into the office.

"Hey, man, glad I caught you," said Drew.

"Yeah. It's getting stifling hot in here, so I was about to head home. Want to come over? Have a beer and maybe dinner downstairs later?"

Drew signed heavily. "Shoots. Sure. I just wish I hadn't come all the way up here. I should have called." He paused while Pancho closed his briefcase and began walking toward the door. "But I do have some news."

Pancho stopped and looked at him. He knew Drew well enough to see from his face that it was good news. "Let's save it for when we're more comfortable then."

***

Twenty-five minutes later the two were sitting on Pancho's lanai overlooking the ocean. It was a calm day and the water, with no surf swells, was glassy, blue and inviting. Sans Souci Beach below the condo was still crowded with Sunday beachgoers, and the mingled sounds of people talking and of children playing provided a pleasant white noise.

"So, what you got?" asked Pancho, opening a Stella Artois and handing it to Drew.

"Two things. First, since we're paying Keani to sit around and babysit Booger, I figured we may as well put him to work, so I asked him to do some checking on Scotty Gouveia." Drew took a long pull on the beer. "Ahhh. That's good. Anyway, he came up with two pretty interesting things. First, Gouveia is married to a woman whose name is Alexis Kanakaole, who happens to be the *hanai* daughter of Margaret Kanakaole."

Pancho held up his hand to interrupt. "When you say *hanai,* do you mean formally adopted or just taken in by the family?"

"From what Keani could find, she was formally adopted when she was ten. He couldn't tell when she'd been taken in by the family."

"Okay, go on. So why is this important to us?"

Drew picked up his beer again, but he didn't drink. "Because Margaret Kanakaole is the sister of Nappy Makuakane." He drank.

"And Nappy Makuakane is?"

Drew put down the beer and smiled at Pancho. "Nappy Makuakane is Bobby Lopaka's long-time lieutenant."

Pancho ran his right hand through his hair, thinking. "So what does that give us? All I can think of off the top of my head is that Gouveia's relationship with Nappy, and therefore Lopaka, may have been the reason why he got such a sweet deal on the security agency. What am I missing?"

Drew chuckled. "That's all I could think of for the longest time. But then I went back through what we've learned. We know from Booger that robbing Auntie Irene was Gouveia's idea. We now know that Gouveia had an inside track into the Lopaka syndicate. Gouveia had to find out from someone that Irene was going to be in possession of something worth stealing. So, my friend, doesn't it make sense to assume that the information came from Nappy?"

Pancho nodded slightly, tentatively. "I can see that. But what I'm struggling with is why both Nappy and Gouveia would double-cross someone who had apparently been good to them and who's probably one of the most dangerous and powerful men in Hawai'i?"

Drew's smile widened. "And that's where the second piece of news from Keani comes in. Booger was right about the gambling. It seems that ol' Scotty Gouveia was in debt big time to a couple of Vegas casinos. Keani has an old NFL buddy who played for Denver who now works as a so-called collection agent for a firm that exclusively represents casinos. So Keani called this dude and learned that Gouveia is about a quarter mil into the casinos and his account had been turned over to 'collection.'" Drew made air quotation signs. "All the deadlines and non-violent extensions for Gouveia to pay up are expiring and things are about to get seriously rough."

Pancho took a sip from his beer and stared off at the ocean. After a moment he nodded and gave Drew a small, crooked smile. "So Gouveia panics and convinces his wife to get her mother, Nappy's sister, to help."

"Mmm," grunted Drew, swallowing some beer. "Only instead of helping out by giving or loaning Gouveia money, Nappy shows him how he can make some money by doing a low risk snatch from an elderly woman by the name of Auntie Irene. She must have been doing something illegal, which would mean that she couldn't even report the mugging to the cops." Drew bent over and rubbed his right knee.

"A perfect crime, so long as it doesn't get back to Lopaka that the perps are really his own people."

Drew sat up and let out a low chuckle. "Or so long as things don't go horribly wrong and Auntie Irene gets killed, and the money, or whatever, goes missing with a perp who wasn't even supposed to be in the game."

"Yeah. Or that," said Pancho wryly.

The two sat silent for several minutes. They watched the slow migration from the beach as the afternoon turned into a lazy dusk.

"There's more," Drew said finally.

Pancho turned to look at him. "Good?"

Drew shrugged. "A good start. I found Sammy Lee, the guy Marcus' girlfriend, Amy, said might have introduced Marcus to the dark skinned dude called Rash."

"And?"

"And nothing yet. I didn't want to scare him off by calling him, so I'm going to intercept him when he gets off work tomorrow after I go to Pupukea and have another visit with our boy Booger."

Pancho picked up his beer and inspected the bottle to see how much was left. "Well," he said, putting the empty bottle down on the side table, "just understand that I don't have many tomorrows left in this trial."

Thirty-Three

Pancho was at his office desk early on Monday morning when the phone rang. Susan wasn't in yet, so he picked it up himself. It was the Sheriff's Office calling to tell him that Jackson had asked to see him before court began. Pancho told them to bring Jackson to the attorney conference room at eight-fifteen, then he sent a yellow Post-it note to Susan's computer desktop telling her to call both Amy Park and Scotty Gouveia to let them know that their subpoenas required them to be in court that day.

Once he finished with the good doctor this morning, other than Jackson himself, he was out of witnesses. Pancho figured he could use Amy to describe Rash, a slightly built dark man whom Pancho would try to give to the jury as an alternative to Jackson. Gouveia would be problematic, and Pancho hadn't actually decided to put him on yet.

Pancho was windblown by the time he got to the courthouse on Punchbowl. The trade winds had whipped up with a vengeance overnight and pushed down from the Ko'olau mountains through the downtown skyscrapers with unusual ferocity. Pancho knew he must have looked like a wild man as he walked into the courthouse rotunda and put his trial briefcase on the conveyor belt to go through the scanner. He smoothed his hair as best he could and pulled his red tie from off his shoulder before retrieving his case and heading to the elevators on the Diamond Head side of the rotunda. Three minutes later he was sitting in the small, freezing, attorney conference room with Jackson.

***

Jackson stunned Pancho immediately by saying he thought they should make a deal with the prosecution.

"Why? Are you telling me you're guilty?" Pancho's heart was racing and his throat felt constricted. He'd placed so much faith in Jackson. Had it been misguided? Was all of his gut wrenching fear of failure nothing but self-inflicted mental anguish?

Jackson seemed to shiver. He covered, then rubbed his face with the palms of both hands. He made rare eye contact with Pancho. "No. I still don't think I killed that Auntie lady. It's just that some of the guards tol' me that a lot of people could get killed or hurt 'cause of me. They said that if I get off, even the Judge and all them people who work for him, gonna die." Jackson looked away for a second, then back at Pancho. All Pancho saw now when he looked at Jackson was a young, vulnerable, scared, and brave kid. Jackson was prepared to go to jail to protect people he didn't even know.

"Look, Jackson—" Jackson held up his hand, cutting Pancho off.

"Pancho, I knows you is working real hard for me. Nobody's ever treated me as nice as you. And Drew," he said. He looked down, breaking eye contact. "My whole life people either seem to look right through me, like they don't even see me at all, or else they ack like they scared of me and get away from me fast as they can. It's like I tol' you before. I wasn't even 'sposed to be borned."

Jackson had been staring down at the tabletop as he spoke. Now he looked up again and Pancho could see tears forming at the corners of Jackson's eyes.

"I wonder if those guys who go into movies and schools and shoot people feel like that. Like they think nobody knows them or wants to know them. Like they don't even exist on the earth. So they gots to go and prove to everyone that they're real by making other people suffer." He shook his head in bewilderment. "I don't understand that at all. I don't need people to know I'm real. I don't mind being nothin'.

"Pancho . . . " He swiped at his eyes. "I ain't worth all the time you spendin' on me. I don' want to be the cause of people gettin' killed or hurt or whatever. I already caused my mama to live with the memory of the man who raped her—my daddy. I already caused too much pain." He paused for a beat. "Way too much pain for someone who don't even really exist. I used to be . . ." He scrunched up his face, looking for the word. "Unvisible. Now everybody lookin' at me and hatin' me and blamin' me."

Pancho reached across the table and put his hand on Jackson's arm. "Stop it, Jackson." His voice was firm, brusque, and loud for the small room. He took a breath and spoke in a softer tone. "I don't want to hear you talk like that. You're a good kid who's had a rough life. You didn't kill anyone and I'm not going to let you plead guilty and spend your life in prison. No one's going to get hurt because of you." He took his hand off Jackson's arm and leaned back in his chair. "I mean it, Jackson. We'll get you through this, then I'll help you start a new life."

Pancho wasn't sure he knew what he meant when he said that, but at that moment he knew that when, *if*, he got Jackson out of this mess, their relationship would not just end.

***

Dr. Singer's direct examination was emotional. Harry Chang had objected to Pancho asking the doctor to describe the situation in which Jackson had grown up, but at a sidebar conference Pancho explained to the Judge that Jackson's relationship with his mother and aunt were critical to the doctor's diagnosis of psychologically-induced syncope, and Judge Kingsley had overruled the objection.

As Pancho took the doctor through the story of Jackson's life, even with one eye on the jury he could see the transformation in their faces. He saw two of the women jurors wipe tears from their eyes. A few, whom Pancho noticed had refused to even look directly at Jackson, now openly studied him. The packed courtroom was deathly silent as they listened to Dr. Singer explain how Jackson's aunt had told him about his mother's rape and how her preacher told her she could not have an abortion. There was an audible gasp as the doctor testified that Jackson's aunt told him that he was the devil and would have to pay for the sins of his rapist father.

Finally, Pancho laid the groundwork for the possibility of putting Jackson on the stand to testify about his memory coming back and seeing the guys on a moped.

"Doctor, obviously my client doesn't remember anything while he was passed out in the bathroom, but he told the police that he also didn't remember anything for some time before he entered the bathroom. Would that be related in any way to his syncope episode?"

Dr. Singer absently pulled at his eyebrow and shook his head in the negative. "No, not directly. It's possible, however, that he suffered some transient short-term memory loss from the concussion he suffered when he fainted and struck his head."

Pancho glanced quickly at the jury, all of whom seemed to be paying close attention.

"So the concussion could have caused Mr. Steele to lose his memory of what occurred before he entered the bathroom?"

"Yes, most definitely."

"And that memory loss would most likely have been temporary? Meaning it would be likely for his memory to eventually return?"

Dr. Singer nodded and, seeming to realize that he'd been toying with his long eyebrow, put his hands in his lap. "Yes, and, in fact, it's my understanding that is what has occurred."

Harry Chang jumped to his feet, but before he could say anything Pancho addressed the court, waving Harry off. "In anticipation of Mr. Chang's objection, Your Honor, we will have Mr. Steele testify directly as to what his memory is." Both Pancho and Judge Kingsley looked to Harry, who nodded and sat down.

Pancho wrapped up his direct examination with a few more questions before turning the witness over to the prosecution. Harry Chang made a show of leafing through his notes for a few moments before rising to address the witness.

"Dr. Singer, isn't it a fact that you are basing your opinion as to the cause of the defendant's fainting spells on what he told you?"

Dr. Singer thought for a moment, then nodded slowly. "Yes, it's quite common for doctors to consider the history of the patient as reported by the patient."

"So doesn't the validity of your opinion depend almost entirely on the honesty of the patient, in this case the defendant, a man on trial for murder?"

Again, Dr. Singer nodded slowly. "Yes, that would be true. In many cases, particularly in the field of psychiatry, the patient's self-history is all we have to go on."

Pancho wrinkled his brow, wondering where Harry was going with this line of questioning. Did he know something about Jackson's story that Pancho didn't?

But then Harry abandoned that line of questioning, and Pancho knew Harry was just trying to lay some groundwork for closing argument. Harry probably figured Pancho wouldn't go to the expense of bringing witnesses in from Mississippi to testify as to the rape of Jackson's mother and the murder of his grandparents, so Harry would be able to argue that all of the assumptions of Dr. Singer were based on unsubstantiated statements from the alleged murderer. Pancho had to smile to himself. He wondered if Harry knew that Jackson's mother was uncooperative.

"Now, Dr. Singer," said Harry. "You have testified that the defendant's short-term memory loss for the time frame immediately preceding his entry into the bathroom was most likely caused by the concussion he suffered when he fainted and struck his head, is that correct?"

"It is."

"But again, you have only the defendant's own word for it that he did not remember that timeframe, isn't that correct?"

Dr. Singer again began playing with a long strand of eyebrow. "Yes, except remember he told the police at the scene that he couldn't remember, so it was more or less a spontaneous utterance, which would indicate some measure of validity."

Harry frowned. "So your answer is 'yes,' the history of memory loss comes solely from the defendant?"

"Yes."

"And now you are reporting that the defendant's memory has miraculously returned on the eve of trial, is that correct?"

Dr. Singer smiled broadly. "Well, I wouldn't exactly call it a miracle. It would be expected from memory loss arising from a concussion."

Well done, Doc, thought Pancho.

Harry Chang, being the consummate litigator, didn't miss a beat. "And isn't it a fact that your opinion as to the cause of the short term-memory loss, i.e. the concussion, is just one of many scenarios that may account for the memory loss?"

Dr. Singer inclined his head to one side and nodded slightly. "Yes, there may have been other causes of the memory loss, but — "

"Such as psychological trauma? Isn't severe psychological trauma a possible cause for memory loss?"

"Yes, that's possible, but again — "

"Such as beating an old woman to death? Or watching a friend and accomplice beat an old woman to death? Wouldn't those kinds of events be a possible cause for short-term memory loss?"

Dr. Singer was twisting his eyebrow hair with a vengeance now. Pancho could see the doctor's internal struggle on whether or not to argue with Harry, but Pancho had made it clear to the doctor not to fall into that trap. It would only make him look defensive and biased. He had to trust Pancho to fix things on redirect.

"Yes, those kinds of events could have induced memory loss."

"Thank you, Doctor. No further questions." Harry glanced at the jury, a stern look on his face, and sat down.

Pancho was up in a flash. "Dr. Singer, there's no question that my client, Jackson Steele, suffered a concussion from his fall in the bathroom, is there?"

"No, sir. That diagnosis was made at Queen's Hospital shortly after the incident."

"And the medical literature is clear that a concussion can cause short term-memory loss, is that correct?"

"Yes it is."

"So other than conjecture about some kind of psychological trauma, Mr. Steele may or may not have encountered prior to his episode of syncope, would you say that the documented history of a concussion would be the most likely cause of the short-term memory loss?"

"I would say that, based on the evidence we have, my diagnosis of short-term memory loss incident to a concussion is within reasonable medical probability."

Pancho nodded and looked down at his notes.

"Doctor, do you have any reason to doubt Mr. Steele's account of his mother's rape and of his childhood?"

"Not at all. In fact, it's my understanding that you spoke with his mother, who confirmed the account."

"Objection!" Harry Chang's voice was loud and angry. "Your Honor. We're beyond mere hearsay now, we're into double hearsay. I—"

Judge Kingsley raised his hand to stop Harry. "Objection sustained." He turned to Pancho. "We've entered the realm of attempting to prove the truth of the matter in question, which does bring the hearsay issue into play."

Pancho nodded respectfully. "I understand, Your Honor. I have no further questions of Dr. Singer."

"Let's break for lunch and resume at 1:30," said the Judge.

Thirty-Four

Pancho checked his cell phone as he walked quickly back to his office for lunch. There was a call from Drew, but Pancho decided it would be too windy to hear anything, so he resisted the temptation to call back. The palm trees were whipping, and Pancho noticed more than a few large fronds hanging precariously, thumping a hollow drumbeat against the palm trunks in the wind. A yellow McDonald's wrapper slapped into his right arm, hanging there for a moment before releasing itself and resuming its aimless journey down Alakea Street.

There was a note on his outer door that the office was closed for lunch. Pancho let himself in and immediately called Drew.

"I've got a name." Drew sounded excited. "Rashad Ranatunga. That Sammy dude said he hadn't seen him for some time, but he confirms that Rashad and Marcus were friendly. I'm hoping to get something from my HPD sources soon."

"Where are you now?" asked Pancho.

"Heading up to Pupukea to talk to our boy, Booger, some more. I talked to Keani this morning and told him our thoughts. We're going to threaten to cut the kid loose if he doesn't come clean."

"Okay. Do what you gotta do. I'm done with the doctor, and I've got to put Gouveia on the stand when we go back. I can't put Amy on to talk about the slim black guy who was friends with Marcus until I lay some groundwork for the question. I'll be shooting from the hip with Gouveia. Text me if you get anything I can use."

Pancho put the phone into his pocket. He knew he should eat something, but he was too nervous. His stomach was in a knot. He would put Gouveia on the stand and ask that he be classified as a hostile witness so that his examination would be more like a cross-examination rather than the more delicate, technical dance that was direct examination. He needed to be able to lead Gouveia and push him hard, but Pancho knew that without supporting evidence he could be headed toward disaster — and a conviction for Jackson. He pulled over a yellow legal pad from the side of his desk and began making notes.

***

Scotty Gouveia tried to accost Pancho in the hall outside the courtroom as Pancho returned for the afternoon session. Clearly Gouveia was not happy about being subpoenaed to come back and testify.

"Just need to clear some things up. Shouldn't be long," Pancho said as he pushed by Gouveia and entered the courtroom. The spectator section was packed, as it had been since the start of trial. Harry Chang was already seated. He was leaning back in his chair, looking comfortable and confident; more confident than he'd looked at the start of trial.

When Gouveia was called back to the stand, the Judge reminded him that he was still under oath, then turned to Pancho. "You may proceed, Mr. McMartin."

"Thank you, Your Honor." Pancho rose and absently smoothed his hair. He stood by counsel table, holding a legal pad. Scotty Gouveia stared at him, a stern, angry expression on his pock-marked face.

"Mr. Gouveia, can you tell us again why you asked your employee, Marcus Young, to keep tabs on Auntie Irene?"

"Yeah. I think I answered that already. I knew she and her group had a gig at the Center that night, so I asked Marcus to keep an eye on them when it was over. I knew it would be fairly late, and I wanted to make sure they all got to their cars safely."

"So you asked Marcus to keep an eye on all three members of the trio?"

Gouveia was nodding before Pancho had finished his question. "Sure."

"Is it routine for you to assign one of your guards to watch over someone at the Center? Or was there some specific issue involving Auntie Irene and her cousins?"

Gouveia raised and lowered his shoulders in a kind of half shrug. "Not really routine, but not out of the ordinary either. If I hear that someone well known, like Auntie Irene, will be at the Center late, meaning around closing time for the stores, I would often ask a guard to make sure everything is okay."

Pancho nodded. "So there was no specific threat to Auntie Irene that you were aware of."

"Correct." Gouveia smiled and looked at the jury, and Pancho could see that the anger was waning as Gouveia's confidence in his testimony grew.

"Were you aware that Auntie Irene was carrying quite a lot of cash?"

There was some murmuring from the gallery, and Gouveia's expression changed immediately. Pancho could see that he was trying to look surprised.

"No. How would I? Was she?"

Pancho ignored Gouveia's questions. "Were you aware that Auntie Irene was also carrying drugs?"

Gouveia was shaking his head. His eyes narrowed. His voice sounded indignant when he answered. "No, of course not."

Pancho looked down at his legal pad and pretended to read something. He wanted the jury to see how uncomfortable Gouveia appeared to be. After a few moments Pancho looked up at Gouveia and smiled affably. "What is your wife's maiden name, Mr. Gouveia?"

Gouveia was caught off guard. He looked confused and looked at Harry, then up at the Judge. "What does my wife have to do with any of this?" he finally asked.

Pancho shrugged good-naturedly. "Maybe nothing, maybe a lot. Can you answer the question please?"

"Alexis Kanakaole," Gouveia said tersely.

"Thank you. And what is her mother's name?"

"Objection." Harry Chang stood. "What's the relevance of Mr. Gouveia's wife's family tree?"

Judge Kingsley nodded and looked at Pancho. "Mr. McMartin?"

"If Your Honor will give me a little leeway here, I think I can show the relevance in a few more questions."

The Judge looked back at Harry Chang. "Objection overruled, for now." Then he turned back to Pancho. "But let's move things along, Counsel."

"Thank you, Your Honor." Pancho had been watching Gouveia closely during the exchange, and it was clear Gouveia was agitated. His eyes were flitting in all directions, and he was repeatedly licking his lips as if he had cotton mouth.

"Mr. Gouveia, please answer the question. What is the name of your wife's mother?"

"Margaret Kanakaole."

"Do you know who Margaret Kanakaole's brother is?"

Gouveia looked at Harry Chang with a look that was obviously pleading for Harry to do something, but Harry ignored him and wrote or doodled on his legal pad.

"Mr. Gouveia? Can you answer the question please?"

"We're not real close to my wife's side of the family. She was adopted."

Pancho loved the fact that Gouveia was making things worse by not answering the question. Everyone in the courtroom could now see he didn't want to respond.

"Come, come, Mr. Gouveia. I didn't ask you how close you are to her family. I asked if you know who your wife's uncle is. Surely you know that."

Gouveia sighed heavily. "Yeah. It's Nappy Makuakane."

Pancho smiled to himself when he saw Harry Chang's head snap up at the name, but the courtroom remained silent.

"Thank you, Mr. Gouveia. Now, can you tell the jury what Nappy Makuakane does for a living?"

Gouveia shook his head vigorously. "No. I don't know what he does."

Pancho gave Gouveia a half smile and a nod. "Yes, I can understand that. But you do know who he works for don't you?"

Gouveia rubbed his left eye. "I think he works for the rancher, Bobby Lopaka."

This time the spectators reacted. Most everyone who had lived in Hawai'i for more than a few years knew who Bobby Lopaka was. Judge Kingsley called for quiet and turned his attention back to Pancho. The

Judge seemed to be as fascinated as everyone else with where Pancho was going with the examination.

"That's right," said Pancho, as if Gouveia had won a prize. "In fact, isn't Nappy Makuakane Bobby Lopaka's long-time lieutenant?"

"Objection. Vague and ambiguous. What does that even mean?"

Pancho raised an eyebrow and faced the Judge. "Pick a synonym. How about 'assistant'?"

"Overruled. Answer if you can, Mr. Gouviea."

Gouveia's mouth was turned down at the corners and he rubbed his eye again. "I don't know. I guess he's something like that."

Pancho nodded as if he was satisfied with the answer. He looked down at his yellow pad again and let the courtroom think about the connections he had just made, then he looked up at Gouveia as if he had just thought of another question.

"Who did you buy your business, Paradise Security Systems, from?"

"I bought it from a corporation."

"Yes. And who was the sole owner of that corporation?"

Gouveia hesitated before answering. "Bobby Lopaka."

Pancho was pleased to see that even some of the jurors reacted to this news.

"Since you're related to one of Mr. Lopaka's closest advisors, I assume you're aware of the fact that Auntie Irene was Bobby Lopaka's cousin?"

The courtroom erupted into conversation. Judge Kingsley gaveled the spectators back to order. Pancho simply stared at Gouveia, waiting for an answer.

"Yes, I think I'd heard that," Gouveia finally said.

Pancho's next question appeared to knock the wind out of Gouveia.

"Mr. Gouveia, how much money do you owe to casinos in Las Vegas?" Pancho could see out of the corner of his eye that Harry Chang started to stand, presumably to make an objection, but he must have thought better of it as he sat back down without saying anything.

Gouveia looked panic-stricken, but despite his plaintive looks, he was getting no help from any quarter. He finally inhaled deeply, then exhaled and said, "I don't know the exact amount right now. But yeah, I owe some money in Vegas."

"More than fifty thousand dollars?"

Gouveia nodded.

"You need to answer out loud, Mr. Gouveia. Do you owe more than fifty thousand dollars?"

"Yes."

There was some brief noise from the spectators which ended without Judge Kingsley having to call for order.

"More than a hundred thousand dollars?"

"Yes." Gouveia's response was barely audible. The court reporter spoke up.

"I didn't get that," she said.

Gouveia nodded again. His face had turned a light shade of purple. He licked his lips and his Adam's apple seemed to bob up and down. "Yes."

"More than two hundred thousand?" asked Pancho, cutting off the spectators' reactions.

"Yes."

This time it took several moments for Judge Kingsley to restore order.

"More than two hundred fifty thousand?" asked Pancho when he could be heard again.

"About that."

Pancho picked up a pen and wrote something on his pad. He let the moment linger. When he asked his next question, his voice was soft, almost sympathetic sounding.

"You don't have the money to pay off your debt, do you, Mr. Gouveia?"

Gouveia looked down at his hands, which were clasped together, resting on the witness stand. "No."

"Your Honor." Harry's voice sounded weary. "This is all very interesting, but can we get an offer of proof from counsel as to where this is going? I'm having a difficult time trying to figure out what any of this has to do with the brutal assault and murder of Irene Kamaka."

Judge Kingsley gave Harry a slight nod and turned his focus on Pancho. "Let's have counsel approach the bench."

Pancho and Harry walked to the Judge's bench on the opposite side from where the jury sat. They waited for the court reporter to join them.

"It's almost three o'clock now," said Judge Kingsley. "I'm inclined to stop early, and we can then have Mr. McMartin give us his offer of proof in chambers. How does that sound?"

"I would strongly object, Your Honor." Pancho spoke in the most forceful whisper he could muster. "I'm at a critical point of my examination of Mr. Gouveia. I believe that he must know where I'm going with my examination and, if we stop now, it gives him time to figure out how to respond. Furthermore, I honestly believe that Mr. Gouveia's life is going to be in danger after his testimony, and he may want to talk to Mr. Chang about some kind of protection."

"What?" Harry's voice rose above a whisper and the Judge's expression told him all he needed about getting his emotions under control. "I'm sorry, Your Honor, but whatever kind of game Mr. McMartin is playing should not be allowed. This is — "

The courtroom's side door opened and one of his clerks bustled in. The clerk's face was pale. Judge Kingsley gave him a harsh look, but the clerk quickly approached the Judge and whispered into his ear. Pancho could see the Judge's jaw tense as he listened to what his clerk had to say. When the clerk was done, the Judge nodded solemnly and, with counsel and the court reporter still standing at the bench, he turned to the jury. His tone was harsh and brusque.

"This court will adjourn for the day. As always, you are admonished not to discuss this case with anyone, including your fellow jurors. Unless you are notified otherwise, we will resume tomorrow morning at nine." He turned back to Pancho and Harry. "In chambers, Counsel." He looked at the court reporter. "I don't think we'll need you, Felicia, but stay close for a while just in case." With that he was gone.

Pancho and Harry looked at each other with quizzical expressions. What had just happened? The noise of the jury and the spectators taking their leave brought Pancho back to the moment. He looked at the witness box and saw that Scotty Gouveia was still sitting there. He looked like a deer caught in the headlights. Pancho walked over to him. Gouveia's expression slowly changed from that of abject fear and shock to pure hatred.

"What the fuck are you trying to do to me?" he said, making a kind of hissing sound as he did so.

Pancho leaned in close, resting his arms on the witness bench. "I know everything, Scotty. I know about you trying to get Nappy to bail you out, and I know   he tipped you to the fact that Auntie Irene was going to be carrying drugs and cash. I know you recruited Marcus Young to do a snatch. But Marcus got someone else involved and it all went wrong."

Gouveia rubbed his face with both hands. "You can't prove —"

Pancho cut him off. "Come off it, Scotty. As soon as any of this gets back to Lopaka, you're in deep shit. Let me set up a meeting with Harry Chang. If you come clean with him, I'm sure he can arrange protection for you."

Gouveia was shaking his head. "Fuck. Oh fuck. You motherfucker. What have you done?"

Pancho backed off. "I have to meet with the Judge and Harry in chambers. Why don't you sit here for a few minutes and think about it. I'll let the Judge know so he'll keep a sheriff close by. You'll be safe here for now. We can talk if you want, when I come out." Pancho turned and walked toward the door to Judge Kingsley's chambers. For some reason he felt a knot in his stomach. He could feel his heart pounding, and he silently prayed that we wasn't about to have a panic attack. Something bad must have happened for the Judge's clerk to interrupt court like that, then for the Judge to suddenly adjourn for the day.

Harry was already seated when Pancho entered the chambers. The Judge's face was stern and solemn, but Pancho could tell at a glance that Harry was still in the dark.

"Sit down, Pancho," said the Judge. His voice was soft and kindly. "My office got a call from your secretary, Susan." The knot in Pancho's stomach tightened its grip, and he could feel the blood rush to his brain. His temples suddenly throbbed.

"Is she okay? Is Drew okay?" Pancho asked before the Judge could go on.

Judge Kingsley nodded. "They're both fine. But Drew's partner, Keani Sefo, has been shot and is in a coma, and some young man by the name of . . . " The Judge looked down at a piece of paper. "Davis Bogarty, has been killed. Also shot." Judge Kingsley lifted his gaze back to Pancho. "Susan says Drew is shook up. She also says that all this has something to do with this case."

Pancho's emotions were all over the place. The sense of relief at learning that Susan and Drew were safe was overwhelming, yet he now had to process the information that a kid he was responsible for was dead and that Drew's partner and friend was in a coma. He nodded dumbly to the Judge.

"Take your time, Pancho, but you do need to tell us what this is all about. I assume it relates somehow to wherever you were going with the examination of Mr. Gouveia?"

Pancho took a deep breath, then exhaled. He rubbed his hand through his hair, then left his hand on his neck, unconsciously rubbing it; then he told Judge Kingsley and Harry Chang the story.

Thirty-Five

When Winston Lopaka shot the big Samoan man who opened the door to the Pupukea house, he had no idea it was the famous and much revered ex-football player, Keani Sefo. All he knew was that the big man had a gun. Winston reacted without thinking. He shot Keani in the chest and assumed he'd killed him. He kicked the front door closed, stepped over the body, and walked into the living room. A tan, lanky man in his twenties was sitting on the couch holding a pillow in front of his bare chest. He wore only a pair of long, baggy swimming trunks. The expression of fear on his face was almost comical to Winston. He was wimpering.

It didn't take Winston Lopaka long to get the whole story out of Booger. When Winston was convinced he had it all, he calmly put the gun to Booger's head and pulled the trigger.

***

Scotty Gouveia hung around the courtroom until the chambers conference was done, but he refused Pancho's offer to meet with Harry Chang and ask the police for protection. Pancho watched the man walk slowly out of the courtroom. His shoulders were hunched and his head was pulled into his body. It was a demeanor reeking of defeat and fear.

Pancho felt impotent. He couldn't help but think that Scotty Gouveia was a dead man walking.

***

Rigger Lopaka ended his call with his son, Winston, as he walked into his father's study. Bobby was sitting behind his big desk as usual. A lit cigar sat in an ashtray and curled bluish smoke into the air. A tumbler of bourbon and ice sat next to the ashtray. Buddy and Nappy were lounging in a couple of easy chairs. The smoky room was warm and cozy, and the three old friends had obviously been having a friendly conversation. *Probably talking about old times some more,* thought Rigger. *That's all they seemed to talk about lately.* Rigger glanced at Nappy as he walked into the room and took a seat next to his father's desk. The three older men watched Rigger, saying nothing in expectation of whatever news he had to convey.

Rigger looked at Nappy again. "You carrying a gun, Nappy?" he asked.

Nappy looked surprised, but shook his head no.

"Why would you ask that, Rigger?" his father said in a gruff tone.

Rigger turned back to face Bobby. "Because Nappy betrayed us. He betrayed *you*, Dad." Bobby started to say something, but Rigger held up his hand, cutting him off. "Nappy told Scotty Gouveia that Auntie Irene would have heroin and cash on her that night. Scotty's in deep shit debt to Vegas and his plan, apparently orchestrated by Nappy, was to rip Auntie off and pay off his debts. No one was supposed to get hurt. But the asshole Scotty hired to do the job, that Marcus Young fuck-brain, brought another guy into the picture, a *popolo*, who went crazy and killed her. We're not sure if it's the black kid on trial or someone else. I'm thinking it was someone else."

The room was deathly silent for almost a full minute. Rigger watched as his dad and Buddy turned to stare at Nappy. The normally vibrant looking man had turned an ashen gray and he stared down at his lap. Bobby picked up his cigar and took a puff before speaking.

"Is this true, Nappy?"

Nappy raised his head and looked at his oldest friend. The pain he was feeling was written on his face. He nodded slightly. "He's fucking family, Bobby. My sister begged me to help the motherfucker. I tried to refuse. I swear it. But she was on my *okole* to do something to help. So I finally said I'd tell him when Irene was making a delivery for us. He could arrange a simple snatch. No one would get hurt." He closed his eyes for a second, fighting back tears. "No one would get hurt." His voice was soft and sad and resigned to whatever was to be his fate.

The room was silent again for several seconds.

"What the fuck, Nappy?" Buddy muttered.

"I'm sorry, guys. It was family. You know how it is. I'll pay it all back. Whatever you want me to do, Bobby, I'll do it."

Rigger watched his father physically cringe as he listened to his oldest and closest friend, the great Napolean Makuakane, whine like a guilty child. Rigger watched the anger in his father literally work its way through his large body and explode into the capillaries of his face.

"And *I'm* not family, Nappy? *We're* not family?" Bobby gestured around the room. "We've been more fucking family to you than the deadbeats you betrayed us for. I thought of us as brothers, man, you, Buddy, and me." Bobby choked on his raging emotions and swiveled in his chair to face the windows behind him. He stared out at the wet fog and shivered.

Rigger cleared his throat. "That's not all, Pops. Scotty is back on the witness stand and that *haole* attorney, Pancho whatever, is going after him hard. He knows what we know, and he's drawing the connection between Scotty and Nappy and you in open court. He was about to get into the plan to steal the shit from Auntie when the Judge suddenly adjourned court. I think he'd just been told about the shooting."

Bobby swiveled violently back around. "What shooting?"

Rigger sighed heavily. "We know all this because Winston followed the private investigator, Drew Tulafono, to a house up in Pupukea. Drew's partner, Keani Sefo, was guarding a guy who'd been friends with Marcus Young, the security guard Scotty killed. This guy, a *haole* kid in his twenties, knew the story and told it to the attorney. That's how the attorney had the ammunition to go after Scotty on the stand."

Bobby shook his head, a 'what the fuck' gesture. "Please, God, tell me Winston didn't go in and kill these people."

Rigger's face told it all. "Apparently Keani had a gun when he answered the door, and Winston felt he had no choice but to shoot him. Then he had to torture the kid for a few minutes to make sure he had the whole story from him. He felt he had no choice but to off him when he was all *pau*."

They all heard Buddy mutter "Jesus Christ," but no one seemed to pay him any attention.

Bobby took a sip of his bourbon before he spoke in a calm, neutral tone, which the other men knew to be Bobby at his most menacing. "So let me get this straight. My best friend sets up my favorite cousin and our best courier, Auntie Irene, to be ripped off so Scotty Gouveia can get his ass out of debt. Irene gets murdered in the process. Scotty gets ripped off and tries to track down the money and smack and ends up killing this Marcus guy. But he still doesn't have the shit. Marcus had an accomplice who killed Irene and must have ripped Marcus off. Maybe it was the *popolo* kid on trial or maybe it was someone else.

"Marcus had a friend he told about the deal gone bad. This guy tells the attorney. Winston finds the guy and gets the story out of him and ends up shooting one of the most famous athletes ever to come out of Hawai'i, then kills the witness. In the meantime, the whole fucking world is learning that Scotty and Nappy are related and that Nappy works with me, and therefore whatever drugs and money Irene was carrying came from us. Which means that whoever killed the witness kid was also probably us. Which means that if we kill Scotty before he gets on the stand again, the authorities will know it was probably us. Which means if we give Nappy here what he deserves, the authorities will know it was probably us." He paused. "Does that about sum up the situation?" he asked sarcastically.

Although no one reacted, Rigger knew his dad and Buddy must have heard the whimper from Nappy.

Thirty-Six

It was heartbreaking for Pancho to see his big friend cry.

"Obviously the killer followed me to the house," Drew said hoarsely. He was sitting on the couch in Pancho's office. His large body sagged with sadness. He made no attempt to wipe away his tears. "I killed that kid and put Keani in a coma as surely as if I'd pulled the trigger myself."

"C'mon, man, you can't blame yourself. That's bullshit." But even as he said it, Pancho knew his words sounded hollow. The fact of the matter was that Pancho was having a hard time not blaming himself. They should have foreseen that the Lopakas would be looking for the guys who stole their stuff and killed Auntie Irene. Tailing a private detective who had the same goal was a good strategy.

"What do the docs say about Keani?" Pancho asked.

Drew sniffed and roughly wiped his arm across his eyes. His voice was soft and exuded deep sadness. "He's critical. They're not sure if he's going to make it or not."

Pancho exhaled heavily. The two men sat in silence. Pancho heard the phone ringing almost non-stop in the outer office. Susan's voice was muffled, indistinct.

"I should get back to the hospital," Drew finally said. He began to push himself up off the couch.

"Did you find Rashad?" Pancho asked.

Drew finished the obviously painful task of getting to his feet before he answered. "Not yet. I found where he lived, but no one has seen him for months now. I found a guy he used to hang and drink with who I finally convinced to give me a list of places Rashad was known to frequent, but it sounds like the dude is in full hiding mode."

"Which he damn well better be now that the Lopakas know about him," said Pancho. "We need to find him first."

Drew stared at Pancho for a moment. His eyes were red and moist. "I don't know if I'm up to anything right now, Paunch. I'm kind of fucked up here."

Pancho got up and walked to Drew. It was hard to hug such a big man, but he did the best he could. "I know, man. I know. But we still have other lives we're trying to save. Let's not let what happened today be for nothing." He patted Drew hard on the back and stepped away. "I'm going to set up a meeting with Harry Chang and the cops and try to convince them to find Rashad. In the meantime, go to the hospital and check on Keani. When you feel up to it, do what you can to keep tracking that shithead. Unless I hear otherwise, I've still got to go ahead with the trial tomorrow, and I'm about out of time. I'll be surprised if Gouveia shows up tomorrow."

Drew nodded sadly and limped out of the room.

***

It was almost six in the evening before Pancho was able to sit down with Harry Chang. They were at the bar at Ferguson's in the Dillingham Transportation Building, an historic office building next door to the high-rise where Pancho had his office.

"I'm sorry about Drew's partner," said Harry after he had ordered a Michelob Ultra. "Any more news?"

Pancho shook his head. "No. It looks pretty bleak. Poor Drew is all buss up." He paused and took a sip of his Patron. "Which is why I need your help."

Harry chuckled. "I figured you didn't ask me here to do a deal. You're one stubborn *haole*, Pancho."

Pancho feigned hurt feelings. "Hey, I've dealt a lot of cases with you, Harry."

"Yeah, but pretty much only when your clients' own mothers would have convicted them. So what's up? There wasn't anything I heard from you in chambers today that convinces me that your client wasn't the accomplice Bogarty referred to."

"I know. But what I didn't tell you is that we learned that Marcus Young had a friend he was hanging out with who fits the description of the accomplice. We even have a name, Rashad Ranatunga."

Harry laughed. "What the hell kind of name is Rashad Ranatunga?"

"Sri Lankan. And I'm serious Harry. He's lean, dark, and had short cropped hair at the time of the murder. He and Marcus were friendly. I have witnesses to support that. Drew had tracked down Rashad's apartment, but no one had seen him for months. Sounds like pretty much since the murder. The guy's disappeared. He's our man, Harry, I'm sure of it."

Harry took a sip of beer and appeared to be thinking about what Pancho had said. Pancho gave him time. The buzz of the other drinkers at the long, narrow bar washed over Pancho, and he was struck by the normalcy of it all, but there was nothing normal about the web of murder and deceit defining his life at the moment. Jackson's life was in his hands and, despite knowing with absolute certainty that Jackson was innocent, Pancho felt like he had little control over the course of events.

"So you want me to get the cops to find this Rashad guy, is that it?"

Pancho nodded. "Assuming you won't dismiss the case against Jackson Steele without finding the real killer, yeah, that's what I'm asking."

"And the basis for me asking the police to put a dragnet out for this guy is that you talked to some guys who knew that Marcus Young had hung out with Rashad some time before the murder of Irene Kamaka. That right?"

Pancho leaned in close to Harry. "C'mon, Harry. People are dying here. I won't be surprised if Scotty Gouveia turns up dead before we can get him in to finish his testimony. This Rashad is also a walking dead man if the Lopakas find out about him. As far as I know right now, unless Marcus Young told his killer more than he told Bogarty, the Lopakas don't know about Rashad."

Harry sat back on his stool and looked around the room before looking back to Pancho. "Okay. I'll talk to Bryson Wong. He's the detective on this case. I'll see if they can find your Rashad Ratatunga, or whatever his name is."

Pancho smiled. "Write it the fuck down, Harry. Rashad Ranatunga. Sri Lankan."

Harry smiled back. He tapped his skull. "I've got it, Pancho. I've got a brain like a steel trap." He took a last sip of beer and began to slide off his stool, not looking particularly athletic as he did so.

"What do we do if Scotty Gouveia doesn't show up in court tomorrow?" asked Pancho.

Harry, now standing, shrugged. "That's your problem, Counselor."

***

Pancho held Paula in a tight spoon on his bed. They were both naked, but they hadn't made love. Pancho just needed the close contact with someone he loved. After leaving the bar with Harry Chang, the events of the day seemed to crash down on him. He threw caution to the wind and asked Paula to meet him.

As they cuddled, he filled her in on the awful and stunning developments. She had met Keani once or twice before and had already heard on the radio that he'd been shot, but the newscaster had few details. Now, as Pancho finished bringing her up to date, she lay silent as Pancho stroked her arm and breathed into her neck.

After a while Pancho sighed and turned onto his back, putting his hands behind his head. Paula turned over to face him.

"So what do you do now?" she asked softly.

He huffed through his nose. "Not much I can do except hope Gouveia shows up tomorrow and keep plugging away at him."

Paula put her head on his tanned chest. "And if he doesn't show?"

"I put Amy Park on to testify about the existence of another man who fit the killer's description, then I put Jackson on."

"Can't the Judge order the police to bring Gouveia in?"

"Sure. He can issue a bench warrant. But if he doesn't show, I reckon he'll be long gone. What the Judge does then is anybody's guess."

Paula was silent, but continued to gently rub Pancho's chest. Pancho felt a surge of love for her, and he could feel his body begin to relax. Both had been married before. Pancho's wife had left him because she didn't want to play second fiddle to the law. Paula's husband had left her because his ego couldn't handle the fact that she was a strong woman who was the major bread winner in the family. The two lay there, saying nothing, doing nothing, for another half hour. When Pancho finally felt like some of the weight of the world had eased off his shoulders, he kissed Paula, a long and soft kiss that he hoped would convey the depth of his love and gratitude.

Thirty-Seven

When Pancho crossed Punchbowl Street on Queen Street and the courthouse steps came into view the next morning, he could see that the press had figured out Keani Sefo was Drew's partner. The usual number of reporters and television crews seemed to have doubled in size. When they spotted him, they rushed toward him, yelling questions.

"Was Keani working on this case with your investigator?"

"Who was the other man in the house? Was he a witness?"

"Are these murders related to this case?"

Pancho ignored them all and pushed his way into the building and through the security station. He quickly walked across the rotunda, his boots echoing off the floor. The criminal courts were on the third floor, and when he stepped out of the elevator and began walking toward Judge Kingsley's courtroom, he saw Amy Park sitting on a bench with earpods stuck in her ear. Her head was down and moving slightly to whatever music she was listening to. When Pancho walked by she looked up but said nothing to him. Her glare told him how irritated she was at spending her valuable time sitting around the courthouse waiting to do something she didn't want to do.

As Pancho passed from the rotunda walkway into the hallway where the courtrooms were located, he felt an involuntary lurch in his stomach as he spotted Scotty Gouveia. Gouveia looked like he'd aged ten years. He also looked like he had slept in his clothes, which were the same as he'd worn to court the day before. Pancho figured Scotty had been too scared to go home. Gouveia was unshaven and had dark circles under his eyes. He stared at Pancho with abject hatred.

Pancho's elation at seeing Gouveia was short-lived. A man in a suit and tie who'd been sitting on the far side of Gouveia stood and Pancho saw it was Charlie Hampton, an old-time attorney who had been a prosecutor several decades earlier and now handled pretty much anything that walked into his office.

"Hello, Pancho. Howzit?" Charlie's voice was raspy from years of smoking, and Pancho quickly discerned from the smell that emanated from his shabby gray suit that Charlie still smoked.

Pancho shook Charlie's proffered hand. "Hey, Charlie. Long time. You here on business or are you a spectator today?" Pancho knew what the answer would be, but he tried to harbor some hope that this was not what he thought it was.

"I'll be representing Mr. Gouveia."

Pancho nodded. "Will he be testifying?"

Charlie gave Pancho a wan smile. "What do you think? No, he'll be taking the fifth from here on."

Pancho glanced at the miserable looking Scotty Gouveia, who was still sitting and glaring. He nodded to Charlie. "Got it." He turned and walked into court.

***

Pancho sat at counsel's table and desperately tried to think things through. Jackson had sensed that there had been a big change of some kind and tried to ask Pancho what was going on, but Pancho had put his hand on Jackson's arm and told him to sit tight. He needed to figure things out.

The courtroom was buzzing, and when the jurors were brought in, Pancho could see that the more insightful jurors had picked up on the fact that today felt different. Judge Kingsley demanded silence. His face was set in a stern expression. *Everyone's on edge today,* thought Pancho.

The Judge ordered Scotty Gouveia to return to the witness stand and admonished him that he was still under oath. Then he turned the witness over to Pancho.

"Mr. Gouveia, before the break yesterday, we established that you are in debt to some Las Vegas casinos in an amount in excess of two hundred fifty thousand dollars, is that correct?"

Gouveia looked past Pancho to Charlie Hampton, who was sitting in the front row. Pancho made a show of turning to see where Gouveia was looking just in time to see Charlie nod. Gouveia then looked down at a piece of paper in his shaking hands and said, "On advice of counsel I am exercising my Constitutional right under the Fifth Amendment against self-incrimination." His voice sounded shaky and weak. Pancho could see the man was terrified.

Judge Kingsley had to bang his rarely used gavel to quiet the courtroom.

Pancho plowed ahead. "When you realized that you couldn't pay your gambling obligations, did you turn to your uncle, Nappy Makuakane, for help?"

Gouveia looked down at the piece of paper. "On advice of counsel — "

Pancho interrupted him. "Mr. Gouveia, may I assume you'll be asserting your right to remain silent from here on out?"

Scotty Gouveia looked confused. He stared helplessly at Charlie Hampton, who finally rose.

"Your Honor, if I may. For the record, I'm Charles Hampton and I represent Mr. Gouveia. It is his intention, on my advice, to assert his Fifth Amendment privilege to remain silent as to all further questions."

Judge Kingsley nodded and turned to the jury. "Ladies and gentlemen of the jury, I'm sure you're all aware that under our Constitution every citizen has the absolute right to remain silent as to all questions which may be self-incriminating. That is what Mr. Gouveia is doing here today. Mr. McMartin, and then Mr. Chang, will proceed to ask Mr. Gouveia all the questions they want to ask and Mr. Gouveia will presumably decline to answer." He turned back to Gouveia. "In the interest of time, from here on out, Mr. Gouveia, instead of reading the whole statement your attorney has given you, why don't you just say something like 'I remain silent,' or 'I decline to answer.' It will be noted for the record that you are asserting your Fifth Amendment rights."

Gouveia nodded to the Judge and then looked back at Pancho, who had remained standing. "Did you ask Nappy Makuakane, your uncle, for help with your gambling debts?"

"I remain silent."

"Did your uncle, Nappy Makuakane, tell you that Auntie Irene Kamaka was a courier for Nappy Makuakane's boss, Bobby Lopaka?"

"I remain silent."

Pancho ignored the murmuring from the spectators. "And did Nappy Makuakane tell you that on the day of her gig at the Ala Moana Center, Auntie Irene would be carrying a large amount of cash and heroin?"

"I remain silent."

"Did you and Mr. Makuakane devise a plan for you to have Auntie Irene's purse and ukulele stolen so that you could use the cash and drugs to pay off your gambling debt?"

"I remain silent."

Pancho glanced at Harry Chang, who was getting to his feet, clearly fuming. "Objection, Your Honor. Assumes facts not in evidence."

Pancho had been expecting this. "May we approach the bench, Your Honor?"

Judge Kingsley nodded and said, "Yes, please approach."

When the two attorneys and the court reporter were huddled in front of the Judge, Pancho pointed out that there was a sufficient thread of facts to entitle him to this line of questioning. "Your Honor, Mr. Gouveia has admitted that he was in debt to Vegas casinos in an amount in excess of a quarter million dollars. He has admitted that he did not have the funds to pay that debt. He has admitted that he asked his security guard, Marcus Young, to follow Auntie Irene. He—"

The Judge held up his hand and cut him off. "I agree. I'll allow the question and further questions that follow that thread." He looked at Pancho. "But please let's not go too far into the realm of speculation."

When the attorneys were back at their respective tables, Pancho continued. "Did you hire one of your security guards, Marcus Young, to rob Auntie Irene?"

"I remain silent."

"In fact, wasn't it the plan that this would be a simple snatch and that Auntie Irene was not to be injured in any way?"

Pancho could see from Gouveia's expression that he desperately wanted to answer that question, but he looked at Charlie Hampton, then said, "I remain silent."

"Isn't it true that after you learned that Auntie Irene had been murdered, Marcus Young disappeared and you were unable to find out what had gone wrong?"

"I remain silent."

"And you didn't have the money or the drugs to pay off your gambling debts?"

"I remain silent."

"Isn't it true, Mr. Gouveia, that you eventually found Marcus Young hiding out at a friend's house in Ka'a'awa?"

"I remain silent."

"And you tortured Marcus Young for information on what happened and where your money and drugs were?"

"I remain silent."

"You killed Marcus Young, did you not?"

Gouveia looked broken and pitiful. His voice sounded like he wanted to cry. "I remain silent."

"In the course of torturing Marcus Young for information, didn't you learn that he had convinced a friend of his to help him with the robbery?"

"I remain silent."

"And didn't Marcus Young tell you that it was his friend who murdered Auntie Irene?"

Gouveia's voice was barely audible now. "I remain silent."

"Isn't it true that Marcus Young's friend was a slightly built dark man who is Sri Lankan and who's name is Rashad Ranatunga?"

There was a low buzz of murmuring in the courtroom as Gouveia said, "I remain silent."

Pancho paused and looked at his notes. Scotty Gouveia's decision to take the Fifth had given Pancho the opportunity to ask questions he knew Gouveia would have denied, which may then have ultimately caused the Judge to start limiting the questions. Even though Pancho was fairly sure that Gouveia hadn't gotten Rashad's name out of Young before Young died, he was able to ask the question as if it was a known fact.

When Pancho finished his examination of Gouveia, the Judge asked Harry Chang if he had any cross. Harry slowly rose to his feet and raised his hands in a gesture of hopelessness. "I don't see any point in my attempting to cross-examine Mr. Gouveia, Your Honor."

The courtroom was eerily silent as everyone watched Scotty Gouveia, slumped over and head bowed, walk out of court, followed by his rumpled attorney, Charlie Hampton.

Pancho called Amy Park to the stand. It took but a few minutes to establish her relationship with Marcus Young and the fact that Young had a dark-skinned, slightly built "Indian looking" friend by the name of Rashad Ranatunga. The two had been hanging around with each other prior to the murder of Auntie Irene. She hadn't seen Marcus Young or Rashad Ranatunga since the morning Marcus left for work on the day of the murder.

It was time for lunch.

Thirty-Eight

Pancho was smiling when he met Jackson in the small conference room next to the courtroom. At first he was upset and depressed when he heard Scotty Gouveia planned to refuse to answer his questions, but he soon realized what a great opportunity it gave him to lay out the scenario of Auntie Irene's robbery and death without contradiction. Although the Judge, at the end of the case, would admonish the jury that they could not presume what the answers to the questions posed to Gouveia would be, Pancho knew very well that was exactly what they would do. When coupled with Amy Park's testimony, Pancho was pretty sure he was now in the driver's seat.

Jackson gave Pancho a questioning look. "So you know who killed that Auntie lady?"

"We think we know. We think it's someone who looks a lot like you, although he's not an American black man; he's Sri Lankan."

"What's that?"

"Like an Indian, from India. Sri Lanka is a country just below India. The men tend to be dark skinned and are often slightly built. From what I hear, this guy had short hair at the time of the murder, and it would have been fairly easy for a witness to confuse the two of you."

"So they gonna let me go now?"

"I'm afraid not, Jackson. Just because I think this guy was the murderer and I think I know what really happened doesn't mean the prosecutor agrees. Unless we can find this Rashad person and get him to confess or otherwise tie him to the murder, I reckon the prosecution will insist that your case goes to the jury." Pancho paused and ran his hand through his hair, then he smiled. "But I'm pretty confident at this point that they'll find you not guilty. All we need to do is put you on the stand to say you didn't do it and that you remember those guys on a moped throwing a purse at you."

"You means I still got to testify?"

Pancho reached across the narrow table and put a hand on Jackson's arm. "I need you. We're in good shape now, but I need the jury to hear you tell them that you didn't murder Auntie Irene and explain how your fingerprints got on the purse."

Jackson was silent for a few moments. Pancho couldn't tell what he was thinking.

"But how do I know I didn't kill that Auntie lady? I was passed out. I just think I didn't kill her."

Pancho leaned back in his chair and put his hands on his head. When he spoke, the frustration was evident. "C'mon, Jackson. I appreciate your honesty and all, but you know damn well you didn't kill Auntie Irene. You passed out after those guys threw her purse at you. How could you have killed her if she had already been robbed and murdered *before* you passed out?"

Jackson scratched his head. After a moment he said, "I guess you right. I just don't wanna say somethin' that ain't the truth."

Pancho expelled his breath and leaned forward, letting his arms rest on the table. "And I don't want you to. Just answer my questions with yes or no or in as short a sentence as possible. Let's go through it now."

***

Pancho thought Jackson looked like a little boy as he walked tentatively to the witness stand. As Pancho announced to the court that his client would testify, he had glanced at Jackson and had seen the look of sheer terror in Jackson's eyes. Pancho had a terrible tremor of doubt and fear.

Would putting Jackson on turn out to be a huge mistake? There was a fair chance that he could win an acquittal without Jackson's testimony, but if the jury took the Judge's instructions about Gouveia's reliance on the Fifth Amendment to heart and ignored all of the questions Pancho had stated as if they were facts, they were still left with Jackson's prints on Auntie Irene's purse and an eyewitness claiming he'd been seen running from the direction of the murder.

Pancho watched Jackson settle uncomfortably into the witness chair. Jackson looked at the jury as Pancho had instructed him to do. Pancho hoped that by now, the jury had become accustomed to Jackson's ugly and mean looking visage and would see instead the scared, vulnerable kid Pancho had come to feel so protective of. When Jackson looked back at Pancho, Pancho began taking him through the preliminaries they had rehearsed. Pancho wanted the jury to hear about Jackson's background.

"So, Jackson, when your Aunt told you about how your mother had been raped and her parents had been murdered, what did you think?"

Jackson was silent for almost twenty seconds and Pancho had a moment of panic. They had been through this in rehearsal and Jackson had handled it perfectly. What was going on?

When Jackson spoke it was in a different tone than he'd been using, which had been matter of fact and perfectly audible. Now his tone was soft and there was a slight tremor.

"I was sad for mama. Real sad. She shouldn't of had to go through what she did. An' she shouldn't of been forced to have me and raise me. That weren't right, her havin' to raise up the son of the man who raped her." Jackson stopped and looked directly at the jury. This was unrehearsed.

"But I was scared for me, too," he said. "Aunt Clio said I would go to hell and that I would have to pay for the sins of my daddy. I didn't understand that and it scared me. I didn't think I was a bad person, but both she and our preacher tol' me that I was from bad seed, so I guess I'm bad." He shook his head a little. "I don't know. I still don't know what they was meanin'."

"Did your mother know that your aunt had told you this story?" asked Pancho.

"No, sir. Not that I knows of. She never said nothin'."

"Did your mother treat you bad, like she blamed you for anything?"

Jackson shook his head vigorously. "Oh no, sir. Not at all. She never beat me or tol' me I was goin' to hell or anythin' like that. She hardly ever even yelled at me. She was nice." He paused, like he was trying to find some thoughts. "The only thing I can say about my mama, which I understood once Aunt Clio tol' me what had happened, is that she was never real lovey dovey, if you know what I mean."

"You mean like she didn't hug you and kiss you a lot?"

Jackson nodded and wiped a tear that had formed at his right eye. If possible, his voice was even smaller than before. "She never kissed me and never hugged me. Not that I remember at least."

Pancho stole a glance at the jury. The same two ladies who had cried during Dr. Singer's testimony were now wiping away tears. One woman was shaking her head as if in disgust. Pancho allowed the moment to linger briefly before taking Jackson through his eviction from the house.

"Are you angry with your mother for kicking you out of the house when you turned eighteen?"

Again Jackson shook his head. "Oh no, sir. 'Specially once I knowed I looked exactly like my rapist daddy. I don't blame her at all. Like I done said already, I don't think she should've been forced to born me in the first place."

The courtroom was deathly quiet. Everyone was straining to hear Jackson's diminutive, sad voice as he told his story. Pancho knew it all, but even he was once again moved; not just by the story, but by the complete lack of malevolence in Jackson's words and tone. He glanced at the wall clock and looked up at Judge Kingsley. It was 3:45 and the Judge usually adjourned for the day at 4:00.

"I think this would be a good time to stop for the day, Your Honor."

Judge Kingsley nodded immediately. "Court will stand in recess until 9:00 tomorrow morning."

***

Pancho made his way through the usual throng of reporters and the few diehard demonstrators demanding justice for Auntie Irene, which Pancho translated to mean convict the little black kid. The day was a perfect sub-tropical day. There was a slight cooling trade wind and not a cloud in the impossibly blue sky. Once again Pancho was struck by the surreal transition from the intensity of the courtroom to the ordinariness of the real world.

He slung his sport coat over his shoulder and strolled unhurriedly down Queen Street toward his office, reflecting on the day. It had gone as well as he could have expected. Gouveia's taking the Fifth turned out to be a blessing, assuming the jury didn't take the Judge's instructions too much to heart. Jackson had done great; better than great, but Pancho knew the real hurdle would be Harry's cross-examination of Jackson. Pancho couldn't help but smile to himself. It was the first time in his career that he was worried about a client being too honest.

Thirty-Nine

Nappy Makuakane sat alone in his small ocean-front home in Puako, a residential community between Waikaloa and Hapuna on the Big Island. The house was an older wood frame structure in need of repair. Nappy sat in his worn leather slouch chair facing the picture window looking over the dead calm ocean. The window provided the only light. The house was eerily quiet. Next to the chair was a small wicker side table on which stood a bottle of Dewar's sixteen-year-old Scotch whiskey. He held a small tumbler of Scotch in his right hand. He was unshaven and wore a torn white tee shirt and brown cargo shorts with bleach stains in various locations. He was barefoot.

The sudden sound of music coming from his phone caused Nappy to jerk, spilling some Scotch onto his shorts. He grabbed the phone that had been sitting next to the bottle. The caller ID said 'blocked.' He considered not answering, but the curiosity of who would be calling got the better of him. After all, he had quickly become *persona non gratis.*

"Yeah," he said gruffly.

"Nappy. This is Bryson." There was a pause, as if the caller wanted an acknowledgement.

Finally Nappy said, "Uh huh."

"You're kind of fucked, aren't you old friend?" The tone was not particularly mocking, but neither did it gush with sympathy.

"No shit, Sherlock. What you like? You call for gloat?"

"Fuck no, Nappy. I'm sorry for all the shit you got yourself into. And all for that asshole Scotty Gouveia. I never did like that fucka." He paused for a couple of seconds before continuing. "Actually, the reason I called is to find out exactly what Auntie Irene was carrying when she was robbed."

"This official?"

"Nah. Personal. Did you hear about what happened in court today?"

"Yeah. More or less. Not too many bruddahs are talking to me right now."

"The attorney, Pancho, brought up this guy named Rashad, who apparently looks a little like that *popolo* on trial and who was buddies with Marcus Young. I promised the prosecutor that I'd look for him. I'm thinking that if I can find that kid, I find the stuff he stole."

Nappy was thinking as fast as the Scotch would allow. "You saying the *popolo* is innocent?"

"How the fuck do I know? More important, why the fuck do I care?"

"Jesus, Bryson. You're a fucking cop, that's why."

Bryson Wong laughed. "Yeah, and you're a fucking gangster."

Nappy took a sip of Scotch, then put the glass on the table. He rubbed his face, trying to concentrate. "So why you like know what was stolen if it's not official?"

This time it was Wong's turn to pause. Nappy thought he heard an exhaled breath on the line, then Wong spoke. "I'll be straight with you, man. If this little shithead Rashad has what I think he may have, I can use it. I'll give you a split."

"What am I going to do with a split in Hell?" Nappy said.

There was a chuckle that sounded like a snort on the other end of the line.

"Depending on how much it is, or how much is left from whatever it was, you could use it to get the hell out of Dodge."

Nappy let out a strangled, rough laugh. His voice, when he spoke, dripped with sarcasm. "Yeah, maybe I'll go set up shop in Tahiti or someplace nice where they'll never find me."

"Look, Nappy. Whatever you want. A split or no split. Just do me this favor and I'll look the other way on all the shit you're in."

"You gonna look the other way when they find my body? Or you gonna go after Bobby and his boys who you know fucking well will be the ones who did me?"

Wong let out another big sigh. "What will you want me to do, Nappy?"

Nappy grunted. "What the fuck. What kind of trouble you in, Bryce? Gambling debts like Scotty?"

"Something like that. You gonna help or not?"

Nappy thought about it. What did he have to lose? He was probably a dead man anyway. It was just a matter of time. He knew Bobby and Rigger would wait for the shit storm to pass before they off'd him, but there was no question they would do it. They had to; unless...

"Tell me you'll get to Bobby and demand that I be kept alive or else you'll shit down his throat."

Nappy could hear Wong breathing, presumably thinking. Finally, he said, "Yeah. I can do that."

What the fuck, thought Nappy. *If it works, I get to live. If it doesn't, I'll be just as dead. He spoke into the phone.* "She had thirty-five thousand in cash in her purse and a pound of uncut heroin in her ukulele case."

Nappy heard Wong whistle softly. There was silence on the line after that, and Nappy assumed his old school chum was doing the math. A pound of cut heroin would be worth a couple hundred grand. Uncut would be worth much, much more. Nappy interrupted the presumed math exercise. "You know where this Rashad guy is?"

"Let's just say I've got a bead on him," the caller said.

Nappy picked up his glass of Scotch and took a large sip. He looked out at the ocean. A two-person outrigger went by, heading in the direction of Hapuna. He pushed the disconnect button without saying anything further and took another sip of Scotch. Maybe he needed to get out on the water where an old waterman like him belonged.

Forty

Pancho had packed his notes into his briefcase and was about to leave the office for the evening when Drew limped in. He looked horrible. His normally vibrant brown face had a gray pallor to it. There were dark, almost black, bags piled one on top of the other under his sad looking eyes. Pancho, who had already been standing, came out from around his desk, walked over, and gave the big man a hug.

"You okay? How's Keani?" Pancho asked when they had separated. Drew lowered himself to the couch.

"The doctors say it's still fifty/fifty. He's still critical and in a coma."

Pancho pulled over a client chair and sat opposite Drew. "And you?"

Drew waved his right hand dismissively. "I'm fine. Just feeling old and tired and sad. Need some sleep."

"So why aren't you home sleeping? Why're you here?"

"I know you're running out of time in the trial, so I did some nosing around this afternoon, trying to find that Rashad dude."

Pancho was moved. Drew's friend and partner was in critical condition and Drew was running on empty, but the man was out looking for the probable killer of Auntie Irene. "You didn't have to do that, Drew. You need to take care of yourself. I think I'm in good shape in the trial. Did you hear what happened today?"

Drew nodded. "Yeah. Sounds like Gouveia and Nappy Makuakane are pretty much toast."

"Anyway, I just have to get through the rest of Jackson's testimony tomorrow, then I'll rest. The case should go to the jury tomorrow. I doubt you can do much else before that."

Drew gave Pancho a wan smile. "Not necessarily. I tracked Rashad to a rundown boarding house in Kalihi, not far from here. He'd been there for weeks, hardly leaving the room. He was using the name Cedric Singh. The next door neighbor needed some convincing to talk to me." Drew rubbed his fingers on his thumb, the age-old sign of money. "But eventually told me that the guy looked seriously strung out."

"So he probably has the smack and is shooting up," said Pancho.

Drew nodded again. "Yeah. But get this. Yesterday some older guy came to the boarding house, asked around, and finally found this Cedric guy. The neighbor said the old guy looked like a cop, but he didn't show any identification. The guy was in Cedric's room for about ten minutes, then the two came out together. The old guy had a shopping bag in his hand, which he didn't have when he went in. He was leading Cedric by the other hand. They left the building and no one has seen Cedric since."

Pancho frowned, stood, and walked back to his desk. "Shot of Patron?"

Drew shook his head. "It'd probably put me down."

Pancho sat in his desk chair. "Probably be for the best. You can sleep here on the couch if you don't feel like going home. I'd take you to my place, but I'm having Paula over one last time before the verdict comes out. I'm not sure if the crazies are still out there or not, so I intend to keep her away for a week or so once the verdict comes in."

Drew got slowly to his feet. He stretched. "I'll nose around for another hour or two and see if I can find Rashad, then I'll get some take-out and head home." He turned for the door.

Pancho stood and grabbed his already packed briefcase. "I'll walk down with you."

***

Pancho made love to Paula before they even changed for dinner. He felt an intensity and desperation that surprised and confused him. He came fast, too fast for Paula's own pleasure. He gave her a sheepish grin, like a child caught doing something wrong. "Sorry. I don't know what got into me."

Paula smiled back and pulled him down on top of her. "Nothing to be sorry about. You've been under enormous stress and you needed a release. I'm fine with that." She pushed him off her. "But I think that after dinner we may need to try it again."

Pancho sighed theatrically. "Oookay, if you insist."

They ate at Michel's, not wanting to walk into the craziness of Waikiki. Pancho filled Paula in on what it meant for Gouveia to take the Fifth.

"But how can the Judge expect the jury to ignore the fact that the guy refuses to answer your questions because it might incriminate himself?"

Pancho smiled. "Well, that's the reality of the human condition I'm counting on. Before he clammed up I got him to admit his relationship with Bobby Lopaka's right hand man, Nappy Makuakane, and to admit that he was deep in debt. So that's all in evidence and the jury can consider that. The actual set-up to rob Auntie Irene isn't in evidence, so I'm relying on the jury believing that it's a realistic scenario given the money crisis Gouveia was in."

Paula chewed some of her share of the Chateaubriand with béarnaise they had split. After a moment she said, "But that still doesn't rule out Jackson as the accomplice, does it?"

"No. But for that I have Amy Park, who testified that there's a guy named Rashad who was buddies with Marcus Young and who looks a lot like Jackson. And I have Jackson himself saying that he was tossed the purse by two guys on a moped, one of whom was dark and thin."

"And you got that witness, the Japanese guy, who said that the guy he saw on the moped was definitely not Jackson."

Pancho nodded and took a sip of Cabernet. "So I think there's enough reasonable doubt on the table for the jury to conclude that Jackson was just in the wrong place at the wrong time—and looking the wrong color and the wrong build."

"So he's doing good on the stand?"

Pancho ran his right hand through his hair and looked out at the ocean, which was still calm in the dying light. "So far. He's amazing, in fact. That's in large part because he's so damn honest. He's like a child who doesn't yet understand what a lie is. But that could also be his downfall. If Harry starts manipulating him, who knows what Jackson will say?"

The two ate in comfortable silence for several minutes. When they spoke again, the last of the day's light was gone and the lights of the Waikiki hotels took over as the main attraction. There were a couple of well-lit dinner cruises beyond the reef. They talked about Keani Sefo and Drew and about what an awful toll this case had taken on so many lives.

"Well, it'll be over soon enough," said Pancho.

Paula looked him in the eyes. "Yeah, then your life may be at risk and your main bodyguard, Drew, is barely hanging on."

Pancho looked away. He'd thought of that of course. He'd considered hiring someone in Drew's place, but in the end, for better or worse, he decided there was no one he wanted by his side other than Drew.

After a moment of silence Paula said, "And now, if you're *pau* stuffing your face, shall we go back and see if you remember how to pleasure a woman?"

Forty-One

The word had spread that this would in all likelihood be the last day of trial and, in light of the stunning events of the prior day, the courtroom was packed beyond its capacity. The sheriffs were turning people away and asking some to leave the court. If it was possible, Pancho was harangued by the press more than usual as he walked up the steps to Ka'ahumanu Hale. He smiled and said nothing. He was wearing a light wool blazer over pressed jeans, a starched white shirt, and one of his lucky Lady Justice ties, this one red with small white figures of the blindfolded lady holding the scales of justice.

Lester, Judge Kingsley's law clerk, gestured to Pancho as soon as he had pushed his way into court. "The Judge wants you in chambers, Mr. McMartin. Mr. Chang is already there."

Pancho followed Lester to the Judge's chambers. He smiled at Gladys when he entered. She nodded back, but she looked worried and scared. The taking of the verdict would be the time she and all the rest of the staff were at risk. Pancho looked around and saw a sheriff sitting in the waiting room. *A lot of help he would be if some crazy somehow gets into the building and barges in with guns blazing,* thought Pancho. He walked into the Judge's office and Lester closed the door behind him. Harry was sitting in his usual spot, across from where Pancho was expected to sit. Lester took his seat in the corner.

"Morning, Pancho," said Judge Kingsley.

"Good morning, Your Honor."

"Well, unless you boys have more surprises up your sleeves, today should be the day we get this damn case to the jury. Am I right?" He looked first to Pancho, who nodded, then he looked at Harry. "You gonna have a long cross for the defendant, Mr. Chang?"

Harry shook his head. "I don't think so, Your Honor. Probably a half hour at the most."

"Any more witnesses from either side?"

Since it had the burden of proof, the prosecution had a chance after the close of the defense case to put on rebuttal witnesses, but Harry shook his head. "No, sir."

Pancho spoke up. "Just in the interest of clarity, Your Honor. As you heard in the testimony, there's a person by the name of Rashad Ranatunga whom we believe to be the actual murderer. We understand the police are looking for him even as we speak. I also have my investigator looking for him. In the unlikely event he's found before the case gets to the jury, I just want the record to be clear that we'll subpoena him to testify."

Judge Kingsley nodded in acknowledgement and looked at Harry, who shrugged. "Whatever."

***

Pancho took Jackson through the rest of his testimony slowly and deliberately. He wanted to leave as little room for cross-examination as possible. He had Jackson explain when his memory of the moped coming at him came back and why he panicked when he was thrown the purse. It was good testimony, with Jackson retaining his simple air of honesty throughout.

"No more questions, Your Honor," said Pancho when he was done. He smiled at Jackson, who smiled back and began to rise from the witness chair. Pancho put up his hand. "Stay seated, Jackson," he said. "Mr. Chang now has a chance to ask you questions."

Jackson sunk back into his chair. "I'm sorry." He turned to Harry. "Sorry, Mr. Chang. I knew that. I jus' forgot." It was a disarming moment that could not have been rehearsed.

Harry Chang was forced to be polite back to Jackson. "That's okay, Mr. Steele. You aren't the first one to forget about me." There was light laughter from the crowded courtroom.

"Now, Mr. Steele, let's go back to the moment when you woke up from your blackout and walked out of the bathroom."

"Yes sir?"

"You pretty much walked right into a policeman, is that correct?"

"Yes sir."

"And that policeman asked if you had just beaten up and robbed a lady, is that correct?"

Jackson scrunched up his face, thinking. "Well, first he asked if I was all right, since my head was bleedin'. Then he asked me if I'd just robbed someone. After that he tol' me someone had gotten murdered."

"When the policeman asked if you had participated in a robbery, what did you say?"

Jackson's eyes never left Harry's. He didn't look over at Pancho for apparent help. He answered promptly. "I said I didn't know, 'cause I couldn't remember nothin'."

Harry paused for dramatic effect. "Why didn't you just deny it?"

Jackson looked confused, like he had said something wrong. "How could I deny somethin' if I didn't remember? That would be lyin', wouldn't it?" There was some murmuring in the courtroom which Pancho hoped to be murmurs of approval.

"So if I asked you the same question today as the policeman did on the day of the robbery and murder, your answer would have to be the same, wouldn't it? That you don't remember if you participated or not?"

Jackson scratched his head and then looked up at the ceiling, a gesture Pancho had come to appreciate as Jackson's personal deliberations. After a pause of about ten seconds, Jackson looked back at Harry. "I'm sorry, Mr. Chang, but I kind of have to answer that question yes and no."

Harry let a look of impatience cross his face. He was clearly hoping that the jury would now see Jackson for the prevaricator he really was. "What does that mean?" he asked with a tone dripping with disgust.

"It means that, yes, I would have to say I don't know for sure what I did while I was passed out. But now that I know someone else had the Auntie's purse before I passed out in the bathroom and that they threw it to me, it don't make a whole lot of sense that I robbed the lady. If I had done that, wouldn't I already have the purse?" Again, there was a short burst of murmurs from the crowd.

Pancho was watching Harry. He looked nonplussed for a moment, but Harry was a pro and quickly cleared his face of emotion and plowed ahead.

"And, of course, we have only your word for the fact that you got your memory back for the time before you got to the bathroom and that two men tossed a purse to you during that time frame. Is that correct?"

Pancho could see that Jackson didn't seem to have followed the question. He prayed that Jackson didn't try to answer it.

"Mr. Chang, could you ask me that again? I'm not sure I understood what you is askin'."

Good job, thought Pancho.

Harry tried a theatrical sigh, but Pancho could see it was more a sigh of frustration. He wasn't making any headway.

"Mr. Steele, you've testified that at first you didn't remember anything from the time you entered the Ala Moana parking lot to the time that you got up off the floor of the bathroom. Is that correct?"

Jackson nodded. "Yes sir. That's right."

"And later you testified that suddenly your memory of what happened before you got to the bathroom came back, but that you still don't remember what happened in the bathroom. Correct?"

Pancho could see Jackson literally mull the question over in his mind, then he gave Harry a nod. "Yes sir, that's right, too."

"So when you suddenly got your pre-bathroom memory back, you also suddenly remembered seeing two guys on a moped coming at you, and you suddenly remember one man who looked similar to you toss a purse at you as they drove by. Correct?" Harry's voice was now heavy with sarcasm.

"Objection, Your Honor." Pancho was on his feet. "The question as asked is vague and ambiguous and is unduly argumentative."

Judge Kingsely looked at Harry. "Sustained. Rephrase, Mr. Chang."

Harry looked at the jury with a 'what can you do?' look before turning back to Jackson.

"Mr. Steele. Sometime before this trial started, you claim that you now remember walking in the parking lot before you got to the bathroom. Is that correct?"

"Yes sir, it is."

"And that as part of this miraculous memory recall, you now claim that you remember two men on a moped coming at you. Correct?"

Pancho saw Judge Kingsley look at him, obviously thinking he would object to Harry's use of the term *miraculous*. Pancho gave the Judge a slight shake of the head. *Not worth it*, he thought. His sense was that the jury's sentiments were with Jackson right now and the meaner Harry came across, the better it would be for Jackson.

"That's correct, sir."

"And one of those men looked kind of like you?"

"One of those men was dark-skinned and pretty skinny and had short hair. So if that looks like me, then yes sir, that would be correct." Someone in the audience chuckled.

"And that skinny, dark-skinned man threw a purse at you?"

"Yes sir."

"For no reason?"

Again, Judge Kingsley looked at Pancho to object, but he didn't.

Jackson visibly shrugged. "I guess he had a reason since he threw it. He probably wanted to get rid of the purse." More chuckles from the courtroom. Pancho looked at Harry, who was clearly out of sorts.

"And instead of calling the police or a security guard when you suddenly had the purse in your hands, you ran toward the bathroom and threw the purse into the trash? Is that your testimony now, Mr. Steele?"

Jackson had been nodding even while the question was being asked. "Yes sir, it is."

Pancho smiled to himself. He realized that even he had underestimated Jackson. Just because he looked mean and ugly and spoke with an accent that many people might associate with ignorance, it didn't mean Jackson himself was ignorant. Pancho was reevaluating Jackson's intelligence with almost every answer now. *The kid may be uneducated, but he sure as shit's not dumb*, Pancho thought.

"Did you realize the purse must have belonged to someone?" Pancho knew Harry was going to push too far.

"Yes sir. Most purses do. It sure didn't belong to me." More chuckles.

"Yet you threw the purse into the trash." Harry paused for a second. "Not only did you throw the purse into the trash, you *ran* to throw the purse in the trash. Could you explain to the jury how those actions are the actions of an innocent man?"

Jackson didn't hesitate. "I don't know 'bout actions of how an innocent man would be. But what I did are actions of a man who knew darn well he shouldn't be walkin' around wif someone else's purse." This time there was outright laughter in the courtroom. Pancho saw that even Judge Kingsley couldn't repress a small, fleeting smile.

Harry fumbled around with a few more questions, but he made no inroads into Jackson's credibility and finally gave up. Pancho couldn't remember when he'd seen a Harry Chang cross-examination go so poorly.

Pancho wasted no time in resting the defense case. He glanced at the clock. It was 11:30. Judge Kingsley dismissed the jury for lunch, then ordered the attorneys back to settle jury instructions at one o'clock. He wanted the closing arguments to start no later than 2:30.

Forty-Two

Pancho was dismayed to find the outer door to the office unlocked. Susan was at her desk looking harried as she handled one call after another.

"Mr. McMartin will have no comment on the trial until after a verdict is rendered," she said in a voice that sounded both tired and impatient.

Pancho locked the outer door behind him and made a half-hearted scolding gesture to Susan, who promptly flipped him off. He smiled and went to his office. It was another picture perfect Hawaiian day, and Pancho stopped a moment to stare out the floor-to-ceiling windows. A huge cruise ship had docked at Aloha Tower that morning. The ship dwarfed the building that for four decades had been the tallest building in Honolulu. Pancho thought about taking Paula on a cruise. God knows he and Paula both deserved a break after the emotional roller coaster of this case; but not on a ship of such enormity, he decided as he turned from the window. He'd stick to the weekend on Maui he had planned.

He noticed that Susan had put a sandwich and a bottle of water on his desk. She probably couldn't lock the door behind her as she carried their lunch into the office, then had forgotten to do so. He dug into the chicken sandwich with relish. As he ate, he thought about his closing argument. It would be short and sweet. He thought he had the case wrapped up. He couldn't conceive how a jury could convict Jackson. As he thought it, he felt an involuntary shiver. *That's just the kind of thinking that could go horribly wrong,* he thought; *bachi,* as they say in Hawai'i.

Susan stuck her head into his office a few minutes later. "Need anything, bossman?" Her gravelly voice was raspier than usual, which Pancho assumed was from too much phone time.

"No, thanks." He paused for a moment while he finished chewing a bite of the sandwich. "And thanks for the sandwich, by the way. Why don't you lock up and go home as soon as I head back to court. The case should get to the jury this afternoon and, with Drew out, I don't want you here by yourself."

Susan looked surprised. "You sure? Shouldn't someone be here to answer the phones? I'll be all right with the door locked."

"I'm sure, Suse. There's been enough tragedy surrounding this case lately and I don't want some *lolo,* some crazy, decide he's going to hold it against us if Jackson's acquitted."

Susan came the rest of the way into the office. "So you think you'll win?"

Pancho smiled. "I don't want to jinx it. But, yeah, it's looking pretty good right now."

Susan seemed to think about things for a moment, then finally nodded. "Okay. I'll head home when you leave. Just promise to call me if you need anything or if a verdict comes in. What do you want me to do tomorrow morning?"

Pancho, who was just about to take another bite of the sandwich, put it down. "Come on in. I'll make sure Drew is here. I'll call you if there's a change of plan."

When Susan was back in the outer office, Pancho leaned back in his chair. His sandwich was forgotten for the moment. There was a tightness in his stomach that made him no longer feel hungry. He recognized it as fear. What if he didn't win and Jackson was convicted of murder? What would happen if he won and the lunatic who threatened everyone involved in the case decided to carry out his threat? What would happen to Scotty Gouveia and Nappy Makuakane? Pancho knew he had to expose them as he did, but had he handed them a death sentence? They had crossed one of the most powerful and vicious crime bosses in Hawai'i history.

Pancho rolled his head around his neck and felt a small crack. He felt tight and anxious. He knew he should finish his sandwich, but he couldn't seem to get his appetite back. He closed his eyes, took slow, deep breaths. He could feel his body begin to release some of the tension. Suddenly the intercom jolted him out of his meditation.

"Drew's on line one," Susan rasped.

Pancho sighed and picked up. "Yo, big man. Everything okay?"

"I've got a lead on Rashad. I'm heading out to Kane'ohe now. I just wanted you to know."

Pancho unconsciously leaned forward in his chair. "Do you have any kind of back-up? Remember, the guy is probably a cold-blooded killer."

"I'll be careful. I couldn't think of anyone to use as back-up, so I'll take it nice and slow."

"Maybe we should just call the cops and let them handle it." Pancho could feel the stress returning with a vengeance. He couldn't bear the thought of something happening to Drew.

"Thought of that, but frankly I don't know who to trust. The neighbor dude I talked to the other day said the guy who took Rashad away seemed like a cop."

Pancho was silent for a few seconds. "Okay, but just be super careful, man. By the way, I told Susan to go home when I leave for court this afternoon. I don't want her here by herself if a verdict comes in today. I'd like you to be here with her in the morning if possible."

"Sure. Of course. I'll text you if anything important happens this afternoon."

"Let me know you're all right no matter what."

Pancho could hear a little of Drew's old self as he chuckled. "Yes, dad."

Forty-Three

The two closing arguments were short and sweet. Pancho had never participated in a murder trial where both closings were done inside fifty minutes. They were predictable. Harry Chang went first and focused on the purse, Jackson's prints on the purse, and Jackson's failure to deny his involvement when he was first confronted. His attempt to mock Jackson's 'miraculous' return of memory seemed to fall flat, at least to Pancho. Harry reminded the jury of the eyewitness and repeated the prosecution's theory that Jackson's accomplice had knocked him out and taken off with the stolen goods. Harry finished with a blatant attempt to inflame the jury's emotions with an impassioned and redundant recitation of the brutal way Auntie Irene was robbed and murdered.

Pancho focused on the lack of any evidence on or near Jackson other than the purse. He hit hard on the flawed eyewitness and line-up. He reminded the jury that Mr. Hasegawa had seen two men on a moped, one of whom looked something like Jackson, but who Mr. Hasegawa said was definitely not Jackson. Then there was Amy Park, who knew that there was a friend of Marcus Young who was dark and slim and could easily be confused with Jackson Steele, at least from a distance.

"That man," ladies and gentlemen, "was Marcus Young's accomplice in the horrible robbery and murder of Auntie Irene. That man, dark complected, slightly built, with short-cropped hair, is who should be sitting where Jackson Steele is sitting now. That man and Marcus Young were doing the bidding of Marcus Young's boss, Scotty Gouveia, whom you heard, before he took the Fifth Amendment right to remain silent, testify that he was deeply in debt to Las Vegas casinos. You also heard him testify that his wife's uncle is Nappy Makuakane, the longtime right hand lieutenant of Bobby Lopaka." Pancho paused, watching the jury.

"The Judge will instruct you that you are not to draw any inferences from Mr. Gouveia's decision to remain silent. That's his Constitutional right. But you can certainly draw inferences from the facts that are before you, and I submit that none of the reasonable inferences or scenarios surrounding the tragic death of Auntie Irene involve my client, Jackson Steele, other than having the misfortune of being a black man in the wrong place at the wrong time."

Judge Kingsley and the two attorneys had worked out the jury instructions earlier, so the Judge was able to give the instructions and send the jury off to begin deliberations well before three-thirty. Pancho decided to hang around, hoping there would be a quick verdict. He had Jackson taken to the small conference room and the two sat across from each other in tense silence. Pancho checked his cell phone to see if there were any texts from Drew. There was nothing.

"You did good, Pancho," said Jackson after a few minutes. "Thank you for working so hard for me. Nobody else ever believed in me like you do."

Pancho gave Jackson a small smile. His stomach was in a tight knot and his throat was dry. He hated waiting for a verdict. There was always initial relief whenever he sat down from his closing argument, knowing that there was nothing more for him to do, nothing more he could do but wait. Today he felt the additional relief at having finished the trial without having a public anxiety attack. In the rush of relief, he realized how worried about that he'd truly been.

Inevitably and gradually the relief would give way to anxiety and, in this case, even fear. "Let's hope the jury agrees that I did a good job," he said. His voice sounded dry, hollow, and shaky. He wanted to talk to Jackson about life after this trial, but he didn't want to jinx anything. He closed his eyes and leaned back in his chair, locking both hands on top of his head. He wondered if Drew was okay. He wondered if the crazies who had threatened the Judge's staff were lurking nearby or had they abandoned their misguided crusade once it had become clear that Auntie Irene was no angel? He wanted to assure Jackson that everything was going to be okay, but when he opened his eyes and looked across the table he could see that Jackson was in much better shape than he was.

At four-thirty the Judge called Pancho and Harry into his chambers. "I'm going to sequester the jury tonight. I don't want to take any risks." Both Harry and Pancho nodded their agreement, but before the Judge could continue there was a knock on his chamber's door and Lester, his clerk, stuck his head in.

"There's a verdict."

No one said anything for a few seconds, then Judge Kingsley let out a large breath. "Thank God," he said. "Bring them in."

***

Pancho stood next to Jackson, one hand on Jackson's shoulder, as Judge Kingsley proceeded through the ritual of asking for the foreman to identify his or herself, then asking if the jury had reached a unanimous verdict. The courtroom was continuing to fill as word of a verdict had spread.

The Judge instructed Lester to take the verdict form from the foreman, an older Japanese man whom Pancho would never have picked as the probable foreman. Lester then walked the form to the clerk of the court, who handed it to the Judge. The rustling of the filling courtroom settled down until the room was deathly silent. Judge Kingsley's face was impassive and unreadable. He handed the form back to the clerk and asked him to read the verdict into the record.

The clerk's voice was high and reedy. "We the jury in the above-entitled case find the defendant, Jackson Steele, not guilty of the charge of Murder in the Second Degree."

The courtroom erupted. Pancho smiled at the jury, several of whom were smiling at him and Jackson; then he turned to Jackson and saw tears in his eyes. He opened his arms and the two embraced, saying nothing. Pancho was surprised at the depth of emotion he felt. He became vaguely aware of the Judge gaveling for silence so that he could complete the procedural niceties and get the court adjourned. Moments later it was all over. It was agreed that Jackson would stay in custody overnight. It would be safer for him there. Sheriffs had been assigned to each of the Judge's staff. Pancho and Harry declined police protection. They both sat in the courtroom at their respective tables until everyone but court staff was gone.

Harry was first to speak, getting to his feet as he did so. "You did it again, Pancho. Congratulations."

"Thanks, Harry. Your case kind of fell to shit around you."

Harry gave a slight nod. It was Pancho's way of saying that it wasn't Harry's fault he lost. "Yeah, I guess it did. I hope they find that Rashad guy and he confesses so I won't have to feel like I let a murderer get away."

Pancho stood and began packing his briefcase. "Don't worry. You didn't. Jackson's as innocent as you or I."

Harry grunted. "Time to face the press. You coming?"

"Right behind you. You can tell them how disappointed you are in the verdict, then I'll tell them justice was served and blah, blah, blah."

Harry laughed. "See you around, Pancho."

Forty-Four

After a couple of lonely celebratory shots of Patron at the office, Pancho called Paula to tell her the news and to say he wanted her to keep her distance from him for the next few days. He realized while he was talking to her how emotional he was and how much he wished he could be with her. Clearly the stress of the trial, death threats, the shooting of Keani and Booger, and the concern for Jackson had taken much more of a toll on his psyche than he'd realized. He had tears in his eyes by the time he told Paula he loved her and hung up.

A gentle rain was falling when he pulled out of the parking garage, although the sky was blue out over the placid ocean. When he turned left onto Ala Moana Boulevard the rain stopped and he saw a huge, almost full rainbow to his left. The *pau hana* traffic was thick and Pancho allowed his mind to drift. He was worried about Jackson, but he hadn't allowed himself to think much about Jackson's future out of superstitious fear of jinxing the trial. Now he allowed some scenarios to run through his brain as he inched his way toward Waikiki and his condo at Diamond Head beyond.

As he finally passed the Moana Hotel and broke free of the traffic, he felt the vibration of his cell phone in his left front jeans pocket. He ignored it. He'd be home in a couple of minutes. Instead, he inspected the surf to his right as he drove by Kuhio Beach Park and the famous statue of Duke Kahanamoku. The surf was decent, maybe three feet. He thought about taking tomorrow morning off to go surfing, but then remembered he had to collect Jackson first thing. When he pulled into his parking stall and got out of the car, Pancho pulled out his cell and checked the text message. It was from Drew.

'Call ASAP' was all it said. Pancho felt a chill go through his body. What now? Had something happened to Drew and Susan? Or to the court personnel? He hadn't been listening to the radio. He speed-dialed Drew who answered immediately. The feeling of dread felt like an aching hole in his stomach.

"Are you home?" asked Drew, without preamble.

"Just got here. Still in the parking lot. Are you and Susan okay?"

"We're fine," said Drew, "but go upstairs and turn on the news. They found Rashad." There was a pause. "He's dead."

Pancho was walking toward the elevators but now he stopped. "Murdered?"

"I'm not sure, Paunch. I just heard the news. Go and turn on the news, then we'll talk once we both have more information." He hung up and Pancho hurried to the elevator bank.

***

It took a few moments of channel surfing for Pancho to find a station still covering the story. Pamela Young on KITV was on a split screen with a shot of a gurney being wheeled out of a rundown clapboard building.

"The dead man has been identified as Rashad Ranatunga, the man Jackson Steele's attorney, Pancho McMartin, alleged was the actual murderer of Auntie Irene Kamaka. HPD Detective Bryson Wong has told KITV that Ranatunga appears to have died of a heroin overdose, but stressed that the matter is still pending investigation."

The split screen disappeared and Pamela Young's face filled the screen. "Jackson Steele was acquitted of Auntie Irene's murder just hours ago. The contentious and at times racially charged trial had taken a strange turn when the owner of the firm in charge of security at the Ala Moana Center, Scott Gouveia, suddenly retained an attorney and refused to testify further, citing his Fifth Amendment right against self-incrimination." A silent video of Pancho talking to reporters outside of Ka'ahumanu Hale now filled the screen.

"This allowed McMartin to pose a series of questions which speculated that Gouveia was involved in the robbery and murder of Auntie Irene. McMartin's theory was that Auntie Irene was carrying a large amount of cash and heroin, and that Gouveia intended to rob her to pay off his Las Vegas gambling debts. But the robbery went tragically wrong when one of the assailants, possibly Rashad Ranatunga, viciously beat her to death."

The television screen returned to Pamela Young at the KITV news desk. "We will have much more on the outcome of the trial and the death of Rashad Ranatunga on our ten o'clock broadcast. In other news, a tourist at Sandy Beach appears to have drowned after a rogue wave—"

Pancho shut the television off and flopped onto his couch. His mind was racing, but his thoughts were interrupted by the ringing of his cell phone. He looked at the caller ID and saw it was Drew.

"What d'you think?" Drew asked.

"I'm not sure what to think. It seems pretty damn coincidental that this Rashad guy would croak now. If he had the smack all this time, why would he overdose now?"

"And who was the older guy who escorted him out of the boarding house yesterday?"

The two friends were silent for several seconds. Pancho spoke first. "Where are you?"

"I'm just leaving the hospital. I stopped by after dropping Susan off to see how Keani is and I was just walking out when I heard the news about Rashad on one of the televisions, so I went back to Keani's room and watched the coverage. Want to grab a bite in a while? I assume you're keeping Paula at a safe distance for now. You should have your crippled bodyguard with you." He paused for a second, then said, "And, of course, you need someone to celebrate with."

"Sure," said Pancho. "Give me a call on the cell when you're heading over. I think I'll go down and sit on the beach for a while. It looks like it'll be a nice sunset."

"Mmm," grunted Drew and hung up.

Forty-Five

Rigger hadn't felt nervous or scared in his father's company for many years, so he was surprised when he found himself feeling the way he had so many times as a kid and even as a young man. Bobby Lopaka was in a rage the intensity of which Rigger hadn't seen in decades. The two were in Bobby's study at the Waimea ranch. Bobby had been in a terrible mood since his best friend, Nappy, had confessed to his betrayal, so it didn't surprise Rigger that his father's boiling point was low.

Bobby was sitting forward in his desk chair. His arms rested on the desk and his right hand was holding his cigar so hard that Rigger could see it was about to snap. Bobby's rugged face was red. His eyes were narrowed and his mouth was turned down.

"You and Winston have fucked up every motherfucking step along the way," Bobby hollered. Spittle flew from his mouth as he spoke. "You were supposed to keep an eye on Gouveia and the business, but now we find he'd gambled himself into such a hole that he got Nappy to help him rip us off. Instead of you or your fucking kid finding that Marcus Young first, you let Gouveia find him. Then you fuck up by letting Gouveia interrogate him while you and Winston sit around pulling your puds. So we have no idea what Marcus told Gouveia." Bobby paused to catch his breath. He was talking loud and fast, and the ferocity of his tone chilled Rigger.

"Then, Winston finds that scared kid, what's his name? Booger or whatever. What does he do? He fucking shoots one of the most revered motherfucking athletes in Hawai'i. But worse yet, he doesn't even kill the cocksucker. So is Keani Sefo going to live to identify Winston? What the fuck, Rigger? Did you raise a complete idiot?"

Rigger had sense enough not to say anything. He sat in the large leather chair, watched his father vent and tried not to think of all the times when he was young when his father would yell at him, then beat the shit out of him. Even though he knew his father wouldn't be beating him, he found he couldn't repress the old feelings of fear.

Bobby took a pull on his wet and battered cigar, then spoke in a more controlled tone. "So we finally learned that Nappy betrayed me; Scotty betrayed us; Marcus Young betrayed Scotty; and Marcus Young's accomplice, who obviously wasn't the *popolo* kid they put on trial, betrayed Marcus." Bobby stopped and stared hard at his son. "And now, someone has betrayed Marcus Young's accomplice, assuming it's that cocksucker they just found dead."

Rigger tried hard to maintain eye contact with his father, but after a few seconds of silent staring, he broke off and looked out the window behind Bobby.

"Look, Pops, we did the best we could with what information we had. We were just a few steps behind shit the whole way on this deal." Rigger wiped sweat from around his eyes. "Why do you think this Rashad guy was betrayed? The cops are saying it was an overdose."

The look Bobby gave Rigger was withering. "Jesus, Rigger. Are you as dense as your boy? If Rashad or Rashid or whatever the fucking foreigner's name is was Marcus Young's accomplice, he had the money and the heroin all this time, right?"

Rigger nodded tentatively. "Yeah, I guess that would be right."

"So, one, if he was doing the junk, he would've been cutting it and not shooting up pure shit that would kill him. Two, where's the shit? There's no word that anything of value was found in his room where he died, and there's no fucking way he could've shot up a pound of uncut heroin in the few months since the robbery." Bobby sat back and sucked on his cigar again. "No, someone found him and found the shit, then killed him."

Forty-Six

There were no incidents of violence against any of the court personnel or the attorneys overnight. Nor were any further racial threats made. Pancho knew one night of quiet was not enough to breathe easy, but he also knew that if there was going to be any kind of violent reaction to the verdict it would most likely come sooner rather than later.

Jackson walked out of O'ahu Community Correctional Center wearing one of the new court suits Pancho had bought for him. Except for his face, Jackson looked good. He wore the suit well. Pancho put his arm around Jackson as they walked to the car. Jackson leaned into Pancho like a child leaning into his father's hug. They said nothing as Pancho began to drive toward Waikiki.

"Where we going?" Jackson finally asked.

"My place," said Pancho. "You can stay with me for a couple of days while we decide what you're going to do."

Jackson said nothing for a couple of blocks. He stared out of the window.

"You don't have to take care of me no more, Pancho. You done more'n enough. More'n anyone's ever done for me already. I'll be all right."

Pancho shook his head. "No way. It's like when you save someone's life. You become responsible for them. I'm not letting you on the streets again. We're going to figure out a plan for you. Besides, I've got a surprise for you."

Jackson was silent again. Pancho had become used to Jackson's periods of silence while he thought about what had been said and thought about what he would say next.

"But that's what you do, isn't it, Pancho? Save lives? You don't take care of all them people you get off, do you?"

Pancho smiled to himself, once again surprised at Jackson's astuteness. "Good point. But I have to admit that some of the people I get off are actually guilty and those who weren't already had lives they could go back to. You're different. You're a good kid who's had some bad breaks. You need a little help."

***

When the two entered the condo, Pancho gestured toward the couch. "You can sleep there." He took the small valise he'd given Jackson to carry his few other clothes and sundries and put it on the closet floor. Jackson wandered over to the glass door to the lanai. The view out toward the ocean with Waikiki off to the right was spectacular.

"Wow," was all he said.

Pancho came up behind him and unlocked and slid open the glass door. "Come on out and have a seat," said Pancho. "I want to show you something."

Jackson sat in one of the brown resin wicker chairs. He was still in his suit, and he put his hands in his lap like a child who had been told not to touch anything. In a moment Pancho reemerged from the living room holding some papers. He sat in the other chair.

"Jackson, I want to do something for you, and I hope you'll agree to it." Pancho put some papers on the table. "These are forms for you to fill out which would authorize one of the top plastic surgeons in Honolulu to do some facial reconstruction on you."

Jackson looked down at the papers, then back up at Pancho. There was a blank look in his eyes. "What that mean?" he asked. "What that facial recon, thing?"

Pancho gave him a broad smile. "It means that the doc will make you look pretty. He'll get rid of that permanent sneer and fix the scar, and when he's done, you won't scare people half to death just by looking at them."

Pancho watched as Jackson went to what Pancho called Jackson's 'thoughtful place.' Jackson's right hand went to his face and seemed to trace the line of his mouth, then the scar on the side of his face. When he turned his face up to Pancho, his eyes were moist. "An' I won't look like my daddy no more," he said softly.

Forty-Seven

A week after the verdict, Judge Kingsley, with the consent of his staff, released the sheriffs from their protection duties. There had been no reprisals and no more threats. Clearly the information about Gouveia and Rashad had convinced even the loonies that Jackson Steele was innocent.

"They'll just crawl back into their angry little holes until the next time they decide to overreact and beat their chests," said Drew. He, Pancho, and Paula were sitting on towels on the beach in front of Pancho's condo. There was no surf, but it was an otherwise glorious day. The ocean was like glass. They watched a canoe from the Outrigger Canoe Club glide gracefully out toward the reef. The paddlers worked as one unit, responding to the commands of the helmsman.

"Still, it makes me angry that these people can get away with terrorizing others, then just skulk away scot free when they realize they've made asses of themselves," said Paula.

Pancho laughed out loud. "You mean kind of like the absurd political pundits on television who say all sorts of crazy things which turn out to be wrong, yet not only do they never apologize or even acknowledge being wrong, they're allowed to stay on the air and continue to hold themselves out as experts?"

Paula smiled. "Yeah, like that."

The three sat in amicable silence, watching the people on the crowded beach.

"How's Jackson doing?" Paula asked after a while.

Drew answered, "He's great. The bandages come off in another week and he's looking forward to seeing his new mug."

"He's not too much of a bother?" asked Pancho. Jackson was staying in Drew's extra bedroom while he recovered. There wasn't enough room in Pancho's one bedroom condo.

Drew shook his head. "None at all. The kid thinks he's my personal butler or something. I can barely get a last bite off my plate before he whisks it away and washes it.

Paula chuckled, then said, "Don't get too spoiled."

"Too late."

"What's the latest on Keani?" asked Pancho.

Drew's shoulders made a small shrug. "Conscious. I think the doctors are going to allow the police to show him some mug shots to see if he can identify the shooter."

"Well, tell them to start with the Lopaka family," said Pancho in a bitter sounding voice. "I hear Rigger's kid, Winston, is a mean son-of-a-bitch."

"Did you hear Ala Moana canceled the contract with Paradise Security?" Drew asked. "I hear no one has seen nor heard from Scotty Gouveia since his encounter with you in court."

"Mmm. No surprise there," said Pancho.

Suddenly a Frisbee struck Paula in her right leg. A local looking kid of about fifteen ran up and picked it up without saying anything.

"Hey, brah," hollered Drew as the kid started walking away. "You hit this woman. How about an apology and how about taking the game down to the water's edge?"

The kid turned, looked at Drew, then at Paula and Pancho. "Fuck you, old man," he said, then he turned and walked away, flipping the Frisbee to his *haole*-looking buddy twenty yards away.

The three friends sat in shocked silence for a couple of seconds before Drew finally chortled. "How'd he know my knees were so bad that I couldn't get up to kick his ass?"

Forty-Eight

On the evening after the bandages were removed from Jackson's face, Pancho took him, Drew, Paula, and Susan out to dinner to celebrate. They were at 3660 on the Rise in Kaimuki. Chef/owner Russell Siu had made a special three course dinner for them, starting with the *ahi katsu,* which he knew was Pancho's favorite.

"You look great, Jackson," said Paula as she gently kissed him on his still bruised cheek. The perpetual sneer was gone. There was little sign of the scar. The nose had been built up just a bit.

Jackson smiled self-consciously. "Thank you, Miss Paula. I feel real different."

Drew raised his glass of wine. "We have two things to toast to tonight. The first, of course, is to Jackson, who's on his way to looking like a movie star." The group smiled and laughed as one, then sipped their drinks.

"The second," continued Drew, "is to Keani, who gets out of the hospital in a couple of days and who has definitively identified Winston Lopaka as his shooter. The police arrested Winston this afternoon."

"To Keani," said Pancho. "And to justice."

***

The next morning the body of Nappy Makuakane was found floating in the choppy waters off Puako, on the Big Island. His two-person outrigger canoe was found capsized not far from the body. The authorities speculated that a rogue wave had capsized the canoe and that Nappy struck his head as the canoe overturned. Those who knew the famous old waterman privately doubted that version of events, but everyone who knew the story of his betrayal of Bobby Lopaka was expecting Nappy to turn up dead one of these days anyway. The death was not investigated further.

Epilogue

Jackson Steele left Honolulu a little over a month after he'd been acquitted of the murder of Auntie Irene Kamaka. His surgical scars had healed, and Pancho told him over and over that he was now a fine-looking young man. Pancho wanted Jackson to start developing some self-esteem for the first time in his short life. It looked to Pancho like it was starting to work. Maybe it was just his imagination, but Pancho thought Jackson was holding himself differently — more erect, more assured. Paula had taken Jackson shopping and bought him a wardrobe of cargo shorts, khaki pants, five Aloha shirts, and soft brown leather loafers that could be worn without socks and with either shorts or the long pants.

On the day after the small shopping spree, Jackson announced to Pancho and Paula that he was leaving Hawai'i.

"You and Miss Paula and Drew and Miss Susan been so good to me I don't know what to say or how to say thank you," he said. He wiped at his eyes with his right hand. For the first time since he'd met his former client, Pancho was able to clearly see the emotions in Jackson's face. "But I ain't gonna let myself be a burden on you anymore than I already been," he continued. "You saved my life, Pancho." Jackson's voice broke. "Now I gotta go on out in the world and finish what you done started."

Pancho told Jackson that if he wanted to stay in Honolulu they would help him find a job and an apartment, but beyond that, he didn't try to talk Jackson into staying. He felt like he understood what was going on inside Jackson's head and, although he was scared for the young man, he approved.

"Where're you going?" Pancho asked.

"If y'all can get me just to Los Angeles I'll head off from there."

Pancho bought Jackson a ticket to Los Angeles and he, Drew, Paula, and Susan had all kicked in various amounts of money which Pancho put into an envelope and gave to Jackson on the morning of his departure. It contained five thousand dollars.

At the airport security check Jackson stood tall and proud and looked Pancho directly in the eyes. Without saying a word, Pancho opened his arms and Jackson stepped into a hug. The two men stayed like that for almost a full minute, unaware and uncaring that other travelers stared at them as they hurried by; then Pancho patted Jackson's back and stepped away. Both men's eyes were wet with tears. Jackson nodded at Pancho, turned, and was gone.

***

Pancho thought of Jackson Steele many times over the course of the next two years. He'd heard nothing of or from the young client who had moved and touched him in so many ways. In his most pessimistic times Pancho feared the worst. Had Jackson gone through the money and was back on the streets? Had he been arrested again, or worse, had he been killed? Pancho admitted to Paula that he had a hard time envisioning a world where all was well for Jackson Steele. A change in looks would have made a huge difference for him, but he was still a poorly educated black man with no skills and no support system.

"The odds of life turning out well for him are too low," Pancho said to Paula. "And frankly it kind of makes me sick to my stomach to think about all the bad things that could've happened to him."

"But not knowing can allow you to think that great things have happened for him," said Paula. "Think about the fact that he came into your life for some reason. Think about the impact you had on his life before sending him out in the world to make his own way." She paused and took a sip of the wine she'd been drinking. "The only possible outcome has to be good."

She'd said that with such conviction that Pancho couldn't help but smile, take her hand, and tell her he loved her. He so much wanted to believe that what she said was true.

***

One bright and hot day in August, almost two years from Jackson's departure from Honolulu, Pancho walked into his outer office and automatically took the handful of mail Susan held out for him as he headed to his office. He casually tossed them onto his desk as he took off his sport coat and hung it up, then he ran his right hand to smooth his long, wind-blown hair and sat at his desk. He needed to finish a brief this morning, and he had a preliminary hearing this afternoon. Idly riffling through the mail as he thought about whether he could get through with the hearing in time to get some surf time in, he stopped suddenly. He was holding a plain white envelope with no return address. What had gotten his attention was the handwriting of the address. He recognized it immediately as that of Jackson Steele. He felt his stomach flip. Fear or surprise or just anticipation; he couldn't tell what he was really thinking; probably a little of all.

Pancho tore open the envelope and two pieces of paper fell out. One was a check drawn on a Wells Fargo Bank account from Santa Fe, NM, made out to Pancho McMartin in the amount of six-thousand dollars. The other was a handwritten note.

Dear Pancho: I know you was from New Mexico and so I figured if it was as full of good people like you it would be a good place for me to live. I like it a lot. I'm doing real good. I got a good job doing construction. The doctors have me on medicine so I won't faint no more. I'm taking classes at night to get my GED. I been saving lots of money, so here's what you all lended me and some interest. I think you and Drew and Susan and Paula would be real proud of me. Thank you. I love you all.
Jackson

End

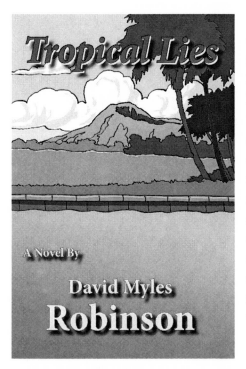

If you enjoyed this story of Pancho McMartin, we are sure you will also enjoy David Myles Robinson's previous Pancho McMartin novel, *Tropical Lies*. Pancho's client is a former mercenary, accused of the brutal murder of the man who was once Honolulu's most sought-after investment counselor. *Tropical Lies is* an edge of your chair legal thriller of nervewracking suspense and surprising twists. Available from BluewaterPress LLC at www.bluewaterpress.com.

Another really great read by David Myles Robinson is his novel, *Unplayable Lie*. It is a great golfing tale involving a young college graduate destined for the pro circuit, only to be derailed by witnessing a murder on on the back nine of the Congressional Country Club in Washington—by the man who will probably be the next President of the United States. Also available from BluewaterPress LLC online at www.bluewaterpress.com.